Dead Time Story

Richard Sanders

To Laurie with love.
I'd be dead without you.

>>>>>>

If you hide the universe in the universe itself, there is no place where it can be lost.

_The Japanese Poet Soshi, 1421-1502

CHAPTER 1

THE APP OF MY EYE

How many tragedies and comedies, memories and blackouts, devils and angels, obscure philosophies and trembling ecstasies have been born during a night of heavy drinking? How much love and hate, happiness and sadness, darkness and light? How many plots and plans, laughs and tears, hook-ups and fuck-ups, conceptions and deaths? Or, in the case of Rj Delgado, fuck-ups *and* death?

Rj Delgado was a freelance software developer who'd been hired as a consultant by *Real Story* to help us build a mobile app. He was a pudgy, puffy, amiable man, and despite his habit of Skyping in the nude and carrying a portable scale wherever he went to keep track of his weight, I thoroughly enjoyed the few months we spent working together. Not a handsome guy, no—he looked a lot like a blobfish, in fact, same blank-to-sad expression—but he knew his apps. I still have the wireframes he produced somewhere in my office.

One of my jobs as a top editor, one of my too many fucking jobs, was to liaison with Rj, provide editorial oversight on an app that would give your average mobile user instant access to the *Real Story* archives—to years of web content, plus decades of stories, photos and whatnot from the magazine. The thing was coming along nicely. We still had a few kinks to work out on functionality, but the app was testing well—testing *phenomenally* well—with focus groups.

One night he left my office to meet up with friends at a bar on Ludlow Street called Sweaty Cindy's. He was running late, no time to stop off at his apartment. I remember it was a cold late-winter night. He was wearing that big fur coat and that cowboy hat that made him look like a Kodiak bear prowling for dinner at the O.K. Corral.

As soon as he got to Sweaty Cindy's Rj started drinking barrel-aged Martinez cocktails—gin, vermouth, bitters and maraschino—occasionally cutting their sweetness with shots of Jose Cuervo Gold. He drank so much he could hear his liver splashing.

Not much of the evening remained in his memory. He remembered the place was packed. He remembered a 90s retro band—Death To Arugula, he believed they were called—playing a few sets. He remembered the bartender's name, Jenna, remembered her throwing a nickel at a customer who'd left it for a tip. He remembered his friends talking heatedly about something at one point, saying *the body count keeps going up*, but he had no idea whose bodies were being counted. He remembered showing a woman the self-built smartphone he used for testing, remembered showing her the *Real Story* app. He remembered going to the bathroom and weighing himself after he peed.

And that was it. He couldn't remember what happened after that.

He couldn't remember what happened to the self-built smartphone and the *Real Story* app.

Rj told me all this the next morning when he called from his apartment-slash-studio on Mott Street. At least he'd made it across the Bowery and home. He sounded guilty, groggy, ashamed and awful, like a Kodiak who'd stupidly stumbled into a trap and been taken down by a hundred tranquillizer darts. I felt bad for him. My own days of happy inebriation were long gone, and I would've given him some pre-AA advice, some 12-step prep, if he'd wanted it, but he didn't.

As messed up as he was, though, he didn't have a vast number of regrets about losing the app. He was confident we'd get it back. Developers, he said, were losing prototypes for apps and phones all the time. It was so common, in fact, that a whole retrieval ritual had sprung up. Whoever found the missing device would do a teardown, trace the name of whoever'd registered the app and try to sell it back for a few thousand bucks. If the developer balked at paying, the finder would sell it at a reduced price to one of the techie websites, who'd feature the device as the latest leaked-data, sneak-peek product development.

Losing prototypes was so universal, Rj added, some companies were doing it on purpose. They'd deliberately leave devices in bars or restaurants or other public places, hoping to get free publicity on the websites for their upcoming product. Some companies would leave dummy prototypes around, trying to throw the competition off track.

It was all SOP, Standard Operating Procedure, and the *Real Story* app was no exception. Nothing to worry about. Someone would find his tester phone, identify the app, get in touch with him and sell it back for a couple thousand bucks. Chump change, really, in the larger scheme of things.

He was almost right.

Someone did get in touch—but with *me*, not him. I got a call from a guy—a call on what turned out to be an untraceable number—saying he wanted to strike a deal. Why call me? He'd found two names on the patent application, Rj Delgado and mine, Quinn McShane. When he searched on me and found out who was, who I worked for, he figured I'd be the richer source.

Which was probably wise, because what the guy was asking for wasn't a couple thousand or even a few thousand bucks. He was trying to bleed me for a quarter million.

"Little steep, don't you think?"

Well, this is potentially a highly actionable piece of commerce.

The fuck was he talking about?

I put a high value on *Real Story*'s archival content, but getting access to it isn't worth any $250,000.

I asked Rj for an explanation. In person. I went to his place on Mott Street to talk to him, so I saw firsthand the guilty, wriggling-worm look on his face as he told me what was going on. The app, he admitted, didn't just provide access to the *Real Story* archives. It also contained a bit of a secret ingredient, a little sweetener, a little software magic known as MIXEX.

I won't bore you with the details of how MIXEX works, mostly cause I don't understand them. But basically it's a program that analyzes a group of people's responses and thought patterns in real time, locates the hidden connections between them and writes an instant script to make those connections stronger. MIXEX, in other words, mixes minds, melds them together, nudges people into agreeing with each other.

"You can actually predict the curve," said Rj, "plot out the future momentum."

MIXEX, he added, was similar to software the Pentagon was developing to train troops by computer, fuse solid bonds between them. *That's* why the app had tested so incredibly well in the focus groups. Their minds had been merged into one.

You gotta be fucking kidding me.

"Before we get in to the ethics of this thing," I said, "which I think is going to take some time..."

"Oh shit—I'm sorry."

"...what do I do about this guy? I'm not paying him a quarter mill."

"I'll take care of it. When he calls back, have him get in touch with me. It's my fault, what can I say? I should've..."

"Yeah, you should've."

"Just push him in my direction—least I can do. I'm sorry, I'll handle it. I promise."

Done. I gave the guy Rj's contacts, then sat back and waited to see what would happen. Did my job, earned my keep. Meetings, stories, layouts. Added stuff to my To Do list, where things can be safely ignored without being forgotten.

I felt on edge the whole time, felt on edge when I left work. Didn't get much sleep that night. Kept texting Rj, emailing, calling. No response.

I didn't hear anything that night, didn't hear anything until the next day, when somebody in the office said *hey, that developer you're working with? They found his body.*

Found it, to be exact, in the Mott Street apartment. Face up in the living room, dried vomit foam caking his mouth and the floor. No signs of struggle, no signs of break in. Ruled a probable drug overdose.

Bullshit.

Rj was a drunk, sure, but he was no stoner. I'd pumped enough crystal meth in my veins over time to spot all the tells of drug use, and I'd never seen any in him.

They were going to do an autopsy. Okay, wait a little while before jumping to the conclusion that somebody had obitted him.

I remember I was standing on the corner of 49th and Broadway a few days later when I saw the first snowflake come down. Just drifting in the air like a single piece of white soot. It was a warm-weather storm—within minutes we had snow falling on the east side of our building, but fog on the west.

A few minutes after the sky began filling I got a text alert about the autopsy results. OD confirmed. Rj had taken a lethal dose of something called cathidrone, one of those designer drugs that are still legal because the government hasn't seen enough of it yet to declare the shit dangerous. Cathidrone's becoming popular in Europe, the authorities there blaming it for 30 deaths last year alone. U.S. buyers can order the powder online from the U.K., where it's conveniently labeled as plant food, bath salts or pond cleaner.

This was completely off the wall. You've got to have one serious appreciation of the drug market to be getting into shit like that. Rj didn't have a serious appreciation for anything except too much booze. He might put ungodly combinations of alcohol in his system, but not plant food, bath salts or pond cleaner.

It made no sense, and as that keen adjudicator Judge Judy always says, *If it doesn't make sense, it probably isn't true.*

I broke into his apartment that night.

Don't ask how I got through the downstairs door or past Rj's lock (a Keystone double-cylinder deadbolt—a five-minute job).

The walls of his place were thin. I was picking up the hours-old smell of one neighbor's broiled swordfish dinner. His other neighbor was still watching TV at 2 a.m. A commercial—*attention catheter users*. Must be watching CNN.

There were still stains on the living room floor, spots where his vomit had congealed into white threads. This is where they'd found his body, staring up with a stunned, bloodless, what's-happening-to-me look on his face.

I felt twilight sick.

I liked Rj. I'd miss him. Despite the moral lapse with the MIXEX, he was a good guy. I was sorry I hadn't gotten to know him better. Sorry I'd never found out what Rj stood for, why the j was lower case.

I searched the apartment. I found the fur coat and cowboy hat. I found his portable scale. I found out he liked soup. He had enough of the stuff stocked away to supply the world with the second Flood.

I found a huge stash of porn. Rj was fond of playing the one-backed beast, as Rabelais might say.

I found printouts of his financial statements. He kept them in a folder with the bank names crossed off. Every time his bank was sold and changed ownership, he'd blot one name out and write in another one.

I didn't find anything, not in the statements, not anywhere. I didn't find any suggestion that he was in trouble with anyone but me. I didn't find any mention of MIXEX or the guy who'd called about the app. I didn't find any reason why someone would slip him an overdose of a designer drug.

The three or four inches of snow that had fallen during the day had already been matted into dirty gray slush on Mott Street. I headed for Canal, lost in thought and trying to think my way out of it.

They had one of those video newsstands on Canal Street, the LCD screen on its back panel showing news, weather, transit info and commercials. The stand was closed for the night but the video loop was still running. As I passed by, I saw a statue of Jesus silently going up in flames.

Kind of appropriate for a night like this.

I plugged my iPad into the jack. The audio explained that a statue outside a church in Galesburg, Illinois had been hit by a bolt of lightning. The video had been shot by the startled minister. This was second time in less than a year that the statue had been struck by lightning. Residents were wondering what it meant. Why did God keep sacrificing his only Son?

"I don't want to say I told you so."

"Then *don't*. Just fucking *don't*."

"But I *did* say it."

"Don't *say* it. Smug is not a good look on you."

Jesus.

I scanned the street. A young couple was indulging in some three-in-the-morning fight with each other, really going at it. They were coming from the direction of Mott Street and they were *screaming* at each other. They were louder than the newsstand audio.

"Why don't you get yourself one of those *internet* girls? You'd be a lot happier."

"Are you *judging* me? Are you fucking *judging* me?"

"I'm judging you so hard it's giving me a *headache*."

Do you mind? I'm trying to listen to the end of the world here.

I managed to hear that the first lightning bolt out in Galesburg had knocked one of Jesus' arms off. This blast, however, was more direct and all that was left of the statue was a charred skeleton of steel.

"I can't *believe* I didn't say that."

"Well you *didn't*. You're one of those guys, you tie yourself to a fucking tree and then complain you can't fucking *move*."

They were coming this way with their melodrama. Pale, dark-eyed people, both of them, each dressed in deep, Caravaggio black.

The woman had a kind of strange beauty that you can probably get used to after a while. Black hair with a dyed blue horizontal streak running across the front, so that it looked like she was wearing a headband.

The guy, a gleaming-eyed Prince Myshkin type, his small bones strung together with fiber optic wire.

She was getting angrier because he was telling her not to get so angry.

I couldn't hear a thing on the audio. I pulled my iPod out of the jack and was just putting it away as they were passing by.

"Who the fuck *are* you?" the guy was saying. "Who the fuck *are* you?"

Only he wasn't asking her. The question was directed at *me*.

And a second later, after I'd given him a blank *what?* look, he lunged at me and smashed a fist in my face.

It didn't really hurt—the guy had glass knuckles. It was more the *surprise* of the thing that stunned me.

"You think this is seasonally appropriate?" he said. "You think this is, what, the year 2222?"

The little shitbone was standing right in front of me with this ass-cocked, puffed-chest, looky-here attitude, spit flying out of his mouth.

Check that guy's coffee.

His girlfriend, meanwhile, just kept walking away, sadly shaking her head.

"Who're you with?" he said. "*Tell* me. You with Cascadian? Microtek? React? Zero-plus-ex?"

"In fucking English, please?"

Not the answer he was looking for.

He went to hit me again. A telegraphed punch, easily blocked. I countered by going for his stomach, giving him a shot that, yes, had some hair on it.

I didn't mean to hurt him that much, just to stop him, but I may have miscalculated. He *oophed*, doubled

over, staggered backward, lost his balance and fell flat
against the wall of a South Asian fish market. His
expression was dazed, befuddled, like a cyclops trying to
go cross-eyed.

No effect on his mouth, however.

"I don't think you're Cascadian," he groaned. "No,
I don't think so. I'm working with Cascadian right now
and you, you're not registering on the scale. Activate,
maybe? Metritel?"

"Are you crazy?"

"Yes, why?"

"You realize I don't know who you are or what the
fuck you're talking about."

"It's a possibility. Sure it is. I guess the question is
how much does it matter? Is it important that you have a
clear and distinct knowledge of all the elemental strings
being pulled here? Should you be conscious of every
formative process major or minor that's lead up to the
present moment? How much does the totality of events
depend on the totality of your awareness? Who the fuck
knows? Really, I'm asking, *who* the fuck knows?"

"Listen to me."

"Yes."

"Why don't you just calm down and get yourself
together?"

"I've got a different thought."

He took something out of his pocket, some
rectangular instrument. It looked like a clunky, old-
fashioned cell phone.

It wasn't. What it was, I later found out, was the
prototype for an incapacitating weapon that was being
designed for military and law enforcement use. It worked
by releasing a high-powered beam of electromagnetic
radiation, specifically a beam of high-frequency
microwaves.

All I knew, though, was that I'd just been hit by an
invisible, spline-shank rotary hammer, the thing pushing
out enough pounds of pressure to pulverize a concrete
wall. I couldn't move—I might as well've been tied head
to foot. My skin was getting the overheated, rubbery feel

of a very hot day. My body felt like a chain-locked pile of old tires.

"Unpleasant, isn't it?" the guy said, getting to his feet, keeping his finger on the zap button. "What were you doing in there? You know what I mean. Rj Delgado's place. Why were you skulking around in there?"

I could just about move my mouth, get a few words out. "Hate to see...friends killed."

"Friends?"

"Friends."

"Who are you?"

"Quinn McShane...*Real Story.*"

The guy nodded. "He mentioned you. The app, right? He spoke highly."

"Glad...could you...?"

He eased up on the microwaves. Feeling and movement made a gingerly return to my limbs.

He said his name was Roots Randolph, also a friend of Rj's, though any further affiliations were left unstated. Maybe because he was too busy examining his belly.

"Hurts?" I said.

"There's considerable discomfort, yes."

"It's go away."

"Feels like Judas' jockstrap." Which presumably was not good, since Roots fell into moody contemplation. "You said killed. You said friends killed."

"Killed."

"I was thinking that too. I mean cathidrone?"

"Did he even know how to spell it?"

"Not unless it was a-l-c-o-h-o-l. Not a chance. That's why I ran a Cellnex on his phone."

"I'm sorry..."

"Forensic tool kit, very decent hash functions. You know someone's number, you can pull the binary content out of the phone without touching the thing. Not legally admissible, but it works. I pulled the data on all his texts."

"And?"

"Some bad news. Your app? He'd coded it with a strange little piece of software."

"MIXEX, I know."

"He *told* you?"

"I found out. He copped to it."

"Did he cop to *stealing* it too?"

"That he didn't mention."

"Well that's how he got it," said Roots. "MIXEX's got thievery heat all over it."

"He lost the app. Left it in a bar, Sweaty Cindy's on Ludlow."

"Yeah, I know it."

"Somebody called, wanted $250,000 to sell it back."

"Fair price."

"This guy who called, you think he did the deed?"

Roots shrugged. "More likely whoever he took it from did the deed."

"Who'd he take it from?"

"Well, that I don't know. But I know who developed it. Zero-plus-ex."

A familiar name, even to a know-nothing like me. "That's the security company? Big firm? Corporate paranoia?"

"That's them."

"With that guy?"

"With that guy. MIXEX is proprietary—*extremely* proprietary. They own it. They'd want it back,"

"Wish I knew that for sure."

"So do I. Rj was an old friend."

"So how do we find out?"

Roots looked at me, nodding to himself. "I know how to get inside. I do work for them."

"Wait, I thought you said you work for somebody else."

"Cascadian, the competition."

"Well which one is it?"

"Both. Plus."

Jesus.

He went silent for a moment, sadly contemplating the mass of shadows stretching along Canal Street. Or contemplating sadness itself.

Black sky above, only distant noises. Funny how sometimes you can feel like you're standing in a graveyard in the middle of the city.

"I'm gonna trust you on this," I said. "I see you've got some talent. Your fight with your girlfriend? You had me fooled. That was a nice routine."

"*What* routine?" His hands went ulcer-fast to his stomach. "Shit."

"Still hurts?"

"It's so fucking crapulous."

"It won't last forever."

"Oh I know it won't."

He took out a foil packet, ripped it open and slapped a pain patch on the punch site.

"Morphine," he said. "Low grade. Thirty milligrams."

"You *are* a trip, aren't you?"

"It's *safer* this way. Safer passing through the skin than the digestive system."

"Sure, you don't want to damage your liver."

"Damage," he repeated, thinking to himself. "You know something? I should've known Rj was a thief when I first met him. Moment I laid eyes, I should've known."

"You can tell?"

"Absolutely. I can tell—mile away I can tell. All you got to do is look. I can tell by their walk and their talk and their attitude. And by the way they're looking at me."

CHAPTER 2

NOTHING BUT NETS

Wavefunctions

One balmy afternoon on the campus of MIT, Professor
Emeritus Bruno Ashoori stood on the stage of the Kresge
Complex, making a long, effusive, over-detailed
introduction to the day's distinguished guest speaker. The
topic, *Hexidecimal Resonance Advances in Quantum
Cryptography*, promised to be an enlightening and
entertaining one, Prof. Ashoori assured the audience of
graduate students, because the speaker—the painfully
intense man seated on the stage behind him—was Lukas
Lister-Bertozzi, the founder of [O+X], pronounced Zero-
plus-ex, an individual known for his brilliant, even daring
work, his aggressive proclamations, his grandiose
pronouncements. The introduction finally over, Lukas
Lister-Bertozzi stood up as Prof. Ashoori returned to his
chair on the stage. But Lukas stopped him halfway,
suddenly reached down for the professor's crotch and
forcibly yanked up his open zipper. "Someday," the
speaker announced, "you can tell your grandchildren that
Lukas Lister-Bertozzi fixed your fly *on this spot.*"

   The incident was typically characteristic of Lukas
Lister-Bertozzi and, by extension, of [O+X]—
unconventional, surprising, fearless, ruthless, debatable,
controversial, grandly off the wall. I guess it's a measure of
the company's reputation that even a techno-duffus such as
I knew [O+X] was a big player in corporate intelligence and
counterintelligence. The research I did fleshed it out:
[O+X], in fact, was one of the world's leading purveyors of
security encryption, pulse code modulation, collision-
resistant algorithms, null ciphers, jargon code, 128-bit hash
values, certificate validation, steganographic concealment

and revealment and a thousand other ways of mapping the hidden digital landscape of corporate cybercrime.

The story: Lukas was the only child of Margo Lister, an actress, and Oliver Bertozzi, a stage director, both zealous nonconformists who insisted their son called them by their first names. Dedicated to spreading the liberating effects of radical theater, Margo and Oliver traveled around the country, putting on small, obscure productions in small, obscure locales.

By the time Lukas was 10 the family had moved 43 times, which made school attendance a bit of a problem. Didn't matter, though, because his parents didn't believe in institutionalized education. It was a system, in their view, designed to crush the spirit, destroy the ability to learn and engender a dangerous fear of authority.

Homeschooled, allowed to follow his own interests, Lucas developed an early and voracious fascination with science, especially quantum mechanics. He read on his own, took online courses and spent a lot of time at libraries studying how quantum wavefunctions contributed to the invention of lasers, semiconductors, microchips, electron microscopes and magnetic resonance imaging.

Over time, his wunderkind grasp of physics enabled him to become a very sophisticated hacker. By 12 he'd built an underground reputation as a wise-child genius who, using only Margo and Oliver's ancient, battered Dell, could break into some of the most secure systems in the world.

At 14 he rebelled against his parents. From now on, he informed them, he would address them as Mother and Father—they were no longer on a first-name basis. Shaken to their philosophical cores, Margo and Oliver tried a compromise. How about Mom and Dad? Not happening—it's Mother and Father. They hated him.

At 16 Lukas filed for declaration as an emancipated minor, and he enrolled himself in his first school. Six years later he had a masters in physics from Princeton and a doctorate in quantum cryptography from Caltech. His fanatical devotion to one realm of thought had given him gifts that were prodigious, effortless and almost magical.

And a fluke of fortune had given him money. Back when he was 15, the family had been renting an apartment in the West Bank area of Minneapolis, where Mother and Father were putting on a silent production of *Waiting For Godot*. One of the neighbors in the building was a star shooting guard at a local high school, Melvis Burningham. Melvis approached Lukas one day, saying he needed help. He'd gotten his girlfriend pregnant and needed to get her fixed—he couldn't have a baby derailing his basketball career. Melvis had tapped into his own money but was still $300 short. Could Lukas come up with the money? He swore to God he'd pay him back.

Lukas hacked the 300 out of an ATM, but, dubious about the repayment prospects, he made Melvis sign a promise. If Melvis ever made it to the NBA, he'd give Lukas 10% of his signing bonus.

Five years later Melvis Burningham signed with the Dallas Mavericks for an $8.5 million bonus. Lukas tracked him down and asked for his share. Melvis refused. Lukas took him to court, convinced that even though they were minors at the time of the loan, he could make a case.

He started [0+X] with the $850,000. Barricading himself in a rented garage, Lukas began writing code and flow charts for camouflaged compression programs, covert field-testing programs, anti-pilfering programs, numeric overwriting programs, code-decoders (codecs), decoder-codes (deccos), leak detectors, prototype protectors, disinformation spreaders, fake authenticators, audio and video encryption, spread-spectrum steganographics, challenge-response and other varieties of reverse Turing tests.

His first client was a small media company, a firm that wanted to protect its trade secrets—and discover the competition's—using [0+X] software. Next he took on a midsize telecommunications network, then a nuclear power plant operator, then a contract from the military.

Running his company with a Jesuitical intolerance for imperfection, a ready willingness to humiliate and fire subordinates and a rabid demand for secrecy that made the CIA look like loose-lipped crack addicts (visitors sometimes had to wear blindfolds when passing through the offices), Lukas transformed [0+X] into a master of the confidential strategies, the paranoid plotting and the conspiratorial huggle-muggle of corporate espionage.

A few other things I'd found in my research:

• Lukas never kept a personal phone number or email address for more than a week. That's how worried he was about being hacked.

• By one estimated and conservative account, his clients had scrapped $100 billion worth of projects after they'd gotten peeks at other companies' projects and had to switch directions.

• The head of another corporate intelligence outfit was once asked if [0+X] considered him a threat. "In Lukas' mind," he said, "his only competition is God."

• Whenever he went to speak to prospective clients, Lukas asked to have a plate of raw, fresh, undried areca nuts—with all betel leaves removed—waiting for him. And then he wouldn't touch them. In fact, he had no interest in areca nuts, fresh or dried. It was simply a way of gauging a company's attention to detail and willingness to work with him.

• Introduced at a reception to Sir Francis Fitch, who'd won the Nobel prize in physics that year, Lukas pretended to mistake him for a small-Midwestern-college professor who'd just lost his tenure, and spent the rest of the evening going up to Sir Francis and telling him to buck up, you'll find *something* somewhere.

• As another physicist said of Lukas, "The surface of the Earth isn't dense enough to support this man's ego."

>>>>>>

Oh yeah, there was one other thing that turned up in my research: [0+X] was the Mecca of suicides. Over time its employees had developed an unfortunately pronounced habit of taking their lives. There were two incidents in first few years of rapid growth—one person died by a self-inflicted gunshot wound, another by a drug overdose. Then the pace picked up as the company continued to expand—

slashed wrists, self-asphyxiation, jumping off the [0+X] building—until it built into a bona fide wave.

Two years ago eight staffers killed themselves (two gunshots, two carbon monoxide poisons, one pesticide poisoning, three workplace jumpers). Last year the number rose to 12 (three gunshots, two slashed wrists, one intentional car crash, six workplace jumps). The company installed safety nets around the building, which managed to discourage the leapers. But this year alone [0+X] had already seen seven suicides (two gunshots, two drug overdoses, two hangings, one jump in front of a train).

Such rash behavior naturally raised a few questions and brought a good deal of scrutiny to the secret-keeping company. Since [0+X] had gone public several years ago, Lukas had to calm his board's concerns. "We're running a thorough review," he told them. "We're reappraising workplace procedures, everything, and we've taken significant steps to raise morale. We'll leave no stone unturned until we find a way to stop this waste of valuable assets.

"My own feeling is that success is the root of the problem. Success carries a burden, and increased success carries increased burdens, increased stresses that can assume the proportions of contagious disease. It's not for everyone.

"Now it may be true that we ignored the toll for too long. It may be true that we were so blinded by our economic accomplishments that we lost sight of the price they demand. But look at the situation from another perspective, a less hysteria-prone perspective, and I'm sure you'll realize, the high number of suicides is simply another quantifiable measure of our achievements."

Night Traders

We were talking about Rj Delgado as the B61 bus rolled into Red Hook, Roots Randolph saying he hadn't been looking all so good the last time he saw him. At least we *were* talking about Rj at one certain, definable point, then suddenly we were—or *he* was—talking about his neighbor's wife dying and how much it pissed him off.

"You were close with her?"

"Hardly knew her."

"Okay."

"But now, every time I run into him, I'm gonna have to think of something to say. I can't just pass him by. The obligation, you know? It's too fucking much."

We got off on Van Brunt Street, and Roots led me into the South Brooklyn night with a stream of insane muttering. Something about "all these naturoquackic processes and everybody's asking is it *really* organic? No, it isn't, but they *think* it is and that makes them feel better. But what nobody's asking is where does it end? How does it resolve itself? Where are the fucking songs of spring? Don't ask."

"I didn't."

We were heading for the Upper Bay, Governor's Island visible across the water, on a rumble-stoned street lined with piles of garbage, shattered windows, broken outlines of misty buildings. We passed a group of yawning dealers selling $10 bags of heroin—the local March of Dimes. We passed a raunchy bunch of sidewalk drunks, swapping bottles of Mad Dog and Richard's Lemon Gin. We passed a sickly group of people with shaking hands and bristling hair. Flashblooders—shooting up with another junkie's blood, getting just enough of a taste to keep withdrawal away.

I wasn't sorry I was carrying my Glock under my jacket.

At the end of the block was an abandoned house bent over like an old woman with stenosis. The side door took us into a small space of cement walls blackened with mold and down a set of water-rotted stairs. We came to an ancient steel door that looked like it had been salvaged from *The Titanic*.

Except for the magnetic strip on its side.

Roots swiped a card.

Loud music. Disco lighting. Lots of alcohol. Maybe a hundred people packed inside wearing *fabulous* clothes and *fabulous* shoes. It was a club—but one with a bingo wheel on one side of the room and a caller and everyone standing around filling out their cards with markers.

One of those underground bingo clubs, an illegal enterprise even though its patrons weren't competing for money but for free-drink coupons redeemable at the bar.

"Why're we here?"

"We're not," said Roots.

We worked our way through the crowd and the smoke-filled air. Cigarettes, pot, even cigars—really testing the limits of liberality.

We came to another steel door with another magnetic strip. Two women were standing nearby.

It comes in odorless form too, one was saying.

So what? said the other. *I just put it in my mouth. I don't stick it up my nose.*

Roots swiped another card.

Quiet. Soft chatter. Long, low tatami tables with maybe two dozen guys sitting on bean-bag chairs, yakking with each other or hunched spellbound over their laptops and tablets. Every guy looked like a lonely girl's first boyfriend. It was a study hall for nerds.

The tables were filled with platters of cupcakes and cinnamon buns, Red Bull, cold soda, hot coffee and other liquid sources of caffeine. The air was filled with talk of flagged tags, trapdoor functions, spectrum analyzers,

Vietnamese spam mimics, Russian litter loads, tribal shifts, hypothetical focuses, Rule 30 block ciphers.

Someone came up to Roots and said hello. Roots asked how his project was doing. Coming along—I'm in Seattle tomorrow.

"Seattles's hilarious," said Roots. "I like it there."

Someone else came over, asked if he'd heard about Freddy. He'd been picked up downtown, taken right off the streets. Not even a half-hour ago. How's that for a shot in the gut?

"Why is it," said Roots, "somebody does something good, it takes hours to hear? Somebody fucks up, it takes minutes, seconds."

We walked on.

"All right," I said, "what is this?"

"A group. A loose group of like-minded professionals. We call ourselves night traders."

"As opposed to day traders."

"Right. Day traders deal in things that are open and public. We deal in things that are secret and private."

"And by deal you mean..."

"We steal shit. We find out what the market wants, we go out and get it."

"So that's how you can work for Zero-plus-ex *and* for Cascadian."

"And for whoever. We're freelancers. We're only loyal to each other. We're not, you know, *amoral*, but these companies? When it comes to business, they're all the same."

"You're not amoral, but you steal?"

Roots shrugged. "Every one of us, in the world, we're all descended from a pair of apple thieves."

The room kind of reminded me of the old Café Society club, which billed itself as *the wrong place for the right people*. This was the right place for the wrong people.

We headed for a table on the far side, walking past screens displaying graphics I couldn't possibly understand. Though some I could. One guy was reading a post titled *How Acai Berry Colon Cleanse Saved My Life*. Another was watching some variety of porn featuring naked Japanese women throwing up all over each other.

Humani nihil a me alienum puto, said Terence. Nothing human is alien to me.

Though this—I wish I could say it in Latin—was really tugging at the edges.

I'm talking, of course, about the Acai Berry Colon Cleanse.

We stopped at the workspace of a guy wearing baggy cargo shorts with, oddly, a starched white dress shirt and a rep tie. Friendly sort of schizo. Roots introduced me to Robbo Fragaruccio. He had a sign next to his laptop: *There's A Blind Spot Right Behind You.*

Robbo was playing some game involving all kinds of waves and patterns and digital doodles. Roots said it was based on the Wolfram cellular automaton.

"He's a champ at it. Robbo holds the record for most consecutive games. He's on it all the time."

"I guess he'd have to be."

"It's totally addicting," said Robbo.

"I've got a friend, he's in the mob?" I said. "He's addicted to *Mafia Wars*."

Robbo considered this. "Is that a good thing or a bad thing?"

"That's the problem. Who knows?"

Roots asked if he was still running scopes on [0+X]. Goodbye Wolfram cellular automaton game. Robbo called up a set of schematics.

"Running all the time," he said. "It's like voting in Illinois—do it early and often." He switched through five or six frames, selected one and zoomed in. "You know what the problem with buildings is? They always have doors." Zoom again—lines, labels and circuits filled the screen. "They installed new systems on their doors a few weeks ago. But this one? ED8, northeast side? Its connections to the mainframe keep flaming out. Past couple of days it's been happening. It's a definite vulnerability, a definite uncertainty."

"ED8," said Roots. "Excellent. Excellent coaching up."

Time for me, though, to watch out for my own ass. "You're sure about this?"

"Sure as sure," said Robbo. "Foolproof sure."

"How can it be foolproof?"

"I put a tap kit on one of their fiber optic lines. Clamped it on myself one night."

I was astounded. "A tap? An old-fashioned, wire-on-wire tap?"

"Fully insulated, yeah."

"It's a little throwback, isn't it? A little old school? How do you pick up the signal? With rabbit ears?"

Robbo and Roots exchanged smiles.

"Things've changed," said Robbo. "There's too much cyber security these days. Everything's being watched, everything's being tracked."

"Every person who's using the internet," said Roots, "average people, they've got about a hundred data-gathering devices hidden on their hard drives."

"If I try to hack into this Zero-plus-ex line," said Robbo, "I'll be busted in seconds. But a tap? Like you said, an old-fashioned tap? They're not even *looking* for that. Everybody working in security today, they know digital. But they've lost touch with the physical."

"That's the advantage we have," said Roots. "We monitor electronically, of course, but when it comes to actual action? We go hands-on. Real-feel. IRL."

"We've been forced," said Robbo, "to resort to reality."

Roots went for a say-it-all, zenlike explanation. "Even change," he said, "has changed."

The Quim

We'd just transferred from the bus to the subway back to
Manhattan when Roots started in again with the manic
rambling. This time it centered—though *centered* is surely
the wrong word—on potash mines and outbreaks of rashes
and ungodly skin conditions and, somehow, aural hygiene.
"People're always saying, clean your ears, clean your ears.
Why? Who's looking inside your ears? Unless, you know,
it's somebody who's *looking* inside your ears."

"Why do you keep doing that?"

"What?"

"The scattered talk."

"Ah, *that*. I'm bipolar. Diagnosed years ago."

Ah, *that*. "But you don't take your meds."

"Can't. They fuzz me out, slow me down. This line
of work? I can't do this with that."

The train squealed to a stop. He checked the signs
and stood up. "Got a minute? Long as we're here?"

Where?

The East Broadway station, downtown. Sweaty
Cindy's, Rj Delgado's last known watering hole, was only
four or five blocks north. But we walked in the other
direction, heading south toward the FDR Drive and the
Manhattan Bridge.

"So, bipolar," said Roots. "That's my story. What's
yours?"

Okay, once upon a time I was a licensed
investigator. Doing all right—wife, daughter—except for a
rather dogged use of crystal meth and booze. Up/down,
up/down, up/down. Still doing all right, despite, until one
night when I got so fucked up on speed, alcohol and rage

that I blew a junkie/child-snatcher's frontal lobe away with a bullet. Goodbye license, wife, daughter, but I caught a break and was allowed to plead to manslaughter.

"Man, you did time?" said Roots, stopping on the corner of a quiet street, checking the time on his phone and gazing up at an apartment building. He was waiting for something.

And here, apparently, it was. One of the windows on the top floor—a light flashed on, held for a second, then flashed off.

"On your way to a rendezvous?"

"Not really. More like a quim."

"Sex?"

"A quick meeting—a quim." He kept moving. "So what happened?"

Well, I did my time in Red Mountain Correctional, caught a break there too. Got sober in the in-house rehab program, got into zen meditation through the Dharma Prison Program. Got out, started a second career in the not totally unrelated field of journalism.

"You were an investigator?"

"What I said."

"So as a former investigator, what do you think about that van?"

A row of cars was parked on the other side of the street, among them a large Chevy Express.

"What about it?"

"Just seems…out of place."

"Like somebody's in there waiting to pop you?"

"Something like that."

"Sometimes a van is just a van. But what about that woman?"

She was sitting on a bench in the dark, all alone on this side of the street, directly across the van. Possibly a hooker, coincidentally placed, but these things don't come with guarantees.

Roots' reaction: "Shit."

"I don't know. Let's make a pass. You watch her, I'll go over there and watch the van. If she waves, nods her head, moves, gives any kind of signal, give a yell."

"And what if you see something?"

I showed him my Glock. "You'll know."

I crossed the street, walking in the road, approaching the driver's side of the Express. And suddenly I'm all caught up in it, adrenaline and dopamine in full flow. It was like a zen mind-blower: What exists does not exist, and what does not exist does not exist.

I began passing the van, hand on the gun. Nothing so far—no heads, no sets of eyes popping up. Nothing from Roots. Nothing, nothing, nothing.

By the time I rejoined him, Roots was checking his phone again. Whatever he was up to, it was meticulously timed. Me, I was still all hopped up.

"She's okay?"

"Paid no attention to me. I think she's stoned, just sitting there tripping out."

We kept walking until we came to the radiation lights of a Pathmark Pharmacy set in the shadows of the bridge. We stood outside, watching the handful of nighthawks inside. "Forty seconds," said Roots.

And 40 seconds later a tiny little old man carrying a Pathmark shopping bag came out of the door. Very short man—he could do chin-ups on a bonsai tree. He headed west, toward the bridge. We followed, Roots sweeping the streets with his eyes.

A block later, about 150 feet ahead of us, the old man took something out of the shopping bag—it looked like a bottle of Maalox from this distance—dropped the bag in a trash can and walked on. Roots picked up the pace, looking around, lifted the Pathmark bag out of the trash and kept moving without breaking any stride.

Two blocks later he finally opened it up. Inside was a package of Ponds towelettes, a box of Bounce fabric softener and a jar of SlimQuick protein shake. He unscrewed the SlimQuick jar and shook out its contents: Chunks of dark red gems. Rubies. Pigeon blood-red rubies, the most valuable kind. You could see their needle-fine flaw lines. Meant they were untreated, uncut.

"This is how I get paid," he said. "I don't do money."

"Why not?"

"Same story—too much surveillance. Every transaction you make can be tracked and traced. It's easier for me to spread these around, convert 'em to cash whenever, bury the sources."

"Jesus. All this sneaking-around, Cold War shit, it's really necessary?"

"Trust me."

"Even the light-in-the-window routine? You can't just call?"

Roots looked almost insulted. "On the *phone*? Gotta be kidding. If your phone's not tapped these days, you're *nobody*."

Lost In Space

The [0+X] building rose from the horizon like some humungous, unhealthy, hermetically sealed exclamation mark. It was located in Rocky Crest, Suffolk County, on the grounds of the old Federated Aerospace site. Decades ago, when it was one of the leading employers on Long Island, Federated played a critical role in America's lunar explorations. The optical and electrical guidance systems for the Apollo command modules had been built here. So had the mapping cameras for the Apollo service modules, used to survey the surface of the moon.

I guess it's kind of a tribute to the Space Age glory days that the same ground was now holding up the whitewall tires of a gleaming, fully restored 1959 Chrysler Imperial.

Maybe it was part of the night traders' cutting-edge nostalgia, I don't know, but the vintage car was owned and operated by Mr. Roots Randolph. He'd spent a ruby or two on this Virgil Exner-designed classic, refinishing its wide tailfins, its extruded chrome grille, its swivel-out seats, its pioneering cruise control, its TorqueFlite transmission, its completely operational Hi-Way Hi-Fi record player.

As he piloted the Imperial past [0+X] headquarters, Roots was talking—calmly—about Lukas Lister-Bertozzi's passion for secrecy. [0+X] developers, for example, weren't allowed to talk about projects they were working on with anyone, not even other [0+X] developers. If they did, they were ex-[0+X] developers. Even worse, Lukas wasn't above spreading disinformation about former employees. So while you might've been fired for revealing something, suddenly you're being accused—by unsourced rumors, by internet innuendo—of *stealing* something.

"You get along with him?"

"Enough to work with him, yeah," said Roots. "But I don't like him."

"Why not?"

"Not that big into rabies."

[0+X] was bordered on the north by woods. We parked on a nearby road and got out. Roots took an ultraviolet flashlight out of his backpack and we began picking our way through the spiky silhouettes of branches and roots, the red tints of maple buds, the sweet, rich, almost visible smell of last fall's decaying leaves.

I said I was glad he wasn't talking funny tonight. He said he'd gone to see his psychiatrist that afternoon.

"How'd it go?"

"Not good. She got all worked up."

"Over what?"

"She said I should've made an appointment."

"You just dropped in?"

"I felt the urge. I was in the neighborhood."

We were in the neighborhood of the building now, the ED8 entrance. We could see the anti-suicide nets strung across the walls.

The door was equipped with a BioFreq 2000 lock—an appropriate model number, said Roots, since each one of these things costs around $2,000. According to him, the BioFreq was a complex, two-stage security system, combining a fingerprint reader with an RFID (radio frequency identification) key. Certified at a grade-one commercial security level, it was way beyond my picking techniques.

Way it worked, a [0+X] employee would touch the fingerprint pad and a yellow LED light would flash, indicating that the user was authorized to *try* to gain access. To actually get inside, the employee would then have to insert a [0+X] RFID key in the slot. The lock's RFID reader would scan the key and send the data to a transponder, and if the key data matched the digital information stored inside the transponder, a green LED light would flash. The door handle could now be turned.

That's how it worked. Of course, as we all know, things don't always work the way they're supposed to. Whenever a BioFreq glitched out, it had to be reset. How? Roots crouched, opened a flip panel underneath the door handle and showed me the Firewire port inside. A [0+X] engineer would have to come out here, hook up his handheld with a Firewire connector and reprogram the lock.

Which is exactly what Roots was going to do now.

He took a phone-like device out of his backpack that looked a lot like the microwave thingy he'd zapped me with on Canal Street. But this one came with a Firewire connector, whose other end he attached to the port under the door handle.

"I'm really psyching for this," he said.

He did some finger-walking over the touch pad. Waited. Did some more.

The lock's yellow LED light came on. Yes!

More touch padding. More waiting. And then more padding.

No green light.

His fingers ran all over the pad, recalculating, recalibrating, reconfiguring.

Still no green light.

"This a little bit surprises me," he said.

Un-huh.

He went back in the backpack and came up with another Firewire connector, only this one tapered on one end to a thin filament-like wire. Roots worked the wire into a tiny hole between the pins of the port, plugged the other end into his device and moved his fingers over the pad.

Yellow light, yes.

Green light, no.

"I thought you said you knew how to do this."

"I never said that. Did I say that?"

"Not in so many words."

"Well how many words did I use?"

Jesus.

"What do we do now?"

He rummaged through his backpack, desperation all too evident, kept searching until he found something at the bottom: an old rusty paper clip. He unbent the clip, jammed it into the hole in the port and began a furious bout of poking and prodding.

The yellow light flashed.

He went manic with the clip, trying to push the interior locking pins down, maneuvering it this way, that way, every which way but loose.

The green light flashed like a mother.

"Well played," I said.

ED8 led us into a massive storage area, rows and rows of cantilevered shelving, pallet racks, catwalk systems, conveyor belts, hundreds of shrink-wrapped cartons.

Where to?

"I know where the MIXEX was developed," said Roots. "I know the division. Good place to start."

We carefully walked through the rows, feeling the rush, the narcotic thrill of breaking and entering, and were making beautiful progress until we heard a low, motorized hum, almost a pathetic buzzing.

Roots grabbed me and pulled me behind the shelves.

Seconds later, two little vehicles that looked like vacuum cleaning robots traveled past our row a hundred feet ahead of us.

Security bots. ASSETS, said Roots—Automated Servo-Security Evaluation Team Staff. [0+X] was crawling with the little buggers and their wireless network systems, their coordinate finders, their waypoint navigators, their infrared scanners, their cameras with 360-degree pan and -10 to +45-degree tilt functions.

"Wave of the future," Roots griped once they'd passed by. "On the other hand, they make my job possible."

"How's that?"

"Corporate security's all defense now. Even the human operators, that's all they're trained for. Companies are putting all their money into protective measures, walling it off. There's no one left who can go on the offense. That's where the night traders come in. We're part of the anti-disintermediation process."

"Translation?"

"Bring back the middleman."

Please remain where you are.

The voice, coming from down around our feet, was soft and vaguely British, like Helena Bonham Carter waking up after a long night's sleep.

An ASSET was squatting next to us. There'd been no buzzing—it must've switched into some stealth mode to sneak up on us.

Strobe lights flashed in our faces, over our bodies. A tray slid out from the side of the ASSET. I was instructed to place my Glock on the tray, Roots his backpack. *Oh yes, and the weapon you have in your pocket*—Roots' electromagnetic incapacitator, the one I'd tasted on Canal Street.

Please place some form of identification in front of my scanner.

"Fuck you!" Roots lost it. "What kind of shit is this? Real estate won't appreciate, oysters are dying from hepatitis infections, pleaplods are withering on the vine, and you think we have time for this?"

What did you say? Something about oysters?

"You heard what I said."

After a moment's calculation, the ASSET responded. *Mr. Lister-Bertozzi wants to see you.*

"*Bullshit.*" Roots turned to me. "*Can't* be. It must be malfunctioning. It's just giving us standard responses."

No, no malfunction. I analyzed the content-patterns of your speech. Mr. Lister-Bertozzi wants to see you, Rudolph Randolph.

"That's your real name? Rudolph?"

"I don't want to talk about it."

>>>>>>

Radioactive

In the elevator, the ASSET scanned my fingerprints, my irises and my driver's license, paying special attention to the serial-killer photo the DMV had snapped of me. Roots was doing alternate-nostril breathing to calm himself down. The door opened on the top floor, into a mango hued corridor that despite its 12-foot ceiling still looked and felt like a cave.

Activity ahead of us, people in lab coats coming in and out of a sidedoor. We looked inside as we walked past, slowing down but not seeing much more than a huge space and dozens of researchers milling about. The wall sign near the door said *Gengo*.

Please keep moving.

"What goes on in there?"

"I don't know," said Roots, "but whatever it is, I helped. They're using celesium-137 in there, thanks to me."

"Radioactive material?"

He nodded. "Got it from a hospital that was going out of business, from their blood irradiator—they use radioactive isotopes to sterilize blood. Easy snatch, container was about the size of a soda can. I got there just before the Department of Energy."

The ASSET prodded us along until we came to an unmarked door at the end of the corridor. Couple of strobe-light bursts on its security panel and the door opened up.

We were in some hallucinogenic light show. Neon tubes bouncing with every conceivable bright color in the Skittles spectrum filled the space, and every time we moved the tubes bled a different color, like they were reacting to our heartbeats, breathing rates and body

warmth. If you took the people who design those neon
Times Square spectaculars, fed them peyote, tossed them
off a bridge with bungee cords and kept them in an
isolation tank for 48 hours, this is what they'd produce.

"Janiva does some wonderful things."

The voice wasn't the ASSET's. It belonged to a
woman who was slipping out from a mouth of multi-
colored shadows.

She'd had an angel's beauty at one point in her life,
but not anymore. Her eyes were sunken, her expression was
fogged and her skin was a bride-of-Christ pale. She seemed
to be focusing on some image she couldn't quite see but
was too haunting to forget. The room's neon colors
changed as she moved close to us—blues, whites, purples.
Winter colors.

"This is one of her most beautiful pieces," she said.

"Fantastic," Roots replied without a whole lot of
enthusiasm.

The woman nodded, then stared off at the lights. Or
not at the lights, but some void between them.

You're expected.

The ASSET herded us through the room.

"Who's that?" I whispered.

"His wife. Mrs. Lukas."

"And who's Janiva?"

"My girlfriend. You met her, remember?"

"With every brain cell I still have left."

Who designed this place? Frank Gehry and the Phantom of
the Opera? We were in an office, or a study, or a retreat, or
a chamber with walls that were flamboyantly curved and
distended, all high dramatic flair, as sweeping as a
conviction, all mash-upped with a thousand goth touches—
filigreed wrought iron, black stone work counters,
infectious nightshade colors.

A tapestry of mathematic signs and symbols
covered one wall from floor to ceiling. A legend at the
bottom read: *The Schrödinger Equation, 1926.*

He was standing in front of a nine-leaved lacquered screen, the video monitors on each panel showing surveillance coverage. But not current coverage. The views from outside the [0+X] building had been shot in daylight, with fresh snow falling. He was enraptured by old surveillance footage.

In the flesh, Lukas Lister-Bertozzi lived up to his advance billing—sullen, lanky, intense, impatient, exacting, forensic, disconnected, hugely filled with himself. He had slate gray eyes, a scraggly beard and long wealthy-hippie hair parted in the middle and growing down to his shoulders. He was wearing a tattered knee-length coat—I think it actually might've been a frock coat—that looked like it'd been skinned off an old dead dog. He was eccentric enough for membership in the House of Lords.

"How did I know you, or someone very much like you, was on the premises?" He spoke without taking his eyes off the falling snow. "I assume that's among your first questions."

"Be nice to know," Roots confessed.

"First let me reconstruct your possible perspective. Either you or one of your night trader friends somehow discovered a vulnerable point in ED8. You decided to exploit it. Sadly, for you, the vulnerability was finally repaired 26 minutes ago. Your information was outdated. So while you were able to disable the fingerprint ascertainment and the RFID—and I wouldn't mind knowing how you did that, I'll pay for the information— you were unable to disable the lock's audit trail. I became aware of an unauthorized access the moment you opened the door."

"Shit," said Roots.

"Yes, shit. Such is the age we live in, rife with shit. No one can be trusted. Here, look."

He walked over to the slab counter of a workspace, called something up on its screen. A headline: *Special Panel Appointed To Investigate Ethics Commission.*

"Even the watchdogs need watching," he said. "So your break-in, I suppose, is simply par for the moral course. Still, it leaves me surprised. After all the commerce I've had with you—mutually beneficial business—why are you violating my lab, my home?"

"We were just trying to find something out. We weren't out to steal anything."

"Well yes, you were—you were trying to steal *knowledge*. I'm almost tempted to say you're walking down a very slippery slope. But this isn't a slippery slope—it's a straight plunge into hell." Lukas finally turned to look at us. "And may I ask, just FMI, what you were looking for?"

"It's about the MIXEX. The prototype."

"Hmm. Interesting."

"A friend of ours, a developer, kind of found himself in possession of it."

"Who's this developer?"

"His name was Rj Delgado."

"I know his work. *Was?*"

"He lost the prototype one night. Somebody tried to sell it back to him. Next thing, he's dead. And not naturally."

"I understand, yes, and let me say this about that." He began jabbing the air with his finger, lecturing Osama bin-Laden style. "I'm very fond of the MIXEX, and the prototype was indeed a good one. But I can always build another. I played no part in attempting to secure it back. And while I'm fond of the MIXEX, it's not an essential part of my portfolio. I doubt I would've taken someone's life for it."

"We're just trying to get straight on this."

"If that means you're looking for a suspect, I'd suggest looking at someone who'd be trying to hurt me. Someone who might use the MIXEX against me."

"Well, that's why we—"

"We, we—what's with the *we?* Who *is* this, by the way?"

He was referring to me but not expecting an answer from me. Instead he went over to the ASSET and pressed three of its buttons. The ASSET replied by feeding him a long, narrow printout that looked like a supermarket receipt.

What he read seemed to startle him. *"Real Story? You're an editor with Real Story?"*

"A *top* editor."

His eyes kept returning to the printout and then back to me, studying the paper and yours truly with equal fascination.

"You have a sizable audience," he said. "You have *quite* a sizable audience, both in print and online. You're one of the few media franchises that've continued to build a base."

"Well, we've tried to focus on brand mark—"

"I want to talk to you."

He was becoming animated now, almost *excited.* Something in the room had shifted. Some mysterious script had just been flipped.

"I want to make a public announcement," he said. "A maximum-impact announcement, plus proof of my claims. I've been looking for the right media venue."

"Maybe we can work something out." I thought I was being generous.

"No, you don't understand." He came close to me, stood right in front of my face. "I can put you on the map."

"We're already on the map."

"A bigger map. The biggest map possible. I can make you part of the most unforgettable moment in history."

Time Squared

The ASSET was gone now, replaced by a male human who'd just handed Lukas a freshly poured glass of Diet 7-Up. Lukas tasted it, tasted it again, handed it back. "Take this downstairs, have it analyzed. Third floor. They've changed the carbonation formula, either the CO_2 values or the pressurization levels. It's much more powerful now. The bubbles keep exploding in my eyes. Find out why."

That left him, Roots and me sitting in ornate, straight-backed Brewster chairs. Not very comfy.

"Since broad consumption of the internet began," he said, "one category has remained consistently popular. Besides porn. Genealogy. The many, many, almost *infinite* profusion of genealogical sites. The reason for their appeal is not complex. We all want to trace our connections to the past. We all want our lineages, our linkages, our family trees or what have you. We all want our stories, our *full* stories. Am I right?"

Roots and I nodded, glanced at each other, wondering what the hell we'd gotten into.

"We're all intrigued by the past, which is to say we're all intrigued by time. And yet, we ask ourselves, what *is* time? What *is* the past? We all understand the passage of time, and yet what, *exactly*, is passing? Such is the nature of time—everybody knows what it is, nobody knows how it works. And no matter how hard we try, no matter how many birth records and death certificates and land deeds and old photos and letters and diaries and genetic analyses we employ, the past always remains elusive. The butterflies of time always escape even the sharpest collector's pin." He permitted himself a smile. "Until now."

You got me. "Come again?"

"What I'm saying, what I want to make clear to the world, is that I've found a way to return to the past. I've found a way to retrieve the truth from the invisible depths of time."

This was some extraordinary variety of bullshit.

"You talking about time travel?"

He laughed. Frankly a what-an-idiot laugh.

"No, not time travel. Not some mythical transport through gravitational-dilation portals. Not something that raises all those embarrassing hypotheticals about changing past events. What happens if I go back and kill my father? Do I therefore not exist, and thus can't go back to kill my father in the first place? So therefore he's alive and helps conceive me and one day I decide to go back and... No, not time travel. Time *capture*. A genetically based reconstruction of the past. A passive, non-interactive observation of the faithfully re-created past. Do you understand?"

We just stared at him.

"I've accomplished many things in my life, I think we can all admit to that, but all my accomplishments pale in comparison to this—a way of discovering once and for all the infallible truth of the past."

I had many questions for Lukas, but none more pressing than, Exactly what *is* your relationship with reality?

"This is quite a departure," I said instead, "from corporate espionage."

"Not a departure. An *extension*. What, after all, is espionage? A quest for information hidden in the databases of your competitor. This is a quest for information hidden in the databases of time, in the secret archives of the past. Same principle, but on a grander scale. This is an act of resurrection, of taking dead time and bringing it back to life."

"And you want to use *Real Story* to make your announcement."

"I want to release it through one single outlet, yes. Based on what I know of the media, if you give everyone unlimited access, no one will be interested. But if you restrict access to one channel, suddenly everyone else gets thirsty. Competitive envy is a wonderful tool."

"True enough, good plan. Telling you the truth, though, I don't know how much I can push this."

"Are you serious? I'm proposing a fundamental shift in human worldview. I'm proposing to answer the mysteries of history."

"Yeah, but it's a little…"

"Mr.…." He checked the printout. "Mr. McShane, suppose I won permission—to give you just one example—suppose I won permission to take DNA scrapings from the Shroud of Turin? Suppose I did that? I could prove whether the face stained on the cloth really belonged to Jesus. I could prove whether Jesus really existed. I could prove what Jesus really did. I could prove what Jesus really said. And you don't think, Mr. McShane, in your infinite media wisdom, that there wouldn't be some *small* market for this?"

>>>>>>>>>>>>>>>>>>>>>>>>>

CHAPTER 3

SKULLS DON'T LIE

Debunkered

One of the enduring controversies of World War II is whether Adolph Hitler ended his cracked, tortuous life by killing himself. Even the accepted version of events is complicated by stumbling contradictions, bizarre gaps, fissured facts and the black scars of genocidal horror—crisscrossed by so many twisted branches it's impossible to see the sky.

Most experts believe Hitler had taken his life and that of his mistress, Eva Braun, on April 30, 1945, as the Third Reich was collapsing. Allied forces were invading Germany from the east and west. The Soviet Army had already entered Berlin and was battling its way to the center of the city, the site of the Chancellery and its underground bunker, where Hitler and Braun had locked themselves away for the past four months.

Knowing defeat was inevitable, Hitler had decided to commit suicide and asked his doctor for a double dose of cyanide pills on April 22. A week later, at midnight on the 29th, he married Eva and dictated his last will and testament. After 16 years together, the couple lived as man and wife for less than 40 hours.

At approximately 3:30 p.m. on the 30th, a loud gunshot was heard in the lower bunker. Two of Hitler's most trusted aides, Martin Bormann and Joseph Goebbels, found the bodies inside. Eva's smelled of burnt almonds, the telltale scent of cyanide. Hitler had also taken the poison, then given himself a guarantee with a bullet in his right temple.

The couple was taken outside, doused with gasoline, set on fire and buried in a shallow grave—which is where they were found three days later by agents of SMERSH, the Soviet intelligence unit.

At this point the official version takes a dip in murky water. For reasons conjectured but never fully explained, the Russians told no one about the discovery. Instead, Hitler's remains were secretly interred 100 miles away from Berlin. Keeping the skull and parts of the jawbone for analysis, SMERSH hid the corpse beneath the parade ground of a military base in Magdeburg, where it stayed concealed until 1970.

That year, as the Russians prepared to turn the base over to East Germany, the man who would later become leader of the Soviet Union decided to destroy what was left of the body. Yuri Andropov, then director of SMERSH's successor, the KGB, worried that if the location of Hitler's grave became known, neo-Nazis would turn it into a shrine, a monument to anti-Semitic, Holocaust-praising or Holocaust-denying hatred. And so, on the night of April 4, 1970, KGB agents dug up the corpse and set it on fire once again, this time burning it to oblivion.

That's how the authorized version ends, with the ashes of Adolph Hitler dumped into the Elbe-bound waters of the Magdeburg sewer system.

But not everyone bought into the story. For one thing, much of it rested on the accounts of SMERSH and the KGB—scenarios that didn't exactly come with certificates of veracity. For another, there were no high-ranking witnesses to the death scene. Bormann and Goebbels found the bodies in the lower bunker, but Goebbels killed himself the next day. Bormann disappeared and was never captured.

Then there were the sightings, the Elvis-like mirages manifesting all over the Western Hemisphere. Hitler was said to be living in a moated castle in Westphalia, hiding on a hacienda outside Buenos Aires, tending sheep in the Alps, working as a croupier in Evian-les-Bains. He was reportedly spotted in Grenoble, St.

Gallen, off the Irish coast, at the South Pole, in a cave in northern Italy and at the proverbial inn in Innsbruck.

Weird chatter, the stuff of which conspiracy dreams are made, but many took it seriously. Dwight Eisenhower, head of the Allied forces, later president of the United States, expressed doubt that Hitler was really dead. Even Josef Stalin, the Soviet dictator who presumably had the bones hidden in his basement, told his lunch companions at the Potsdam conference he was sure Hitler had escaped.

Many years later, those bones in the Kremlin would spur critical questions about the accepted version. In 2002, the Russians allowed an independent team of scientists to conduct DNA testing on the skull. The hole in the cranium seemed to suggest that, indeed, Hitler had ended his life with a bullet. But the DNA results came to a slightly different conclusion: The skull belonged to a woman between the ages of 20 to 40. Hitler had been 56 in April 1945 and, by all accounts, a man.

The controversy remained. No one doubted that Adolph Hitler had been a human Satan, but what the hell happened to him ?

Buzzing In The Hive

To give you an idea of the marathon madness taking place at the [0+X] complex, people scrambling with nervous-breakdown speed along catwalks inside a three-story-tall aluminum sphere, everything a circus of chaos, when one of the staffers collapsed and appeared to be convulsing, Lukas screamed, "Let the fucker have his stroke! Keep moving! Keep *moving!*"

All this was happening in what's known as The Hive, a house-size basketball lined with quantum cascade lasers calibrated to project holographic images on all 360 degrees of the interior wall.

Lukas, wearing his protective goggles, told me where he'd gotten the DNA sample: From the armpits of a NSDAP uniform personally made for Hitler by Hugo Boss. The collector of Nazi memorabilia who owned the uniform had provided three full notebooks of documentation, authenticating its provenance, its pedigree and its unwashed condition.

Once the sample was obtained, it was processed through an ECI, a Eukaryotic Chromosome Isolator, used to identify and amass the parts of DNA encoded with an individual's memory.

Standard procedure so far, until it came to the next step, which in layman's terms I guess you could say involved putting the encoded memory in reverse. How did it work? Please, later for that. Suffice it to say for now that the DNA went through some digital geekery conception of repressed-memory therapy. It was charged to go backward, and when the appropriate moment of time was reached, the resulting code was etched on a piece of plastic. Shine the lasers on that piece of plastic and you've conjured up a holograph.

Which was just about to happen. People were running, testing, yelling, howling, caught in a visionary dream-frenzy of completion. The staffer who'd collapsed was back on his feet now, ignoring his concussion. The links that would send the live feed to the *Real Story* servers and out to the waiting world were checked and primed. People were pawing for Lukas' attention, but he had the foresight to stop and make sure one of the staffers was getting all this down in the notes for the eventual Lukas Lister-Bertozzi autobiography.

A voice came over the dozen speakers that spanned the echo-free interior of The Hive: Everything was ready.

The Capsule Version

Out of habit, I was expecting to see something like the grainy b/w footage of old *March of Time* newsreels. But no. The go-back, as they called it, was producing hi-def, 3D, full-color images. Damp, cracking, mine-shaft walls became clear, lit by suffocating yellow lamp light. The crumbling stone box of Hitler's personal study in the lower bunker, submerged in shadow. Just looking at it you could smell the crypt.

The furniture was sparse, temporary: a faded couch, a table, a scabby desk, two deteriorating chairs, a file cabinet, a Blaupunkt radio.

It was like an image captured by the Hubble telescope, gazing back into the history of the universe.

The table held the remains of a crepuscular honeymoon feast—champagne, cognac, Valrhona chocolate. But most of the food was raw, including strawberries, figs, blackberries, carrots, celery and radishes. It was a typical diet for Hitler, who, inspired by the composer Richard Wagner, believed only a vegetarian ruler could conquer the world.

Hitler was at the desk, a fierce-eyed old jackal, wasted flesh, severely clipped mustache frosting with gray, 56 going on 1,000. The desk was stacked with towering piles of paperwork, delicately but precariously balanced. Hitler was vaguely looking through a folder he held in his hands.

He spoke. Hybrid translation software instantly generated subtitles. "I should be attending to my files. But everything I read is irrelevant, redundant. False." He looked up and past the piles. "Don't do that."

Eva Braun was sitting on the couch, wearing a stylish black silk dress and a wedding ring, a cigarette and a Ronson lighter in her hands. "Even now?"

"Especially now."

She put the cigarette and lighter down. At 33 she was a robust bleached blond, immaculately groomed but unaffected, still with color in her skin despite four months of living underground, the tone thanks to years of nude sunbathing.

A healthy woman, but with darkness, with vestiges of wounds, in her eyes. She'd met Hitler when she was 17, working as an assistant and model for his personal photographer, and twice in their early relationship she'd tried to kill herself. The first time she'd shot herself in the chest with her father's pistol. The second time she'd taken an overdose of the sleeping pill Phanodorm. Hitler committed himself to her as she was recovering from the drugs. He seemed drawn to self-destruction. Two of the other women he'd dated had also attempted suicide, and succeeded.

"I can't maintain these files," he said, tossing the folder on the desk. "Only swine maintain files."

"Did you put on clean underwear?"

He nodded, took a deep breath of the room's thick air. "I'm sorry. I feel terrible about all this. I feel…embarrassed."

"Don't ask me to judge you. It's not one of my duties."

"Then let the judgment be mine." He stood up, stretched, took two steps and rested himself on the perch of the desk. "You know what I fought. Nocturnal pestilence. Subterranean resistance. Asphyxia by filth."

"Do you want me to forgive you? Fine. I'll forgive you for something. Anina Hauschild."

"Now for the finger-pointing part of the program."

"If I can forgive you for that, I can forgive you for anything."

"I never *touched* her."

A knock on the door. Hitler grunted permission. A fan of light invaded the room as the door opened. A hefty man whose uniform no longer fit him—his bottom button barely had a grasp on its hole—came inside. Facial recognition software added a contextual note to the subtitles: Field Marshal Wilhelm Keitel.

In defiance of his bear-like build, Keitel approached sheepishly and greeted the Fuhrer with only half a straight-armed salute. "My apologies," he said. "For the interruption, and for the news I have to deliver."

Hitler didn't respond, remained resting on the desk.

"The garrison has no supplies left," said Keitel. "Ammunition is running low. Weidling believes his troops will soon stop fighting."

"Which troops?"

"The *city* troops. The *Berlin* garrison."

"Send in more."

"There's no one left to send. I'm sorry, the city will begin to fall in hours."

Hitler shrugged his shoulders. "Very well."

"We've also heard from Rome. The idiot is dead. He was captured near Lake Como, trying to escape."

Semantic paralleling software produced another contextual note: Benito Mussolini.

"He was executed, then strung up by his heels with meathooks. He and his… [Keitel glanced at Eva] and his girlfriend were both strung up."

Contextual note: Clara Pettachi.

"They were hung from the roof of a gas station. An Esso station. No one knows what the future of Italy will hold."

"The future is too late."

Keitel automatically nodded in agreement, got ready to leave. "Oh, and I have a message from your doctor. Blondi and the pups have died."

Hitler looked up, interested. "The pills worked?"

Contextual note: Fearing that his cyanide capsules were fake, Hitler had them tested on his German shepherd and her brood.

"Completely." Keitel hesitated. "I'm sorry, but I hope you know how much those who love you are suffering."

"I know. That will be all. Wait. What's the day like?"

"Gray and moist. Low clouds."

"Good. Thank you."

When they were alone, Hitler let a huge yawn go. "Are you sad?"

"Not really," said Eva.

"I don't want you sad."

"Don't worry about me."

He stood, went around to the desk drawers and removed a Walther PPK pistol and an antique rose pillbox.

"We live in a time of murmurs and whispers," he said, "tribes of lepers and slobbering toads. No poems or songs can save us now." He placed the gun on the table, shoving aside a bottle of champagne, and sat next to her on the coach.

"I want no pain," she said. "Never again."

"That's all I ever meant for you. That's all that will ever happen."

He opened the pillbox and removed two capsules. She stared at them. Stared at them for some time.

"Do you remember when I changed my hair?" she said.

"You made it darker."

"Just a *slightly* darker tint." She laughed. "You were horrified.'

"You looked so strange. You were completely different."

"I dyed it back right away. I made sure I never changed it again."

He laughed for a moment, then turned his eyes to his hand. "Can I get you anything? Another drink?"

"Thank you, no. That's not really necessary."

He took her hand, raised one of the capsules to her lips. "Just bite on it."

"Don't worry about me."

She took the cyanide in her mouth and bit down, and after two or three seconds began to slump away from him. He put his arm around her and held her up. Within 10 more seconds she'd lose consciousness, and within minutes she'd be dead of cardiac arrest.

"Many years ago," he said to her, "I met a man in Essen, a coal miner. He'd been trapped for three weeks in a gas explosion, trapped with eight other people. A Krupps mine, of course. I asked how bad it was down there. He said it was the best three weeks of his life. He couldn't afford to let his spirits sink. He had to keep himself and the others going. But now? Fuck it, he said. Ever since he'd been rescued, fuck it. There were many times, he said, when he wished he was still trapped in the mine."

He took the Walther from the table, bit into the capsule and placed the barrel against his right temple. The explosion of the gunshot in the small space roiled from echo to echo. The gun fell to his feet in his last conscious memory as the blood running from his head and down his chin began to form a stain on the arm of the couch.

Misguided Mumbo Jumbo

Quasars, those gamma-ray cauldrons that live at the center
of galaxies surrounding super massive black holes, burn
with so much energy their light can be seen across the
entire length of the universe. The [0+X] go-back kinda had
the same effect. In fact I don't think the splitting of the
atom was celebrated with as much fanfare. You could hear
the blood rushing to commentators' heads—and other
anatomical areas as well—as they prepared to discuss what
they'd seen.

*Lukas Lister-Bertozzi may be a shadowy figure, but
he's turned a blazing spotlight on the immense gray fog of
history.*

I can only describe what I saw an indescribable.

*[0+X] has hit a home run, and there isn't enough
tape in this world to measure the shot.*

But not all members of the commentariat were so
enthusiastic. Skepticism, in fact, was rampant, especially
among professional historians. In fact, the more steeped
you were in Hitler Studies, the more likely you were to
characterize the effort as

...a criminal assault on scholarly process.

...the most bogus form of digital mumbo jumbo.

...misshapen, misbegotten, misguided.

*...an amateur production in the theater of the
absurd.*

*...something more restrained historians than I
would have to call "a big fat lie."*

*...something only the most gullible 9/11 conspiracy
theorist could believe.*

Even those who supported the accepted version of Hitler's death took pains to denounce the go-back as

...a slickly produced reenactment.

...a CGF—a computer-generated fraud.

...mere shadows playing on the walls of Plato's cave.

But one thing gave all the critics uneasy pause. The name *Anina Hauschild.* The one thing Eva said she could forgive Hitler for was his alleged dalliance with a certain Anina Hauschild. This was curious because in all the well-documented details of Hitler's life, the woman's name had never surfaced before.

Critics first seized on this as proof the go-back was counterfeit—until a respected Hitler researcher discovered that Anina Hauschild did exist and could well have had an affair with the Hit man. Turns out she was a friend of Geli Raubal, the daughter of Hitler's half sister Angela. He was known to have possibly slept with Raubal, which might explain why she killed herself. So if he was getting on the low down with Raubal, why not with her friend Anina Hauschild?

This, *apparently,* was something new—a connection that had never been mentioned in the billions of words written about Hitler. Certainly it was something that not even the most assiduous [0+X] screenwriter could've dug up. Then how did Anina Hauschild appear in the script? None of the critics could explain it. And for all their tortured rationalizations and coincidental explanations, none of them could quite dismiss it.

Roll Over Beethoven,
Anastasia And Tupac

By only giving the go-back to us, Lukas had hit upon a sound release strategy. Media people only get interested in something when they see other media people interested. Once the go-back debuted on *Real Story*, journalists and their audiences pushed the topic into must-talk status. Shares of [0+X], which had suffered some depression from the rash of employee suicides, jumped 12%.

But by itself the strategy wasn't enough. Sure the press is interested, I told him, now they've got to *stay* interested. Toss out a few tidbits for other media outlets, make them feel they're getting part of the story. Otherwise they'll start turning against it and downplaying its importance. Throw the others a few bones before they go find something else to feed on.

So Lukas agreed to do a series of follow-up stories. Say what you want about him, he was an easy interview— ask a question, lean back and let him rip.

Herc's a representative sample of the remarks he made:

...no, you're right, I normally don't respond to my critics, and I've always had many. But their reaction to this project has been so insightless, so blind, so abundantly misinformed, such a masterpiece of titanic stink that it behooves me to answer back. I've always been accused of taking crooked paths—well this time I'm guilty of going straight to the shining mountain. And I'm not surprised that the ticks and fleas of the academic world can't see it. When people are faced with the vision of an infinite mountain,

some begin to scale its heights. Critics hide their faces and wheeze with myopic asthma.

...a process that replicates historical analysis, only it does it approximately 122 times better. The great unanswered questions of the past now have the potential to be answered. What caused Beethoven's death? Did Anastasia survive? Who shot Tupac Shakur? Who built the statues on Easter Island? Who really killed Martin Luther King? For the first time in human history, the sphinx will be able to speak.

...a tolerable level of stupidity up until now, but there comes a point. How can they shut their minds off? How can they ignore the obvious? What about Anina Hauschild? She's the glaring gap in their theories, and instead of trying to address the omission they simply close their mental laboratories down. This is why, generally speaking, the educational system is in structural decline.

...yes, there are other plans, certainly there are other plans. I'll be announcing them in the near future. For now let it be understood that the past is no longer an unfathomable phantom. This is the key.

...not too much to say that this is a pivotal moment in the history of our species, that it's the most significant shift in human consciousness the world has ever witnessed. I don't think that's an exaggeration in the slightest.

Lukas, obviously, wasn't big on sound bites, but his message was still clear. He wasn't just laying his critics to waste. He was serving God with a cease-and-desist order. The universe had a new miracle-maker.

CHAPTER 4

INTERZONE

Let's Say You Live In A Galaxy
100 Light-Years Away

"Everything exists at the same time," said Lukas, off and running. "Everything, the past, the present, the future, simultaneously exists. Each moment of spacetime is like a frame in a filmstrip—doesn't matter if they're sprocketing through a projector or not, they still exist. This is one of the most powerful insights of quantum mechanics, one of the most powerful ideas I know. The moments making up spacetime are timeless, they don't change. Every event in the history of the universe, everything that has happened, is happening and will happen exists right now, even as we're sitting here."

Here being his *Dr. Caligari's Cabinet* of an office, that gothstrocity nesting on the top floor of [0+X] headquarters. I'd come here for a very simple, clearly defined purpose: to find out more of what he knew about MIXEX and, by extension, Rj Delagdo. But after broaching the subject for about 12 seconds, Lukas got himself snared in other thoughts. All juiced up by his media excursion, he decided on the spot to give *Real Story* the Grand Interview—the full and untrammeled explanation of the origin and genesis of the go-backs.

I wasn't gonna say no to that. Sticking to MIXEX suddenly made me feel like Ruth Gordon at the end of *Rosemary's Baby*. Everybody's over there making goo-goo eyes at the Son of Lord Satan, and I'm fussing about the knife scratch Mia Farrow left on the polished floor.

Later for MIXEX.

"Simultaneous time is critical to understanding the go-back," he said. "Once you've grasped it, the rest is easy—though of course I'll try to explain the process in terms you understand."

"You don't have a crayon?"

"When I was young, I spent much of my time thinking about time travel. It was one of the reasons— No, it was *the* reason I became interested in quantum physics."

In his early lonely days, he said, when he was shifting from city to city with his nutjob parents, he was constantly dreaming about shipping himself out to the future. He read everything he could about possible modes of teletransportation. Time dilation. Quantum tunneling. Using rotating black holes as portals. Finding white holes on the other side of black holes. Finding wormholes in the curvature of spacetime. Pulling cosmic strings together to warp those curves of spacetime.

But the more he studied, he said, stabbing the air with that bin-Laden gesture, the more he realized that physically daytripping into tomorrow was impossible. Scientists might be able to theoretically teletransport a pair of simple particles into the future, but a human body? With its billion billion billion particles? Maybe more? Too much entropy, too much decoherence. Too many multiple probabilities. The odds against it were staggering.

Lukas forgot all about time-transgression and accepted his place in the present, settling instead for the arcane sublimities of corporate security.

Then something happened to him. A few years ago. Some kind of breakdown or crisis. Something marked by "confusion, fatigue, fevers, vertigo, anger, danger, buzzing, tremors, sleeplessness, apocalypse. Something lost and terrible was massing above me, congealing all around me, but just out of vision range, and it was so clotted and coagulated I couldn't think about anything else."

"What happened?"

"I think I was being prepared. I think I was in one of those preparatory stages, one of those way stations, where the mind is being primed to receive a vision. I was walking in the wilderness, plunging deeper with no direction, when I came to a dawning in the woods, an opening of strange and radiant light."

The source of the light? The past. A new way of seeing the past. A realization that if the future is increasingly disordered, it's because the past is ordered. If the future is highly entropic and increasingly decoherent, it must have started in a state of low entropy and stable coherence.

"That's when I knew," he said. "The past is real, the past really exists. Do you understand? We have no trouble believing that space is really out there, that space really exists. Well so does the past. It's *really* out there, it *really* exists. Now what do I mean by that."

"What *do* you mean by that?"

"Let's say you live in a galaxy 100 light-years way. Let's say the date is Nov. 22, 2063. You train your instruments with their fine resolution on the planet Earth, on the city of Dallas. You see crowds in Dealey Plaza, a presidential motorcade slowly approaching the Texas Book Depository. You see John F. Kennedy waving with his right arm raised. You see him suddenly look to his right, then lurch and move his hands to his throat as a bullet penetrates his back and exits through his neck. It's the Zapruder film all over again. Only you're seeing it for the first time, as it really happens, as the light reaches your galaxy 100 years later."

There you have the theoretical basis of the go-backs. Not time travel but, again, time *capture*—a way of recovering events that have already happened and playing them back.

"I realized that if I could scan the essential ingredients of the *now*, the essential ingredients of spacetime in its current state, no matter what those essential ingredients ultimately are—whether they're gravity loops or zero-branes or some other articulation of Matrix theory—if I could scan them and reverse their velocity, I could call back everything that has ever taken place."

"Cool."

"Sure, cool. Except it presented a whole *other* set of problems."

>>>>>>

One of the ASSETS served us coffee. [0+X], I noticed, had
its own porcelain mugs and embossed napkins. Sometimes
it's the little touches that really knock you out. Anyway, the
whole other set of problems, Lukas explained, was that the
past is virtually infinite. The dilemma was, where do you
go? Put it this way: Google *the past* and you'll get about
two billion results. That's a lot. So how do you narrow the
scope of your search? How do you find focus?

That's the challenge the prototypical plans for the
go-back faced. Say you wanted to pay a visit to 1927. You
wanted to see Babe Ruth hit his 60th home run, or cheer at
Lucky Lindbergh's tickertape parade, or go to the premiere
of *The Jazz Singer*. Fine, but by going back in spacetime
you're looking at an infinite number of choices. You're
walking into a multiplex showing an infinite number of
movies. How do you navigate your way to *The Jazz
Singer*?

It was right around then that Lukas discovered the
work of Dr. Vivek Rajman. ("Rudimentary research, but
it served my purposes.") A quantum biologist, Rajman was
studying the phenomenon of memory transfer—in
transplant cases, the recipient of an organ often experienced
memories belonging to the donor. Rajman had made
extensive use of ECIs, eukaryotic chromosome isolators,
investigating how people's memories become encoded in
their tissue and DNA.

But he wanted to take it further. He wanted a
panoramic, one-look map of an individual's entire bank of
memory. To do that, Rajman created a piece of software he
called the PIB—the Pangenetic Illumination Beam. In
effect, it took a fast-shutter, freeze-frame snapshot of a
person's entire universe of memory-encoded DNA.
Convert the snapshot into patterns that can be etched on the
surface of hard, durable plastic, hit the plastic with laser
light and you've got a holograph of that person's every
memory.

"I remember the day I read about the PIB," said
Lukas. "I remember the *moment* I read about it. I thought I
was going to fall off the face of the earth."

Rajman's PIB was the answer he needed. By going back with an individual's DNA, he could limit the scope of his search. He could reduce it to a comprehensible, finite field. He could control where he was going.

What Lukas did next, simply put, was invent a way to run a PIB holograph backward. Again, I won't bore you with the details because they're like two or three universes beyond my fucking understanding. But basically, he used the law of time-reversal symmetry—the law stating that any object can be made to retrace its tangent by reversing its velocity. He combined the law with silicon chips and light-emitting diodes and developed processors that transmit data at 50 gigabits per second, each one fast enough to download 100 hours of digital music in less than a second. He fine-tuned the process with quantum averaging and nuclear pixelization and spacetime tagging and created what can only be called a human genome project for the past.

That's what was going on in the *Gengo* lab on this floor, every calibration powered by the celesium-127 he'd bought from Roots Randolph. He was reconstructing the past Plank unit by Plank unit, like someone might recreate Van Gogh's swirling self-portrait of September 1887 short, manic brushstroke by short, manic brushstroke.

"You saw how well it works. You saw what an influx of precision data can do. That's what it all comes down to—precision and persistence. Persistence because no matter how many times people knock you down, you get up again and you—*what?*"

Time out. A staffer was standing in the doorway, telling Lukas the QA testing on a new phase of security software was diaper-full of problems. He was needed on the second floor.

"We have to break off for now," Lukas said to me. "I'm sure you have questions, so—here—let me give you a copy of my book. It goes into the go-backs in greater length and detail."

He downloaded something called *Interzone Quantum Time Differentials6B* into my phone.

"Please. Feel free to explore the grounds," he said. "Read, relax, enjoy yourself. Take a nice walk. Believe me, I'll have no trouble finding you."

>>>>>>

Collapse

I think I can say this without any hesitation, equivocation or doubts of any kind: The last thing I expected to see outside was a game of lawn bowling. But there it was. A dozen men and women dressed in white shoes, white pants, white jackets with [0+X] logos, playing on a rectangular patch of new grass. Trying to roll a green ball closest to a small white target ball. Which isn't as easy as it sounds because the green ball was slightly flattened on one side, so you had to toss it on a curved, biased and occasionally wobbly path.

Really strange thing to see out here. With ASSETS wheeling past on patrol. Other staffers toodling by on Segways. Suicide nets strung from the buildings. A warm, sunny day for it, yeah, dogwoods blooming like snow swirls against the other bare trees on campus. But still. Who'd expect to find a game invented in 13th-century England, favored by Henry VIII and Francis Drake, taking place in the middle of a corporate security complex?

And what a strange way to play it. Lawn bowling is usually a chummy, collegial affair, people standing around sipping whiskey or tea. Not here. These people were dazed and distracted, not looking at each other and, since many were wearing iPods, not talking to each other. Separate islands just gong through the motions. It almost seemed like they were being *forced* to play.

Whatever. I took a bench nearby and began digging into *Interzone Quantum Time Differentials6B*. Which I could see from the first page was going to be a bit of a challenge. Very much like rolling a ball slightly flattened on one side across grass.

We find ourselves standing at the beginning of an historical epoch, an unparalleled moment in time, whose precise nature I shall describe shortly. Perhaps some might expect me at this point to mention my own role in this momentous undertaking. They will be disappointed. This is not the place for a celebration of one's achievements. I should note, however, that the human mind possesses no limits. In analyzing the many-branched problems and vertical obscurities the world presents to us, human contemplation will take the most unimaginable risks. "Our thoughts are our most valuable weapons," as Lucius Magius said when speaking to the Tiberians. And while there's no denying the remark was made in very different circumstances, its meaning in this context, I trust, will be abundantly clear.

Lukas Lister-Bertozzi wasn't just gifted with extraordinary pretensions, he was spectacularly insane.

I skipped a few pages ahead, trying to pick up the good parts.

I find it difficult to go on at this juncture without discussing the current so-called controversy over Stage Two of Schrödinger's magnificent equation. In fact, it's impossible to even begin addressing the subject of this book without touching upon the thorny subject of wavefunction collapse. In connection to which I must draw the reader's attention, if the reader is not already aware of it, to Tollanov's recent work on perpendicular z-yields. Now what, the reader may ask, do z-yields have to do with wavefunction collapse? My explanation will follow in due course, but first let me say that...

I was also finding it difficult, at this conjuncture, to go on. It wasn't just the writing, the digressions, the general incomprehensibility.

There was also the matter of the knife sticking into the side of my neck.

A man was standing next to me, pressing a blade into the flesh over my carotid artery, holding the steel 1/64" away from the puncture-point with the precision of a moyle.

"Can I help you?"
"I think so," he said. "Kill me."

Nailed To a Bad Cross

He was one of the lawn bowlers, a scraggy, tubercular guy with pink and mealy skin. His features had a sinking, caved-in shape, like someone had mashed a hand over his face when he was coming out of the womb. A night vision all dressed in white.

"Sorry?" I said.

"I want you to kill me. I'm tired of it. I don't have a clue. Not anymore. I'm just trying to be myself, but I don't have a clue anymore."

I looked across the humorless horizon. The other bowlers weren't paying any attention.

"I'm not into that."

"Please, my life doesn't want to live anymore. I can't stay put. I can't... Just take this and kill me."

His blade was made with a Loveless drop-point design. Best hunting knife there is.

"Let's talk instead."

"*No*. Talk, no. Just take this away from me. Take it all away from me."

"Okay. Just hand it over."

He hesitated, thinking. "I don't trust you. If I give you the knife, you won't kill me."

"If you don't give me the knife, I *can't* kill you."

"This is a problem."

"You didn't think this through, did you?"

No, but he had an idea. He placed the knife at the base of his throat, just below the larynx. "Just one good push—shove it in." The blade would slice through his neck and sever the cervical nerves in his spinal cord.

"And if I don't?"

"I'll turn it on you, cut you as bad as can be."

"If I don't kill you, you'll kill me?"

"You got it."

I stood up. "Let me get some footing."

"Good idea." He shut his eyes, waiting for it.

Like taking candy.

I hit him with an uppercut in the stomach, and grabbed his wrist as he was doubling over. I put my other hand behind his elbow and pulled it toward me while pushing his wrist away from me. Three seconds of pretzeling pain and I had the knife.

"You *fuck*," he said, quite betrayed.

"Suicide? You're riding the wrong wave."

"*Don't*. Don't. I don't want to hear it."

"What's your name?"

"Spangler. Cito Spangler."

"Cito, what's wrong you want to take your life?"

"This fucking place. There's no *immunity* around here. It's all whispers, hushed voices. Around here, believe me, nobody's gonna be pulling your daisy around here. That's the truth, and if you've heard that before, believe me, the half of it has *not* been told."

Or the quarter. Or 2.5.

"Suicide's a strange thing, Cito. We want to get away from this world. Thing is, at the same time, this is the world we really want to live in."

"I know, I know—I've heard it all. That's what she always says, the chaplain, always saying shit like that. And you know what I tell her?"

Cito suddenly erupted in a stuttered, staccato *F-U-U-U-U-C-K YOU* and came charging in.

You could see his play a mile away. He swung a feeble roundhouse at my head, a suffering duck of an attack. I blocked it and kneed him in the nuts. He went down hard with a look of great confusion and pain.

"What kind of shitshow is this?"

A woman's voice. I turned, saw at first a long back-length of white hair. Prematurely white hair. The woman only had a few lines beginning to wrinkle her face, and they hadn't been formed by age but by sadness and irony.

She came up to us, spoke to me. "What're you *doing* to him?" An angry tone, though it somehow seemed to breathe grace.

I held the knife up to her. "He pulled this on me, wanted me to kill him."

"Is that too much to ask?" said Cito, holding his balls on the ground.

"Give me that." She took the knife, then looked carefully at me. "Are you the one from *Real Story*?"

"What've you got, a summons or a warrant?"

"Stay away from him. Stay away from all these people."

"Why?"

"If you're part of the go-backs, then you're part of what's destroying these people. He's turned this place into a slave pen, making them work double, triple, quadruple overtime either on go-back research or on security projects to *pay* for the go-back R&D. People aren't hooked up to do that."

"That's what I was telling him," said Cito.

"You can't put people under that kind of pressure and paranoia. You can't nail them to that cross. You're just poisoning them with their own ass breath."

"What excuse can I use?" said Cito. "The dog ate my iPad?"

"I thought he told his board he was taking care of it."

"Right," she said, "and what's he done? Put up suicide nets? Institute mandatory lawn bowling as therapy? Hire me? And do you know what he told me when he hired me? *No matter what gets done, these things are just going to happen.* That's his attitude. *That's* why Zero-plus-ex employees have been declared an endangered species."

>>>>>>

Her name was Belinda Halestre. Lukas had hired her, she said, through a corporate chaplain-placement service. She was supposed to bring spirituality to the workplace, offer an outreach to the burn-outs and the overstressed, run groups and one-on-ones and a suicide hotline and provide just enough moral and emotional support to get staffers to perform their functions in a calm and comfortable frame of mind. I don't know if she was any good, but she seemed to give off light when she spoke.

"Get up," she said to Cito, who wobbled to his feet. "Why didn't you come to me? You're out there on the margins, why didn't you come talk?"

"Why bother?"

"Cause it sounds like you need a brain shower, wash some of that self-destruction out of your mind."

"Right."

"I've missed you the past couple of sessions."

The bitter expression on Cito's face seemed to suggest he'd just been sucking on a used Tampon. "Lot of good they do me."

"Up to you. What do I always say? The water a cow drinks turns to milk, the water a snake drinks turns to poison."

"I could use a drink." He brushed himself off and turned away. "Excuse me, but I'll be getting the fuck out of here." He started walking.

"They did a survey," Belinda said to me. "Eighty-seven percent of all Zero-plus-ex employees believe they're more depressed than the average Zero-plus-ex employee." She yelled out. "Come and see me, Cito. Don't be a stranger."

"I can't help it," he yelled back.

Days Of Time And Roses

I got the hell out of there—*enough*—walked several city blocks until I came to a whole other part of the grounds. Nice, quiet, isolated spot, nothing around but a small lake, a bench, a willow tree dipping its branches into the water. I took another stab, so to speak, at *Interzone Quantum Time Differentials6B*.

I have already made several allusions, albeit in highly indirect fashion, to Wheeler's historic delayed-choice experiment, with which everyone is familiar. I see no need, therefore, to embark on a detailed analysis of the provocative questions it raises about the interplay between events in the past, even in the extremely distant past, and events experienced in the present. Such a discussion would be unnecessary. But let me simply note that in the forward march of our quantum-system understanding, and I am most specifically referring (as the reader, no doubt, has surmised) to the entrencheration of planes-of-simultaneity observations, and to any statistical results at levels of probabilities which sustain such observations, the implementation of new ideas, such as Wheeler's was, in its time, is indispensable.

The brain sprain I was developing was pretty severe. I decided to Google *Interzone Quantum Time Differentials6B,* hoping for some kind of Cliff Notes guide to the epic. I found a number of comments, all by physicists, none flattering.

Lukas Lister-Bertozzi's public statements have always fallen a few shades short of apparent sanity. Perhaps it's comforting to know that his magnum opus is no exception.

I'm not sure if the proper diagnosis for this disease is called oral incontinence or verbal diarrhea.

I finally managed to finish the book and I can say, with some pride, I failed to understand a single word.

Probably the worst book ever written by a member of our discipline, and that, as we can all attest, is saying something.

You won't be the same person after reading it, mostly because much of your life will have already passed.

"How're you finding it?"

Lukas was standing next to the bench, a dozen Cezanne roses resting on his arm.

For me? Acknowledging the difficulties of *Interzone Quantum Time Differentials6B*?

I didn't tell him how I was finding the book. I told him instead about the knifepoint request for assisted suicide.

He didn't seem terribly concerned. "Who was it?"

"I didn't catch the name."

He shrugged. "How do you like the book?"

"I was just getting started when it happened."

"I see." He glanced down at the roses. "Come with me. I want to show you something."

The greenhouse squatted in another part of the compound, filled with cultivated summer flowers—lilies, zinnias, marigolds, bachelor's buttons, six-foot-high sunflowers. A slab of granite was propped against a glass wall just inside the entrance. *Lukas Lister-Bertozzi Was Conceived On This Spot.*

"Here? At Federated Aerospace?"

"No, somewhere in northern California, around Red Bluff or Shasta Lake. I'll move it there once I find out."

He walked to the back, where the flowers formed a circle around another rectangle of rock, this one set in the ground. A small tombstone carved out of veined ebony limestone, the black-on-black texture making it look like it had been cast in gunpowder.

The inscripted name: *Samantha Lister-Bertozzi.*
Only four years separated the dates.

"My daughter," he said. "My seed. My only child."

The greenhouse, I realized, had been built around
the grave, always keeping the little girl warm, always
surrounding her with color and beauty.

"What happened?"

"Fire. A fire broke out in our old residence on the
top floor, where the *Gengo* lab is now. An electrical fire."

"How did she—"

"I don't know. No one knows. My wife was
watching her. Supposed to be watching her. No one knows
what happened. By the time they pulled my wife out she'd
gone into shock. Deep groundswell shock. She's never
really come out of it. Sabreena has amnesia, a particularly
severe case of dissociative amnesia. Whatever happened
remains locked in some subterranean gallery."

I pictured the woman I'd run into with Roots,
wandering like Ophelia among his girlfriend's neon lights.
Ring-eyed and lost, nursing some heirloom grief.

"Has she gotten help?"

"Many treatments. Many long and expensive
treatments. Some of them painful, some of them personally
demeaning. Nothing has penetrated the bottom of the
shadow. I think Sabreena's given up now. Too upsetting,
too traumatic. Or maybe she's too afraid of what she'll
see."

He knelt down, placed the roses in front of the
tombstone, cleared away a few petals left over from
yesterday's dozen.

"I remember everything about her, every moment of
her life. Everything she said. Those words. Daddy, this
movie is so *emotional*. Mommy, Daddy's being too
judgmental."

"I'm sorry."

He kept staring at the grave. "I walked the grounds
for weeks. Blazing sun. Rain storms. Drops dripping.

Fever. No hope, no light. This terrible...*tenderness*." A moment went by. "It was right around then... It was around that time, when I began to consider the possibilities of the past."

"The go-backs?"

"The beginnings of them. Around the same time, in the same place in my heart." He got to his feet. "I made a promise to myself. No more inherited mysteries. No more suffering. No more night, no more emptiness, no more shadow. No more silences that tell us nothing. I'd find a way to find an answer to every question."

"*Every* question?"

"*Every* question."

"Not to sound discouraging..."

"You can't discourage me."

"Aren't there questions that *have* no answers? Truths that can't be known?"

"They will be."

"Even the most fundamental soul-center questions?"

"The future, our *entire* future, depends on answers. It depends on solution, not confusion. The answers will be found. The future will be amazed."

"I don't know..."

He was getting impatient. "Do you have any questions more *directly* related to the go-backs? How about the book? How far did you get?"

Shit.

"You know, I was curious about Dr. Rajman's work with DNA. All that memory-transfer stuff?"

"It's all in the book." He waved his hand— *dismissed*. "I want to talk to you about something else. I want to talk about what you were talking about when you first came today."

"MIXEX?"

"The MIXEX program, and your friend..."

"Rj Delgado."

"I've been giving it some thought. I may have, if you'll pardon the expression, an *answer*."

"Which is?"

"Not here." He looked at the grave again. "Certainly not here."

From Arson To Ashes

The term *The Cenacle*, a derivative of the Latin word *cena*, means *dinner place*, though through centuries of Biblical use it's taken on another meaning—*The Upper Room*, the place where the Last Supper was held. Given his messianic impulses, maybe it's no surprise that Lukas chose the name for his private retreat. His version of the Cenacle was an elevated 15x15-foot cube whose walls and ceiling were made of glass. Like an extravagant tree house it perched 10 feet off the ground on steel beams, and once you took the winding stairs up, it gave you a panoramic view of the complex, the Long Island Sound and the sky above.

He came here, he said, to take his meditations. Or, in this case, to keep on talking.

"They say you're only as good as the people you work with. I believe that, I truly do. That's why I work alone. But it wasn't always so. In the beginning, when I started Zero-plus-ex, I hired a man named Trimshaw Dawson. Old money, old knowledge, old man. Bit of a crackpot, but he knew the security business. I made him my chief adviser, my Number Two, gave him access to all my code books. I believe he had something to do with your friend's death. Quite a *bit* to do with it, actually."

"He's *here*?"

"No longer, I'm afraid. We worked well together at the beginning, our thoughts rhymed and chimed. But dissensions developed over the years, friction over policy and strategy. He became quite combative, a real disruption among the other C-Suite executives. Too much shooting in the tent, as the saying goes. He became quite a thorn in my side."

Could've seen that one coming.

"One day Trimshaw announced his intention to retire. Couldn't take the alienating atmosphere any longer. Fine, good riddance. I had him sign a non-disclosure clause, a confidentiality clause, and a non-compete clause listing each and every company where he was barred from working. What I *didn't* do—and this was my oversight, I candidly admit it—I didn't include a provision for any *future* competing company. But that's what happened. A few months after he left, the old cow joined a consortium of investors and backers and formed his own security company. Cascadian."

Roots had mentioned the name. He freelanced for them too.

"So Trimshaw has gone from the bright lights of Zero-plus-ex to the flickering candles of Cascadian. But he still knows my secrets. He was one of the only people here with access to all my data, and confidentiality and non-disclosure be damned I know he's using it. The old misery is still a thorn in my side. Have some fruit."

A platter of Meissen china, with cherries, apricots, segments of pears and oranges surrounding the [0+X] logo, had been set out on the table, the Cenacle's only piece of furniture. Lukas took three cherries. I took an orange wedge and a [0+X] napkin. The orange was nice and juicy, but with just the *slightest* taste of turpentine.

"You probably don't know this," he said, "but we've been beset by problems here."

"I *do* know. The suicides."

"Those too, yes. But I'm referring to acts of intimidation and destruction—*non*-self-destruction. Zero-plus-ex and its employees are under attack."

He ticked the incidents off. At the current rate, his staffers were receiving two dozen threatening calls a week, both on their work and personal phones. In the last month, three bomb threats had been called into the company. During that same period, eight attempted but unsuccessful hacks had been recorded in the system, as well as three attempted but unsuccessful physical break-ins (not counting mine and Roots'). Of late, 17 workers had their tires

slashed at home, and 11 had their car or home windows
smashed. Two executives' houses had caught fire, arson
ruled in both cases. And the ashes of one executive's
mother had been stolen from a family's mausoleum.

He kept moving around, taking in the 360-view as
he went through the checklist. It struck me how much the
Cenacle resembled a 10-foot-high version of his daughter's
greenhouse.

"You think it's all Trimshaw Dawson?"

"He's a parasite, a dung-sucking termite queen. He
lied to me—he told me he was *retiring*, going to open a
winery or something, I don't exactly remember. The point
is he's a liar, and a liar, as far as I'm concerned, is capable
of anything."

"Yeah, but arson? Stealing ashes?"

"It's a chess match. He's trying to clear my board
and he's intensified his game. The arson and ashes were
two of his moves. So, I believe, was the MIXEX."

"You're serious."

"Always."

"Going on what?"

"I know that when my prototype disappeared,
people at Cascadian became very interested. Their chatter
reached cicada levels."

"How do you know?"

"Mr. McShane, please, I'm *in* the business."

"Right."

"Now as much as I can guess, I frankly don't know
how your friend...again?"

"Rj Delgado."

"The developer—yes, I know his work. I don't
know how Delgado came into possession of the MIXEX,
though we can assume he paid an outrageous price. What I
do know, based on what you told me, is this: Number One,
he lost the prototype after a night of carousal. Number two,
someone who found it called you. Number Three, your
friend said he'd handle the negotiations. Number Four
you know."

"They found his body."

"Let me suggest a scenario. Whoever found the prototype was not very discreet, and once the otherwise routine retrieval process was complete, he boasted about the money he'd made. Trimshaw's people heard about it and paid your friend a visit."

"And injected him with a designer drug?"

"To get his hands on a valuable piece of my software? To stop a project of mine in development? Trust me, he'd do worse."

"Thank God you're not biased."

"His actions have been a long source of trouble. Yes, I'm convinced—about 99.99999 percent convinced—he's conducting a concerted campaign against me. Even these deaths, these *suicides*, they could be part of a Cascadian conspiracy. What I'm telling you is this, instead of you and your friend Roots breaking my locks, I suggest you turn your attention to Cascadian."

"And you?"

"Let him keep the prototype. I'll build another. He can't hurt me. I'm protected against any further attacks. I've taken steps. The complex, the grounds, the building, everything is safe. No matter what he tries, no matter what he thinks he is, he's just like all the others."

"The others?"

"The rest of the people on earth."

CHAPTER 5

MAD LOVE

Shock Waves

We all know the Law of Don't-Say-It, right? A baseball announcer notes that a pitcher has a no-hitter going through the seventh, and you know the next batter up is going to knock a weak bloop single over the shortstop's head. The guy at the shop tells you your car will be running for years, and within a week you're calling for a tow truck. The doctor tells you your numbers are *fantastic*, and within a month you've been diagnosed with some horrible disease. Well, Lukas violated the Don't-Say-It Law when he said he was protected from any further attacks, everything was safe.

The next afternoon [0+X] was hit by a massive cyber blitz, an electric lash-out that invaded the entire complex and paralyzed its systems like a digital drop of curare. Lukas called it an unsophisticated effort, but acknowledged it was the most damaging and widespread attack the company had ever sustained.

Somehow, someone managed to disable the sensors that detect unusual levels of activity, a signal of an impending assault. Since no alerts were triggered, no one knew what was happening. First the network became sluggish and slow, then access was suddenly denied even if you were right in the middle of a task. Thousands of programs crashed at the same time, and moments later the company's entire infrastructure collapsed as its connections to the power grid were severed. Nothing was left but an alarming stillness, a terrible tranquil silence.

Early assessments suggested [0+X] had been the target of a *distributed denial of service* attack, a tactic using thousands of outside computers to mount a simultaneous offensive. Someone who'd discovered a weak link in the company's defenses—or someone who already knew about it—had infected tens of thousands of private computers, infiltrating them by tricking their users into downloading a virus that was nearly impossible to spot and pretty damn impossible to trace back. At a certain point that afternoon, servers in the U.S., Canada and Mexico directed the infected computers to launch a strike on [0+X], overwhelming the company's systems with a single, concentrated, tsunami-strong shock wave.

Once the network was up and running again, Lukas assured his employees that the incident was under review and that immediate steps would be taken to close the security hole.

>>>>>>

I heard about all this from Roots. No word of the blitz had reached any form of media, high, low or in between. So it was up to Roots to fill me in as LSD colors warped around his short, bony head.

It's ironic, I guess, that we were meeting in a place explicitly designed for security—a Romanesque castlelike structure with Gothic arches and round 200-foot-tall towers. We were in the Bedford-Atlantic Armory, on the border of Crown Heights and Bed-Stuy, a fortress built in 1889 so the 13th Regiment of Brooklyn could protect the wealthy from rioting by the indigenous poor and the growing immigrant population.

Ironic too, I guess, that many of the destitute were now living inside these walls. The Armory housed one of New York City's largest homeless shelters.

But community space could be rented out for special events. Like an installation by Roots' girlfriend, Janiva Escobar.

Erotically curved neon tubes sprawled throughout the space, hypnotizing the room with dreamlike wraparound patterns of jewel-colored light. Like the artwork on the top floor of [0+X], this was a biometric sculpture, using surveillance technology to translate the crowd's heartbeat, breathing, voice and movement into images that shifted from voluptuous, sensual, fleshy, vaginal, and phallic to the psychedelic hydrogen swirls of Jupiter's cloud belts.

A well-attended affair. Couple hundred people on hand, 99.99999% of all sexes wearing Jordan Rare Airs, Dior blazers and untucked vintage shirts. Is it just a coincidence that untucked shirts became popular just as national obesity rates began climbing?

Typical artshow chatter, spoken over stompbox-driven dance music:

Where's his head at?

Up his ass as usual.

What's CINAMMON made out of? It's made out of CINAMMON.

If we're having sex tonight, I've gotta adjust my insulin dose.

Robbo Fragaruccio, the night trader I'd met in Red Hook, was standing nearby, telling someone else about someone else getting beaten up and charged for drug dealing.

Roots had said he needed a quim, a quick meeting, with me, so I subwayed out here.

"Lukas wants to see me," he said.

"Why?"

"Can't cipher it out. I got the feeling something happened during the attack, some kind of serious damage was done."

"You couldn't message me this?"

"See, he wants to see you too."

"What did I do?"

"It's what he said."

"When?"

"Right now." He looked up, saw Janiva coming over. "Soon as I break the news."

Janiva still had that dyed headband bluing across her black hair. I still hadn't gotten used to her good looks. Roots reintroduced us. I said I liked her work. She thanked me.

"What I was wondering," she explained, "if you looked at the future with magic eyes, what would you see? I was going for a dynamic, mercurial arena, where you'd never know what to expect. I think of this as realism in advance of reality."

"I gotta go," said Roots.

"You *what*?"

"I've gotta leave."

"Now? You *can't*."

"It's *work*."

For some reason, Janiva made her appeal to me. "I'm sick of him doing this. I'm sick of night trading. I want him to quit. I want him to work with me. Look at that." She pointed to a corner of the installation. "You see the fringing field? The interface instability? He could've *fixed* that for me."

They began arguing about saturation voltage and surface charge and macroscopic fiber-optic contact angles, and somehow their shouting match turned into a snarl-fest about their love life, Janiva saying sex with him was the wildest 12 seconds she'd ever known, Roots saying maybe she'd appreciate it more if she wasn't playing phone Scrabble when he was going down on her. Echoes of their Canal Street combat were ringing through the room.

"I love you madly, despite," she said. "Do you love me as madly as I love you?"

"I guess."

"Fuck *you*. Why am I wasting my thoughts on a sorrow like *you?*"

Off she walked.

He was free to go.

But for a moment after she left, he seemed completely at a loss.

>>>>>>

Vibrational Frequencies

We were in Lukas' office, but not in his office. We were in a small room off the office, a plain room, plain table, plain chairs, plain windowless walls. Utterly gothless, baroqueless or anything elseless. He called it the war room. Because this was war.

"Of course it was Trimshaw. Who *else*? Who else but that vile, crafty, mothbally old man? He was never ready for what I wanted. Or he was *pre*-ready at best."

His dead-dog frock coat was scrunched with tired creases, like he'd been trying to sleep in it. His face looked like someone was already shoveling dirt on it.

"All our data was highly compartmentalized to keep it from leaking out. But I gave him full access to it. I gave this cretin, this scumbagado full open-code-book access. He's the only one who could've walked this walk."

"But why now?" I said. "He's hated you all this time, why blitz you now?"

"Because of the go-back. No doubt about that."

"How do you know?"

Lukas nodded and kept on nodding, brooding in silence. Roots and I decided best not to interrupt him.

"The real purpose of the attack, I believe," he finally said, "was extrication. Something was missing when it was over. My copy of the PIB. You know what it is—tell him."

I explained to Roots that the PIB was the Pangenetic Illumination Beam, the software created by Dr. Vivek Rajman to take a holographic snapshot of an individual's quantum-DNA memory. The PIB was what made the go-back go. It provided a form of spacetime tagging to keep track of an individual's unique vibrational frequencies. The PIB was to the go-back what St. Joseph statutes were to real estate agents.

"I need some of your night trading," Lukas said to Roots. "I'm contracting you to get it back from Cascadian."

"Do you care how?"

"I leave that to your discretion."

"Why'd you want me here?" I said.

"I told you to look at Cascadian for the MIXEX and your friend's death. Here's your chance. Go in on my dime—or on my ruby. Tell Trimshaw you don't like it when people murder your friends."

"You might be right about Cascadian," said Roots. "There's a rumor going around—it's very loose, very unsourced..."

"But."

"Cascadian supposedly has a contract out on you."

"For my life?"

"For your life."

"For how much?"

"A million."

Lukas laughed. "It's not true."

"How do you know?"

"The price is *much* too low."

We were just coming out of the building, on our way to the visitors' parking lot, when we saw some pale, sleepless, fallen angel standing in the dark.

"Shit," said Roots.

It was the missus, Sabreena Lister-Bertozzi. She was reading an iPad, looking very disturbed, like she was trying to keep a shriek trapped in her throat.

She noticed us. "Look at this."

Roots glanced away and kept walking. "I'm getting the car."

"What's wrong?"

"She's a ghost. Which scares the shit out of me because I don't believe in ghosts."

Sabreena handed me the iPad as she watched Roots leave. "Please, look."

She had a news story up about a midwife in Ohio who'd been arrested for murdering six of her own newborn children. Workers digging up her neighbor's property had come across a plastic bag containing the bones of an infant. After obtaining a warrant, Geauga County police began searching the woman's yard. Five more bags holding the remains of newborn children were found. All had been smothered at birth.

Ohio's worst case of infanticide had left the woman's friends, neighbors and former clients in shock. Because of her overweight condition, none of them apparently knew she was pregnant. And none ever suspected she was capable of such alleged crimes. Neighbors described her as "friendly" and "community-minded," though occasionally "a little secretive." Former clients called her a "gifted and caring" midwife who was known for her comforting and compassionate manner. "She helped with my son's birth," said one. "She had tears in her eyes when he was born."

"How could this happen?" Sabreena said in a soft voice. "I don't know what to do about it."

"Not much you can do, outside of pray."

"It gets me right here." She placed a hand on her throat. "I can feel it squeezing right here."

"Are you all right?"

"I don't know."

"Breathe."

"I am breathing."

"Can you take a deep breath?"

She gave this a great deal of thought, as if I'd asked if she knew when Ohio was admitted to the union.

"Lukas is upset, isn't he?" she said.

"Over...?"

"What happened today. The blackout, the attack."

"He is."

"I think he lost something, didn't he? When it happened. I think he lost something, and he wants Roots to get it back. That's why you're here."

"I can't really say."

"What's your name?"

"Quinn. Quinn McShane. I work for *Real Story*."

"I used to read that. May I show you something, Quinn? It's right over here. I think you might be interested."

It was another small greenhouse, around the corner of the building. Who's buried here? But this one was filled with glowing white flowers whose huge petals were in full nighttime bloom.

"Moonflowers," Sabreena said sadly, almost like she was in mourning. "They begin to open when the sun goes down."

"They're really something."

"Very difficult to grow up here, especially in the cold. They're more native to the south."

"You're doing some job."

"Let me guess. Lukas lost the PIB, didn't he?"

Took *me* by surprise. "You know what that is?"

"Of course I know. I know all about PIB. I remember when he stole it from Dr. Rajman."

"He stole it?"

"That's why he's so upset. He can't get another copy."

I decided I didn't believe her. Too crazy.

"You don't believe me, do you? But I have proof. These flowers. Moonflowers wouldn't grow like this if I were lying."

A horn honked. Roots' 1959 Chrysler Imperial was waiting at the edge of the parking lot.

"Well, he *is* upset. Very upset. That's all I can say."

"That's the thing about Lukas," she said. "There are times, every once in a while, you could almost think he was human."

>>>>>>

Going Greene

The chopper pilot must've gotten lost in some *Top Gun-Dawn Patrol* fantasy. He was wearing a leather bomber jacket, Ray-Bans and a white silk scarf around his neck. Bit much, yes, but the man knew how to fly. It took him less than 45 minutes to haul us over Greene County in upstate New York, saving us two hours of drive time.

"That's it," Roots said through his headset, raising his voice above the whirlybird noise. "Salami City." He was pointing somewhere below the blue sky.

"Salami City?"

"Salamanacki. They call it Salami City."

Pushing against the safety harness, I could see a small checkerboard of houses and streets. Only one large, spreading building in the area—had to be the Salamanacki Correctional Facility.

The Eurocopter TwinStar swung to the east, moving closer to Route 87. Twenty seconds later we were flying over a desert of asphalt parking lots and maybe 10 million square feet of warehouses.

"Before the economy went south," said Roots, "everybody thought the trucking industry was headed for gold. They had better supply chains, better warehouse designs, better inventory tracking. So developers came up here, found all this cheap land near the Thruway. Half those warehouses? They're empty now. Cascadian got a good deal on theirs."

We were circling over one of the few complexes with a filled parking lot. Roots rummaged under his seat, came up with something that looked like a camcorder. A Leica tactical scope. I knew the make. Comes with multi-prism-focus and resolution-tightening software. A blurry image of an apartment building, for example, will turn into a clear, sharp, there's-the-guy-in-the-window image of an apartment building. The Leica's only drawback is that it works best with geometric structures. A blurry image of a rock formation, for example, will come out looking like an apartment building.

"I don't see it," said Roots.

"See what?"

"An outbuilding. I've noticed it a few times I've been up here. Can you get us closer?"

The pilot nodded and pulled down on the collective—the control stick at his side—while adjusting the twist-grip throttle control at the end of the stick and using the cyclic lever on the floor in front of him to change the pitch of the twin engines.

Down we went. Gravity tugged on my face.

"You all right?" said Roots.

"Not used to the express."

"It'll be fine. We'll all be fine. Like my father used to say, doesn't matter where you go as long as you get back home. Course he ended up committing suicide, so take it with a grain."

He looked through the Leica again. "Got it. It's a storage shed, right next to one of the doors to the main building."

I took the scope and saw what he was talking about. "What's inside?"

"Don't know, doesn't matter. We'll use the shed for a diversion. Set it on fire, get them to open the main door."

I took another look at the layout. All I could see was the shed, the building and nothing else around. "Where we gonna hide?"

"In the shed."

"But the shed'll be on *fire*."

"I know," he said. "*Exactly.*"

>>>>>>>

Hot-Wired

The stuff had the color and consistency of refried beans. Ice *cold* refried beans. It was a fire-retardant gel, a polyphosphozene blend, according to Roots, similar to the protection stunt actors use when running through flames.

"She's sitting there at the table," Roots said as we stood in the dark brush near the Cascadian warehouse. "She's having her coffee, eating her Cheerios. Nothing's wrong. Suddenly she says, *I hate you and I'm leaving.*" He was talking, of course, about Janiva. "This is the kind of shit, the kind of B.S. Eliot I get all the time. I know, I know, we gotta find a way to find a way. But believe me, we're not *finding* a way."

We were smearing the goop all over ourselves, every square inch of our clothes, skin and hair as the Thruway hummed in the distance. The gel chilled the flesh—I felt like I was layering my head in hands in ThermaFreeze packs. Which somehow made the whole idea seem even *more* insane. But no no no, he'd said, that was the *point*. It was an off-the-hook plan, totally unexpected. Who's gonna be looking for people standing in the middle of a fire? It was the perfect cover.

"She wants me to work with her? Fuck *that*," he said as he coated the back of his pants legs. "Not exactly a happy situation, not what you'd call *fiestal*. She doesn't like what I do? Well I'm doing what I'm doing. I *like* what I do!"

"Watch what you're doing." I pointed to the spots he was missing on his right calf.

"I got it, I got it."

"She really plays Scrabble in the middle?"

"While she's listening to her *iPod*. It's official—you know that. It's been officially designated the worst sex in the history of the world. And she thinks *I'm* the one who needs help? She projects *I'm* the one who needs therapy?"

Sorry, gals, he's taken. Sort of.

The storage shed was a 20 x 50-foot corrugated steel structure with a front entrance big enough for forklifts and a small side emergency door. We headed for the side door, couple of mud men under a cloud-blurred moon. Roots took a handheld out of his backpack, the same one he'd used on [0+X]'s ED8 entrance. Better luck this time.

Inside was filled with cartons. His ultraviolet flashlight picked out the labels: All from Staples. Office supplies, non-critical material okay to store outside the main building.

He began circling the interior, dropping magnesium packs at the base of the plasterboard walls. No liquid fuss 'n muss for the modern-day arsonist.

"In the chopper," I said, "you were talking about your father."

"Doesn't matter where you go?"

"No, the other thing."

"Yeah, shot himself in the car. I found the body. Came home from school one day, gonna meet my friends. Went into the garage, gonna hot-wire the car as usual. There he is in the front seat. First I thought he was waiting to bust me, only he'd fallen asleep. Then I saw the blood..."

"You know, changed my mind. Maybe we shouldn't be talking about this right now."

We stood by a window with a view of the warehouse door 200 feet away. Roots took out a laser ignition wand. He was stylin'. "Ready?"

The air seemed to go stiff for a moment, then silvery-white magnesium flashes exploded all around us. It was like the entire world was filled with paparazzi. The gel was still cold but the heat was magnifying by the second. We held still, waiting, everything overexposed like the ghost images of dilated eyes. We stood there turning well-done, condemning ourselves to burn at the stake.

Finally, alarms from the warehouse. The wild quicksilver sound of circuits rapidly switching on and off. A security crew broke out of the door and charged for the shed. Skull-shaved kneeheads, armed with fire axes, extinguisher tanks and shoulder holsters.

Now.

We ran through the burning door, right through the middle of white moonflower flames.

Shit worked. The shit *worked*. We were uncooked, unscorched, untouched. We'd walked through fire like pair of swamis.

Or not quite.

I was close to the open warehouse door when Roots screamed. He was 15 feet behind me, going limp, his right calf blazing with fire. A tongue of flame was jumping from his leg like an upside-down Pentecost.

From a spot he'd missed when he was bitchin' and moanin'.

I *told* him.

He tried to keep moving but he was losing too much to the pain. His leg buckled and he went down.

One of the security kneeheads suddenly turned away from the burning shed, drawn by the scream. You could see the wolf-tension grabbing him as he spotted the intruder thrashing on the ground. Probably following Cascadian protocol, he drew from his holster and leveled his gun to take a shot.

Dow futures down by 200.

I pulled my Glock and locked on his body. Bits of blood splattered from his chest. He slowly lowered himself down, kneeling like he'd just passed an altar, but once his knees touched the pavement he just kept sinking until he was flat on the ground.

I ran over to Roots, took him by his arms and began dragging him to the warehouse door.

"Are you all right?" he said.

"Fine."

"What about me? Am I all right?"

I think I would've given him a fairly frank assessment of the situation, but I was rudely interrupted by gunfire blasting all around us. The night filled up with shouts and cries, voices pitched over the fire alarms. The bullets were kicking up so much cement dust it looked like it was snowing.

I couldn't see, but I could feel hands yanking at me, snatching my gun away, pinning my arms to my sides while Roots kept yelling, "Am I all right? Am I all right?"

Pruning The Plants

Trimshaw Dawson wasn't anything at all like Lukas Lister-Bertozzi. He was a blue-eyed old man with wispy white hair, suspender-gripped shorts, skinny white legs bottomed-off by red knee-length socks. An amiable slice of aged beef, the kind of geezer who blissfully tells you, though you sure don't want to hear it, that his assisted-living facility is a sexual playground.

"Hard for me to be happy about this," he said. "You come here, you burn down my property, you kill one of my people. It all makes me wonder, Roots. What kind of asshole are you?"

"What're the choices again?"

Roots was feeling a little better now that he'd slapped one of his pain patches on his calf and morphine was leaking through his system. A little better and a little cleaner. The kneeheads had hosed the gel off our faces and hands before hauling us into Trimshaw's office.

Which wasn't anything at all like Lukas' Edgar Allan Poe of an office. Scrubbed, functional, as antiseptic as a mall. Walls a lava of clayish green. No ASSETS running around here, no robotics of any kind. No decorations, either, outside of a huge photo of two spiral galaxies crashing into each other. It was a blow-up of an image taken with NASA telescopes, showing an explosive, tidal-wave intergalactic collision that had been going on for over 100 million years.

"I can't tell you how disappointed I am," said Trimshaw. "I could almost think you don't like me anymore."

"Nothing personal," said Roots. "And that guy who got killed? He was trying to kill me."

"Oh I'm sure, I'm sure, I understand. And I understand how much you cherish your privacy, but I still have to ask. Why are you *here*?"

Roots shrugged. "Just slumming."

"No, the circumstances are too grave for that. I'll tell you, I smell Lukas' hand in this. The whole thing has a ruthlessly obnoxious stink to it."

"No, no Lukas. This is purely on spec."

"You're a young man, Roots. You're young, you're stupid. I'm an old man. Most of my friends aren't on earth anymore, they're under it. I can't pick my nose without throwing my elbow out. At my age I put a *critical* value on truth. I'm sure you're capable of telling me the truth, though you might be out of practice. You're looking for the PIB."

"We're looking for the PIB."

"Of course you are. And of course I have it. How did you like our attack? Impressive piece of action, wasn't it?"

My turn. "Why'd you take it?"

"Simple—to hurt Lukas. To shatter him. Roots here can tell you the history. I took it to demolish that ambitious nonsense of his, his blow-backs, whatever they're called."

"Planning to use it?"

Trimshaw laughed at me. "I'm doing it strictly for destruction. PIB has no practical meaning for me. I'm not trying to recreate the past. I use left-nostril breathing when I want to improve my memory."

"And the MIXEX? Did you take that too?"

"MIXEX. That group-think, mind-meld thing? I have no interest in that particular piece of witchcraft."

"I'm just asking if you took it."

"Ask all you want. Is Lukas saying I have that too? Predictably delusional."

Trimshaw stood up—or stooped up. His spine was frozen at an angle, like he was eternally searching for something on the ground. He shuffled over to the remains of a half-eaten sandwich on the counter. A prune sandwich.

Strained prunes, whipped cream and chopped walnuts between two pieces of bread.

"A friend of ours was killed over the MIXEX," I said. "Rj Delgado, a developer."

"Sorry to hear it."

"Know anything about it?"

He spun around as best he could. "You're suggesting I sacrificed a life, I had an innocent developer killed, just to get back at Lukas?"

"I already know the history. I know you fought some bitter battles. If you hate him enough, why not?"

"We *did* fight bitter battles, yes. Do you know why?"

"Policy differences?"

"*Policy* differences—certainly. Policy differences over the value of human *life*. Policy differences over the *suicides*. Policy differences over the way he pushed and tormented people with his astonishing doses of self-programmed paranoia. I know people suffering through leukemia pain, chemo sickness, three months to live, and you know what they say? *At least I'm not working for Lukas anymore.*"

He left the sandwich and came back to us.

"You know the history? Then you know I was there at the beginning, when the company was a bungled, sloppy, amateurish mess. But that was okay. I believed in Lukas—I was a fan. Eventually I defanned myself. One of the first people to take his life was a man named Felix Pina. He shot himself but didn't die right away. Lukas and I went to see him in the hospital. After we stood at the bedside for no more than a minute, do you know what Lukas said to me? *I'm bored.* Hard to believe we share DNA with that man."

"He's not a smiling guy," I said, "that's for sure."

"Do you know the story of Lu Xun, one of China's greatest writers? He committed a terrible act of treason in 1903, when he was a student. He shaved off his queue, the ponytail Chinese men wore as a symbol of submission to the emperor. That's what I did when I left the company. After years of begging him to show some consideration, some *compassion*, after years of submitting to whatever demons he has raging inside his head, I had enough. I shaved my head—I walked away."

"But you *do* hate him."

"Without question. Shame he isn't sitting here instead of you two. He should be paying the price, not you."

Roots shook himself out of a morphine dream. "The price?"

"What did you expect? You came here on Lukas' behalf, you burned down my shed, you took a life. I can't let Lukas get away with that. The circumstances, as I said, are *grave*."

Fucking incredible.

"You want compassion for the suicides," I said, "but you'll kill us?"

Trimshaw held up his hands—what can I do? "It's just business. All's fair in love and marketing."

"How about we make a deal?" said Roots.

"I'm not interested in your rubies."

"I mean a *trade*. A deal as in a *trade*."

"For?"

"Something of Lukas'."

"*What* of Lukas'?"

"A copy of his all-function analyzer. One of their new projects. You know about it?"

"I've heard some talk."

"Any bug that's planted in an office, it'll pick up on it. It'll sense voltage, capacitance, nonlinear junctions, digital demodulations, frequency—"

"I get it."

"*Then* it links all that data to a GPS tracker, so you know exactly where it is. And *then* it does an analysis of the components—the semiconductors, the transistors, the diodes—crosses that with manufacturing, wholesale and retail databases and tells you exactly who bought the bug and when. It's very advanced, it's the prog of the prog. And it's something you can actually use."

Was this just the pain patch talking? Trimshaw didn't think so. Something was suddenly shifting in his

head. His mind's eye was gazing at a giant invisible
prune sandwich.

"How did you—"

"Don't ask."

"Of course."

"That's the deal. The analyzer for the PIB. And
we live."

The old man weighed the options. "That *would* be a
windfall, no denying that."

"Give you lots of competitive edge."

"And as I said, In have no use for the PIB. I'm not
planning any time-transgressive enterprises. I'm not trying
to make a YouTube of the universe. We might have a
deal."

"You'll let us slide," I said, "on the guy I shot?"

"I'll write it off." Back to Roots. "I have to know if
I can trust you. How soon can you get it?"

"You don't understand. I *have* it."

"Where?"

"Here."

"Here?"

He stood up, unzipped his pants, pushed them down
to his ankles and did the same with his underwear. "Here."

Trimshaw sighed. "I'll get a pair of rubber gloves."

You have to hand it to Roots, so to speak. He'd
come here with a back-up plan. Literally.

>>>>>>

8573304064...

I'm not saying *Interzone Quantum Time Differentials6B* is impossible to read, but it's damn close to it. I couldn't get through more than two pages without mumbling out loud. *The absence of overlapping probability waves in classic double-slit-with-tagging experiments has been called into question, I believe, by the new redaction technology—and, consequently, by the interstitial interference tranches— demonstrated by the recent variation of quantum-erasure endeavors. This is a subject that deserves to be examined at length, and I shall of course do so in a moment. But I find it difficult to resist a brief sidebar comment on the ridiculous, occasionally inane, speculation about the primary frame-of-reference measurement originally used by Scully. A few quick calculations will show that the number, far from being a mystery, is precisely 8573304064322228500135722999997667000001313747566698035555555448306111164444444445181818096557 00200100000066366289012348765000146918341949194 9666661212.*

   With the PIB back in Lukas' hands—and freshly burned, you might say, in my mind—I thought I'd see what *Interzone* had to say about the topic. I was disappointed. Checked the index, did a word search— there were no references to the Pangenetic Illumination Beam or its abbreviation. And there was only one small ref to Dr. Vivek Rajman.

   While the thornier aspects of probalistic decoherence remain a source of contention, I should mention in this regard the DNA-imaging researches done by the quantum biologist Rajman. His work, while in a vastly different field, is not dissimilar to the rectilinear associative theories of Erikson, a man whose Promethean labors and purity of style still failed to prevent him from taking refuge in unsatisfactory conclusions.

That's it. One passing mention in the rush of thoughts, one piss-quick drop in an ocean of words. A curious lapse for someone given to explaining things, re-explaining them, explaining them in new ways, explaining why he's explaining in new ways and overexplaining in general by a factor of 80.

It made me wonder about what his wife told me. He was throwing shit-fits, she'd said, because he'd stolen the PIB and couldn't get another copy. I thought she was wack but I could've been wrong. Wouldn't be the first time. *I have proof,* Sabreena had said. *Moonflowers wouldn't grow like this if I were lying.*

HOW MANY ZERO-PLUS-EXERS DOES IT TAKE TO CHANGE A LIGHT BULB?

Lukas wanted to see me. Urgent. Huge news. *Immediately.* Only once I got out there, one of the ASSETS informed me that Mr. Lister-Bertozzi wouldn't be available for another 45 minutes. He'd been regrettably delayed. All apologies, etc. Would I care to relax in a waiting room? Not for 45 minutes I wouldn't.

Nice day on the grounds—the first day, really, it felt like spring. The air? Like they were pumping it in straight from heaven. Now *this* is weather.

I saw them in a field, just beyond a line of red pines—a dozen or so workers gathered in a semicircle around the chaplain with the long prematurely white hair. Belinda Halestre. They were all sitting on the grass, the workers sad and lost and ashen-eyed, some with their heads lowered between their knees. It was a kind of outdoor quiet room, the chaplain telling them what to do to save their own lives.

"The Bible isn't a collection of dry historical facts," she was saying, "like Wichita was founded in 1863. It's not a textbook—it's poetry. It's meant to *move* you, it's meant to inspire you. You breathe it and take it into your heart.'

I listened, I watched. I watched her. I'd be lying if I said I hadn't thought about Belinda Halestre since the day she told me to fuck off. There was something about her I couldn't describe, some element distilled from water, forests, voices, laughter, horizons.

"We spend all our time trying to know what we don't know. That's what the Buddha said. Instead we should be trying to know what we already know, only we don't know that we know it. We know it, but we've forgotten."

In her own way—the lustrous hair, the trace of lines on her face—she was crazy beautiful.

"If we want to be sure of the road we're on, we have to close our eyes and walk in the dark."

Leave them alone. Get away from here. Close your eyes—no, *don't*—and just walk away.

I was passing back through the pines when someone stepped out from behind a tree. A gritty bag of bones with a caved-in face. Ah yes, Cito Spangler, the lawn-bowler who favored Loveless drop-point knives. He looked sick and soul-shot, like he was ready to announce the end of the world.

"I can't kill you," I said.

"I know. I know I can't count on you for that."

"I just killed somebody. I met my quota for the week."

Cito shook his head. "That's the kind of luck I have."

"Things're still bad?"

"I need to talk to her." He motioned to the chaplain. "Why don't you go over?"

"I can't sit through that. I gotta talk to somebody."

"So? I got ears."

"I already *told* you. This *place*—this mother-suffering *place*. The way everything gets *curdled* around here. Everything gets *congealed* and *diseased*. There's a joke going around. How many Zero-plus-exers does it take to change a light bulb?"

"How many?"

"Just one. And then he hangs himself from the ceiling when he's done."

"That's a *joke*?"

"Around here it is." He moved closer. "You know what it is, nobody *talks* around here anymore. There's no chatter, no everyday back and forth. You say, how're you? Everybody thinks, why's he asking? Who wants to know? Is he spying for the company? Is he spying for *another* company? Everything is suspect. Even in the *bathrooms* there's no talk anymore. No wall talk in the men's, no stall talk in the women's. There's no safe place anymore, and me, I myself? I can't *take* it anymore."

"You sure you don't want to go over there?"

"Will you *talk* to me?"

"Well, you've got a choice. That's what it comes down to. You can scratch your ass all day and complain about the itch, or you can go take a shower."

"What if I take the shower?"

I gave it a shot. You have to learn how to trust your mind, I said, but the *whole* mind, not just your ego. You identify the whole mind with the ego, it's like a swimmer thinking he's the *entire* ocean. Sooner or later, man you're gonna *sink*. But if you can move off the ego, stop identifying with that little flicker of consciousness, riding the waves gets a whole lot easier.

"You want proof there's more to the mind than the ego? *Sleep*."

"Sleep?"

"If the ego is all there is to the mind, then what happens when you go to sleep? Where the hell does that little bit of consciousness go every night? Think about it."

"Are you saying that life isn't as bad as it really is?"

"I...yeah, that's what I'm saying."

"What did I *tell* you?"

A woman's voice. Evangelical anger. Hello chaplain.

Wrong to say she was walking over to us. She was *charging* over to us.

"I told you to stay away from him," she said. "I told you to leave these people alone."

"I was just trying to help."

"He's doing me some good," said Cito. "Not much, but some."

Belinda Halestre was less than convinced. "How can you *possibly* help?"

"I've worked a lot of AA hotlines. Did the same in the Dharma Prison Program."

"Let me ask, what're you doing here today? Did you come here to help these people?"

"I'm supposed to see Lukas."

"I rest my case. You're corrupted. Cito, let's go talk. *You*, go take a flying shit."

There's nothing sexier than a woman who knows exactly who she is.

I could fall madly in love.

Saving Soles

Lukas was just about giddy with excitement. His dizzy,
delirious vibes were making the dark shadows of his office
seem positively sunny and bright. "So sorry to keep you,"
he said, rushing his words. "I had to make sure of what I
had." Was he talking about getting the PIB back? No,
something else had turned Universe Lukas into a happy,
happy place.

"You're okay, right?"

"I'm not unwell. I'm not unwell at all, and I'll tell
you why. I'll be brief. Brevity is a passion of mine, it's
terribly important. I could talk about it for hours."

"What's going on?"

"I've just concluded negotiations with a woman
named Roberta Porter. I suppose you don't know who
she is."

"Right."

"She's a niece of Marina Oswald Porter, Lee
Harvey Oswald's widow. Remember we were talking about
him?"

"Like I'd forget."

"She's giving me access to his shoes. His *famous*
shoes, the ones he wore on the cover of *Life* magazine after
he killed JFK. I just found out—we can get enough of a
genetic sample from the sweat stains in the lining."

"I didn't know you were working on that."

"No one ever knows what I'm working on—that's
part of success' secret. But you see what it means—
obviously. Tell your people to get ready. We're creating
another go-back. We're making another trip to the hidden
library. And this one, I promise you, you won't be able to

get it out of your head."
Right, like a tumor.

Questions And Answers

I made my calls to *Real Story*—everyone was duly
ecstatic—and was heading for the parking lot when I saw
her waiting. White hair, eyes the color of a Moroccan sky, a
midsummer night's dream in early spring.

"Paranoia is rampant around here," she said, "and
I'm afraid it's rubbed off on me. I owe you an apology. I
talked with Cito. I realize you weren't trying to poison his
mind."

"Be hard to make it any more toxic."

"I know. This place isn't exactly the New
Jerusalem. I don't trust Lukas, and I tend not to trust
anyone or thing connected to him."

"He's that bad, isn't he?"

"No, *worse*."

"Then why did he hire you? Make it look like he's
trying?"

"He didn't hire me. His wife did. She insisted."

Did I want to see what Lukas' idea of therapy was?
We sat on a bench, she showed me a questionnaire the
company had been handing out before she got here.

How would you describe your workplace?
_Wonderful
_Frequently rewarding
_Adequate
_I suppose it could be better

How would you describe your co-workers?
_Best friends
_Chummy
_Like everyone else

_Don't know any

If you saw co-workers behaving strangely, would you
_Report them to a superior
_Report them to a superior and all members of management
_Ignore them
_Tell them to stop

If a co-worker says he/she is depressed, that means he/she is
_Not happy
_Tired
_Mistaken
_Hallucinating

How would you describe your homelife?
_Warm and fulfilling
_Necessary for balance
_Not sure
_Does not apply

If the workplace could be improved, would you want
_More training courses
_More overtime
_More choices in the cafeteria
_Parades

How often do you think about death?
_Hardly ever
_Occasionally
_All the time
_Death does not exist

Pretty stunning.
"I'd almost say he wrote this himself, except it's comprehensible."

"I think it explains a lot about the company," said Belinda. "Death comes in three's? How about thirty's?"

She'd just been reading a study about how emotional reactions travel among groups of people, comparing them to the spread of SARS, foot-and-mouth disease and other contagious illnesses. According to the research, happiness follows the same cluster-patterns as the diseases, infecting roughly the same number of people. For sadness, though, the contagion rates were much higher. The cluster-patterns were off the charts. Nothing, not even disease, is an infectious as sadness.

"You can see it happening here," she said. "The more some people walk around in despair, the more other people do the same until despair becomes a core response. The more some people commit suicide, the more other people do the same until they all become fugitives from God."

"There's sure no shortage of victims around here."

"Not only does it get worse and worse, it gets *different*. The last two cases we had? They were overdoses on a drug I've never even *heard* of. Cathidrone. Some designer drug I know nothing about."

"I do. Do you know where they got it?"

"I have enough to do without turning narc."

She asked me how I know about cathidrone. I told her I'd lost a friend to it, which somehow lead to me telling her about my own drug use, about killing the junkie, about the manslaughter break, getting sober and zenned in prison.

"I try to use some Buddhism here," she said. "It's an effective way to reach people, help them quickly find meaning."

"Well, sure. Thing is, with zen, the more you try to find meaning, the less meaning there is."

Well, yes, she said, she knew that. She knew what I meant. If we could comprehend all the mysteries of God, probably no one would ever believe. But she thought zen was good for grasping the darkness of life, because wandering in the dark was a good way to learn about God.

Right, I said, but is it really *learning*? Per se?
Isn't life too crazy to be understood? Isn't that the
beginning of wisdom?

She got a little defensive. The real work of life, she
said, is to grow spiritually, and zen can give you the high
perspective.

But also a low perspective.

It's insanely idealistic.

And totally down to earth.

"It's an eye on heaven," she said, getting ticked off.

"It's two people talking."

"It's a prayer to the universe."

"It's a mother nursing a child."

"It's beyond the beyond."

A beat.

"You realize we're fighting about zen?" I said.
"We're saying the same thing, but we're fighting."

She analyzed the situation.

"I don't like you," she said. "I can't *stand* you."

A second later she was leaning across the bench and
kissing me on the mouth.

My erection was instant and without shame.

I don't know how women sense these things—I
mean her eyes were *closed*—but she knew I could hear a
bell ringing in my balls. She pushed away.

"We're not going there," she said.

"Okay."

"You're cute, except you're not."

"Whatever you say."

"If I ever want to go there, I'll send you a signal."

"Make it a strong one. I'm getting older, I miss a lot
of shit."

Not saying another word she got up and walked
away, a white-hair sway in the honeyed light.

The spirit of Puck was somewhere in the air.
And those things do best please me
That befall preposterously.

>>>>>>>>>>>>>>>>>>>>>>>>>>>

CHAPTER 6

I KNOW WHO YOU KNOW

War Is Hell

Actually, I'm surprised the Lee Harvey Oswald go-back didn't get more attention. Apparently there was a family of five in the Appalachians who knew nothing about it. But for the rest of America, and much of the world, Oswald's reconstructed memories were as interesting as the whiff of blood to a vampire. The total audience who saw the feed was large enough to demand its own seat at the United Nations.

With the PIB kept under heavy security, Lukas and the people working in the Gengo lab prepped for the go-back by first isolating the events of November 22, 1963.

It was all there:

•Oswald arrives at work at the Texas Book Depository. He's carrying a long paper bag that he says contains curtain rods.

•Taking his lunch break at noon, he brings the bag up to the empty sixth floor of the building, overlooking Dealey plaza. He removes and checks a 6.5 mm caliber Carcano rifle. Crowd sounds build in the plaza below as people gather for the presidential motorcade.

•At 12:30, as the noise swells and sirens are heard, Oswald stiffens into a marksman's stance, looks through the scope and fires three rapid shots. He quickly drops the rifle behind a stack of boxes and runs down the rear stairwell.

•On the street, sounds of emergency panic all around him, he catches a bus, but traffic is suddenly snarled by police cars and ambulances and progress is too slow. Getting nervous, Oswald gets off and takes a cab to his rooming house.

•He puts on a jacket, conceals a Smith and Wesson .38 revolver in his waistband and hits the street again. As he's waiting at another bus stop, a police car pulls up. The cop asks who he is, what he's doing out here. Oswald says he's minding his own business. As the cop gets out of the car, Oswald pulls the .38 and fires three times into his chest, then walks over and fires a fatal shot in his head.

•Fleeing the scene, Oswald ducks into the entrance of a shoe store as other police cars rush by, then slips into a movie theater, walking right past the ticket seller's booth and taking a seat in the back. Audie Murphy's voice can be heard as Oswald watches *War Is Hell* for a few minutes until the house lights come up. Police have entered the theater, and after a small scuffle they put Oswald under arrest.

•Taken to Dallas Police headquarters, he's questioned about the killing of Officer J.D. Trippet. As the afternoon goes on, he's also asked about President Kennedy. Don't you work at the Book Depository? Why did you leave the building? Where were you at the time at the shooting? By the end of the day he's been charged and arraigned on both murders.

•The next day, Saturday, passes in a nebula of eating, sleeping, interrogations, perp walks past the press. Oswald yells to reporters that he isn't being given a lawyer, yet each time he's offered legal help he refuses.

•The following morning he's taken to the basement, where he'll be transported to the county jail. With his hands cuffed in front of him, he's led out by an escort of Stetson-hatted detectives into a crowd of bystanders, reporters and network news cameras broadcasting live. Just as he passes through the door, a man in a fedora and a dark overcoat steps forward. Oswald notices the movement, looks at the man and seems to recognize him, but glances away just as the man raises a snub-nosed Colt Cobra .38 and, crouching, fires a point-blank shot into Oswald's abdomen. Slow, confused fade to black. Ninety minutes later, Oswald will be declared dead

at Parkland Memorial Hospital, the same place where
Kennedy was pronounced two days earlier.

It was a fascinating thing to watch, creepily
hypnotic, like watching a tragic documentary you've seen
many times before but from a different perspective.
Lukas, however, wasn't satisfied. It was old news. It
offered no challenge. It wasn't, as he told me, *top of
mind*. It didn't provide any new answers to old questions.
Chief among them, did Oswald act alone? Were others in
any way involved? Was there a conspiracy? What about
the gaps in the official investigations? The
inconsistencies, the contradictions, the oversights, the
mistakes, the changed testimony? What about the
suspicious and/or unexplained deaths of so many key
witnesses? Was Oswald working with the FBI? The CIA?
The KGB? Lyndon Johnson? Fidel Castro? The anti-
Castroites? The Israelis? The Mafia? Why did Jack Ruby,
a Dallas nightclub owner with known ties to the mob, gun
Oswald down that Sunday morning?

What happened *before* November 22, 1963?

Lukas wanted to explore further back in time. He
wanted something stunning and spectacular. He wanted a
go-back with *hair* on it. And so, as his people crawled the
catwalks of the three-story-high aluminum sphere known
as The Hive and turned those quantum cascading lasers
on, here's what the world saw.

I Can't Even Analyze This

A gloomy, grindhouse back room. Flaking gold paint on
the walls, thick red carpet showing signs of leprosy. You
could *see* the smell of old sweat and lavatory disinfectant.
Unintelligible noises came from behind a wall—shouts,
toad-tongue cries, a small bad band playing *You Made Me
Love You*. It was the back-room office of the Carousel
Club, a Dallas strip joint—or as owner Jack Ruby called it,
a burlesque joint.

Ruby sat at his desk. A stocky, pudgy man with
Vitalis-slicked black hair, shaky from Preludin and a
lifetime on the hustle. A dachshund slept at his feet.

Ruby was staring at the man across from him. A
floppy thing, slight and gangly, his bloodless face a wet
yellow color. Lee Harvey Oswald, not speaking but
searching Ruby's eyes, an ex-Marine radar operator
hunting for sonar echoes.

"I'm trying to recall," said Ruby, "but I don't know
you."

"Probably better that way."

"Yeah? Why's that?"

"Cause I think I can help you."

"You can help me."

"Or, if not you, people you know. I think I can help
them, their interests."

"People I know."

"Yes."

"Who do I know?"

"I know who you know."

"How do you know?"

"I asked around."

"Around *where?*"

"It doesn't matter."

"It does to *me.*"

Oswald shifted in his chair, regrouping himself.
"Point is, I can help you."

"You said."

"But I need your help."

"*My* help."

"Or from the people you know."

Ruby sighed and took an oddly dainty sip from an
open bottle of Schweppes ginger ale. "This is a little, you
know, *muddled.* I thought you were trying to help me."

"I am, but once I do, I need help from you."

"What kind of help?"

"I need money. *Some* money. Your connections.
Contacts, whatever. Anything that'll help me get away."

"You wanna leave, is that what you're saying?"

"Yes."

"Causa something you did?"

"*Going* to do."

"What's that?"

Oswald leaned in toward the desk and went to
summon his most serious expression, but the result was
distorted and off-kilter. He looked more like someone
forced to suck on an old Tampon.

"A hit," he said.

Ruby laughed. "A *hit?*"

"Yes."

"A hit. You mean like taking somebody out."

"Yes."

"*You?*"

"I've done it before."

"Yeah, who?"

"A general."

"A general."

"A *fascist* general."

A contextual note appeared at the bottom of the
screen: *The Warren Commission concluded that Oswald
had attempted to kill retired U.S. Major General Edwin
Walker, an outspoken right-wing segregationist, by*

*shooting him on April 10, 1963, with a 6.5 mm caliber
Carcano rifle.*

Ruby was still laughing. "Of *course* he was a fascist
general. And who's your next victim, Martin Bormann?" A
long, long second of silence. "What, you can't say?"

Oswald looked down at the dachshund. "Nice dog."

"Leave the dog out of it."

"Kennedy."

"*Kennedy?*"

"Kennedy."

"You mean the prick Bobby."

"No, the other one. John. The prick John."

"Are you being sarcastic with me?"

"No."

"Excuse me, you're talking about the *president?*"

"Yes."

"Of the United States?"

"Yes."

"I can't even *analyze* this. The fuck *why?*"

"He won't leave my wife alone."

"He's schtupping your wife?"

"He's *harassing* her. Him and his people. The FBI.
They come to the house, they ask her questions. They think
she's a Soviet spy. I met her in Russia, when I lived there.
They think she's passing secrets. They come to the house
and subject her to all these questions. This has been going
on for a number of months. It's been incubating for some
time."

"And you think John F. Kennedy is personally
responsible for this?"

"I *warned* them. I *told* them what would happen. He
should've been informed of the threats. He should know the
consequences of his actions. He should know he's *crushing*
her. Crushing her and crushing me. I'm literally *suffocating*
from this! This is air I'm not supposed to be breathing and I
refuse to put up with it any fucking longer!"

His face had quickly collapsed in a chaotic bundle
of rage. You could understand why he was punished by the
Marines for suddenly and wildly opening fire in an empty
Philippines jungle.

Ruby was leaning back in his chair, eyes fixed on the ceiling. The look on his face: *Why me, Lord, why me?*

"The Russians don't like it either," said Oswald. "They've sanctioned this, they've given me their blessings. But they can't risk helping me get away. That's why I'm here."

"You talked to the Russians?"

"At the embassy, Mexico City."

"Excuse me, excuse me, I *know* some of those people. We get quite a few of 'em in here, when they fly up. They're very careful about what they do. I don't think they'd be getting involved with someone like you."

"It's a co*vert* understanding."

"No, not those people, they got too much class for shit like this. They'd be more interested in staying *away* from you."

"Believe what you want, I can still help you by doing this. You, your people. Lot of government persecution will go away—you can believe that."

"What I believe is that you're driving a real fast car but you got no idea where you're going."

"I know *exactly* where I'm going."

"Yeah? What's your name?"

Oswald stared at him. "Alek."

"So Mr. Alek, exactly how—"

"Hidell. Alek Hidell."

Contextual note: *When Oswald was arrested, two forged ID cards in the name of Alek James Hidell were found in his wallet. It was later learned that the Carcano rifle was purchased by mail order under the name A. Hidell.*

"Okay, Mr. Hidell, can you tell me how you're gonna do this?"

"When he comes here, that's how."

"*Here*? No, not *here*."

"He's coming here, everybody knows that."

"Not *here*. Why the fuck here? We don't have enough problems?"

"It's opportunity."

"Fuck opportunity—not here. Go dirty some other town."

"He's coming *here*. They got his travelogue in the papers. He'll be riding in an open car."

"I know, with his *wife*. You're bitchin' about your wife? What about *his*?"

Oswald shrugged. "Justice."

"*Stop* it—enough. I don't want to hear anymore. This is so fucking *impure*. I heard enough of it."

"Can I assume you're not interested?"

"I don't know where you materialized from, but get your sorry ass outta here."

"Fine, I'll find another way." He stood up. "I got other people to see—don't worry about me."

"I *am* worried about you. You pull this shit, you pull this shit here, no one'll ever forgive you."

"I'm not interested in forgiveness. I just want to be left alone."

"You *won't* be. You'll never be left alone. *Ever*—I can make that promise to you. I won't forget your face, my friend. Anything happens, I'll hunt you down. I'll hunt you down myself."

>>>>>>>

Dinner's Ready And Your Father's Dead

Critical reaction was similar to the Hitler go-back. Some praised it as if the night sky had suddenly filled with meteors, burning angels of truth. The Oswald go-back was an explosion of new intelligence, a revelation of historical importance, one that would finally cast fatal light on those conspiracy theories that had managed to survive under mossy rocks all these years.

As for the conspiracy theorists, they were burning, yeah, but only with indignation. The go-back, they said, frequently in all caps, was a brilliant hoax, an example of technological manipulation, a scam verging on the ridiculous. Nothing about it or its creator could be taken at face value. *Lukas Lister-Bertozzi,* said one, paraphrasing Jean Cocteau, *is a lunatic who believes he's Lukas Lister-Bertozzi.*

One dissenter even constructed a whole theory explaining how the go-back was really produced. Far from using DNA-encoded memory, Lukas had relied on actors and some incredible iteration of digitized news footage and motion-capture software. Lukas invited the theorist to come to [0+X], dissect the process and test the hypothesis. His offer was declined.

Like the Hitler aftermath, Lukas was taking my media advice and giving select interviews. They were all different, yet all the same. He was used to being the target of brickbats, he said, hurled by imbeciles with cat-infested brains. Such attacks didn't concern him—they bored him. They were guaranteed to keep him yawning until the year 2253 at least. But he understood the impulse behind them. These moldy theories were finally keeping their date with

the bulldozers, and there was nothing the conpiracists
could do but sit by their computers with big bottles of their
own urine—a typically eccentric Lukasism—and watch it
happen.

In his appearances, he looked like a man who'd just
put in a bid on the Pacific Ocean and was certain of
success. *The go-backs have no hidden, propagandist
agendas,* he'd say, jabbing his finger at the camera like a
knife blade. *They're completely transparent, they're
dreams whose light can be seen from inside and outside,
and I'll give no quarter in defending them. There's no
surrender in the truth. I don't care what certain members
of the livestock community might say...*

*...their bleating protests mean nothing to me, because I'm
just a marker, a small signpost along humanity's march to
history.*

"Must be a miracle," said Belinda, "that so many
words can come out of a horse's ass."

Lukas' interview was playing on the TVs over in
the bar area, everybody downing his words. We were in the
dining section of the restaurant, having dinner to make up
for the fight—though we both claimed that dinner had been
our idea. What we did agree on was that whatever was or
wasn't going to happen, we'd take a slow, Singapore-math
approach.

She was still looking at Lukas—or, as she called
him, Il Douche. "I love the arrogance of his modesty.
That's what happens when you think your poop is gold."

"How about his genius? Can you give him that?"

"He's a genius at self-deception, I'll give *you* that. I
told him once what he was doing was evil. *But it's GOOD
evil*, he said. He was serious."

She started talking about water fleas. Well who
wouldn't? She'd been reading about an experiment
conducted on laboratory colonies of water fleas. Half were
given steadily diminishing supplies of food, and naturally,
since starving water fleas tend to lose interest in

reproduction, they died out. But what was interesting is that they died long before the food ran out. At a certain point the colonies reached what scientists call *critical slowing down*, where groups lose the ability to adapt to and recover from change. In the case of the water fleas, *critical slowing down* took place when there was still plenty of food available, a full eight generations before the population finally expired. It was as if they instinctively knew in advance—*well* in advance—that they couldn't avoid disaster.

The researchers then took the patterns they'd seen in the water fleas and compared them to other natural systems. They found the same early-warning signals occurring in some very different places. In coral reefs choked by pollution and turned the bleached color of unburied bones. In the teeming vegetation of the Sahara 5,500 years ago as a tilt in the Earth's axis burned the land to desert. In stock markets just before a crash.

Belinda was worried that those researchers would have a field day at [0+X]. The staffers were showing signs of approaching *critical slowing down*, and the cause was the seeping sewage of Lister-Bertozzi pollution.

"He's never given enough of a damn about them, and as far as I can understand it's just gotten worse over time. His ego keeps swelling like an oil spill. His wife told me even his handwriting has grown larger in the last few years."

Yeah, not surprised.

"Interesting woman, Sabreena," I said. "You close to her at all?"

"As much as anyone can get close to her, I guess. I can't really read her all that well. I know she's hurting, obviously, but there's something else going on there. There's something about her, I don't know, it reminds me of Emily Dickinson. *Had I a mighty gun/I think I'd shoot the human race.*"

"Ever talk to her about her daughter's death?"

"Some. Not easy, given the big blind spot in her memory. But some. I think that's one of the reasons she hired me, because of her daughter. When she heard my story, she said, *I think you've got a feel for the woof of the warped.* Part of it, I think, she was thinking about her daughter."

A little jolt ran through me. An almost telepathic sideswipe. *When she heard my story?*

Her mother spent her whole life in park, waiting for the stop signs to turn green. Mom was a garbage head, getting high everyday on a whole pharmacopia of everything and anything—crack, Percocet, Ritalin, heroin, Zyban, Robitussin, diet pills, glue, ludes, coke, Dramamine, Oxy, Wellbutrin, Concerta, Freon, Red Bull or beer. She dropped acid every time she got a migraine. She got a lot of migraines.

A hard down life—single mother raising a daughter, living on some kind of disability, reading Joel Osteen books when she was stoned to find a way out before one of her flash crashes would wipe everything away. Belinda remembered her mother calling to her one night—*dinner's ready and your father's dead.* That's how she found out she had a father. Who was he? Who knows?

The good times came to an end when Belinda was 11. School and the neighbors had been calling Child Welfare for years, and the social workers had never been happy with the conditions of the apartment—the filth, the feces, the neglect. For a reason Belinda never really understood (though it might've had something to do with Mom passing out on the street), things suddenly escalated one week. Her mother found out that Child Welfare was going to arrest her and take Belinda away. For child abuse? Bullfuckingshit. She wasn't going to lose her child. She made Belinda stuff herself into a rolling suitcase and she left the apartment, the snoopy neighbors never guessing she had her daughter hidden inside.

Going ghost—that's what it's called when you take off, switch identities and disappear from the official grid. Belinda could recall drifting through different parts of the country, trying to remember her mother's impossible choices of changing surnames—Bellflower, Moonblood, Lucerne, Jonquille, Roseberry. Eventually they ended up living outside of Vegas, in a place so bleak the town had to ship in weeds just to have something to grow.

One of the downsides of going ghost? No more disability checks. Belinda began shoplifting from local stores, stealing merchandise that her mother would sell on eBay. The idea was her own, Belinda said—she didn't trust her perpetually fucked-up mother to successfully practice the craft. She spent her early teens as a thief. Some irony: The most popular items she lifted included combination locks, motion detectors, ignition kill switches, keypads, steering wheel locks, vibration sensors, hood restraints, alarm systems—anti-*theft* devices.

She was a gifted swiper—few close calls but never getting caught. Until a security guard spotted her walking out of the Freemont House Supplies store with a miniature surveillance camera stuffed inside her raincoat. He yelled. She ran. He chased, caught up with her at a demolition site two blocks away. He confiscated the camera, gave her a blistering lecture, then turned slightly away to call the bust in. A chunk of old rebar was sitting on the ground, steel rods encased in cement. She picked it up, took a swing and caught him in the side of his head.

He went down immediately, huge red gash on his scalp, not moving. But it was *her* life that flashed in front of her. She couldn't believe what she'd just done. She started praying for the man, hoping he wasn't dead, then realized holy shit I've gotta get out of here. She ran, found a bus stop, got on the first one that came along. She ended up in a terminal near McCarran Airport, grabbed another bus and another bus and another bus.

For three days she rode, going she didn't know where and didn't care, just brooding about what happened, praying for the man, deciding what to do next. Three days of thinking there has to be a better way to live than the way I've been living. Sleeping passengers, restroom breaks, vending machine junk food—slowly, very slowly, answers began to come to her. She wanted to go back to school again. She wanted to use her real last name, Halestre, again.

She wanted to make a new start, on her own. She
wanted to find the lit center of her own life. Some new kind
of brain language seemed to be taking over her head. She
wanted stability, some lasting ground. She wanted an
unfailing, long-term relationship with God.

>>>>>>>

"Well, I would've hired you," I said.

"Sabreena liked me. She said I was the best
candidate of all the chaplains they'd sent over. I think what
happened when I was a kid, what I went through, made her
sympathetic. She thought it would help me handle all the
crapazoola her husband had created."

"And Lukas went for it?"

"Nothing ever comes easy with Lukas. He *sort of*
went for it, but first I had to interview with him. I met him
in his lunatic office. He said he was going to give me a
five-word phrase, *This statement is metaphysically
erroneous*, and he wanted me to free associate on it for the
next two hours."

"*What*? What did you say?"

"I really don't know. I think I started by talking
about Aquinas and Wittgenstein, and then— I really don't
know. But apparently it was good enough."

"And now what, you regret it?"

"It's the worst working situation I've ever seen, but
what can you do except what you can do? I try to tell
people you don't have to go through life empty and barren
of spirit. God's power is limited only by our understanding.
The more open we are, the power God has."

"And zen helps you with this?"

"It's very effective."

"Even though it doesn't talk about God?"

"It doesn't have to," she said. "God is implicit. But
zen's just a good way to bring a spiritual smile."

"Or a laugh."

"You think?"

"A belly laugh, actually. That kind of deep laugh
you get when you stumble on the truth."

"Let's not fight about it. For me, zen's relationship with God comes down to this: You can either talk about making love or you can make love. When it comes to God, zen's making love."

"Amen to that."

I looked at the stars outside her bedroom window as if they'd never been seen before, as if someone had just conjured them. We kept taking turns in bed between talking and dozing off, her leg always resting on mine, too exhausted by fuck-love to argue over anything. So much for Singapore math.

I looked around the room again, at the talismans of jade, emerald and amethyst she had hanging on her walls.

She was looking at the sky. "There's so much out there," she said, brushing the white hair from her eyes. "So much we don't know."

"You're talking about…"

"A hundred billion galaxies out there, and they hold more stars than there are grains of sand on all the beaches on Earth."

I can't swear to it, but this might be the greatest night in the history of the world.

CHAPTER 7

MANHATTAN ON FIVE BULLETS A DAY

Today's Special

If you're an inmate on death row in Japan, you never
know when your end will come. It's always a surprise.
The officials don't tell you until the last minute when they
suddenly show up at your cell and say, guess what, your
date with the hangman has arrived. (And they aren't
speaking metaphorically—executions are still done with
the noose.) Even your family, your lawyers—even, God
help us, the *media*—don't know until it's all over and
you're being cut down from the rope. The Japanese say
they pull this ultimate prank to prevent panic in prison and
society at large. I don't know, maybe it's just a way to
avoid the ickiness of last-minute appeals and death penalty
protests. Or maybe it's a cultural thing. They don't care
for suspense. They much prefer the champagne thrill of a
surprise.

Well, not here. As much as we don't like bad
news, we like it even less when it catches us off guard.
Abruptness makes it seem that much worse. Take the riot
in the cafeteria of [0+X] as an example. That was a
complete surprise, and with 28 people injured and one
dead, it didn't go well at all.

In fact it was so much of a surprise no one really
knew who started it. Everyone was sitting in the grids of
row-tables and chairs, eating their meat loaf and broiled
scrod and low-trans-fat fries, when a never identified
staffer began cursing. Not in an angry outburst, just a
random string of obscenities—*fuck, shit, piss, cunt,
asshole*—like a George Carlin seven forbidden words
routine. There was a moment of silence, then a moment of
laughter, then the other lunchers began joining in. People

were taking off their headsets and earbuds and shouting out profanities in a group chant. It was like that restaurant scene in *Curb Your Enthusiasm* where a full crowd of patrons breaks out in curses to show support and solidarity for the Tourette's-stricken chef.

Three ASSETS rolled in to restore order. They motorvated through the cafeteria, instructing the workers in their velvety, vaguely British software-generated voices to *please watch your language* and *refrain from ugly or offensive usage*, sounding like Miss Marple telling people to pipe down.

They were there to prevent trouble. Instead they set more in motion. A bony, bristling, crazy-eyed man with a concave face, Cito Spangler, rushed up to one of the little sophisticated vacuum cleaners and kicked it over. He then began spitting at it and giving it a big time whooping by beating on it with an empty food tray. Alarms went off as the crowd cheered him.

At least the *cause* of the simmering frustration was no surprise. That morning, Lukas had issued an edict banning all expletives in the workplace. Vulgarity, he said in his company-wide email, was too disruptive, too conducive to unrest. Screening software had been installed to monitor all verbal and electronic communication. Even smut words spelled out with asterisks would be detected in texts and emails and punished. *We will maintain ourselves*, Lukas said, *with self-regard and integrity*.

What was that law of unintended consequences again?

A dozen security guards—humans—responded to the alarms, bolting into the cafeteria and charging over to Cito, the downed ASSET and the people who'd gathered around them. Accustomed to passive submission, the employees stepped aside and let them pass, but as the guards began yelling at Cito and ordering him to step away from the automaton, the workers closed ranks behind them. At first the staffers jumped the guards from the back, then from the sides, then from the front. Within seconds a whole screaming kung fu had broken out, the staffers grabbing and cursing and spitting at the guards, beating on them with trays and bottles and chairs.

Everything seemed to blow up everywhere at the same time. Moments later the entire cafeteria had slipped into jerky chaos, hundreds of people tossing food, trays, bottles and cans in the air and overturning the long tables. Red-flag violence ruled, everyone shocked by what they were doing but the shock not stopping them from doing it.

A swarm of workers climbed up on the serving rail and scaled over the counters. Pans of meat loaf and scrod began flying. Dishes were smashed. Cases knocked over. Freezers, fryers and prep tables were battered and destroyed.

It was a full-canvas riot. Some people were running away in terror but most had joined the attack. Bloodied guards were being dragged further into the crowd. Clouds of fryer smoke swirling overhead. Strange crashes coming from everywhere. Paint on the walls gouged with forks. The screams no longer curses but charnel animal shrieks.

There was a pause in one part of the crowd, a sudden hesitation, a note of uncertainty, a realization that something had gone too far. Even chaos has its limits. People stepped aside, moving away from the body on the floor. One of the workers, eyes fixed and staring, a surprised look on his face. First they'd thought he'd slipped on the food-slick floor, but he wasn't moving and threads of vomit were webbing from his mouth. He was giving off the black light of the dead.

Everybody Needs Somebody—To Blame

"Cathidrone," said Lukas. "A designer drug, but an extremely pure compound. Obviously made with complex and refined equipment. It's popular in Europe, but it can purchased here as bath salts."

"Or plant food or pond cleaner—I know. That's why I first came here, remember? With Roots? Our friend died the same way."

"That's right. Yes, you did."

We were standing in front of the lacquered, nine-leaved screen in his office, catching replays of the cafeteria surveillance footage in its monitors. Lukas viewed the rampage with pain and disbelief, the look of a man who's coming close to realizing, *My God, my shit DOES stink.*

"The police are calling it probable suicide," he said. "Intentional overdose. At least they've ruled out homicide."

"A suicide? In the middle of a riot?"

"There's no accounting for taste."

It made sense that he'd called me. He was in terrible need of media commiseration. Nothing travels faster than bad news, and news about the revolt and the death in the cafeteria had spread with astral speed. [0+X], said the press pundits, had reached new heights of headline-making creepiness. The company's stock prices were hurting—the gains made after the Oswald go-back had been wiped out. Bloggers were accusing Lukas of driving his employees to Guinness-worthy levels of self-destruction.

"Everybody's a critic," he said. "*Bloggers*—what gives them the right? I blame Richard Nixon for this."

"Sorry?"

"Nixon—he gave voice to the Silent Majority. He planted the idea that anyone could say anything. There was a reason the Silent Majority was silent. They had *nothing* to say."

Besides the police investigation, Lukas had conducted an internal probe to identify and punish the prime instigators. Dozens of employees had been grilled (I can imagine what that was like), and in the course of questioning Lukas had come to an interesting conclusion: Based on varying degrees of inconsistency, he'd deduced that the riot had been staged.

He reset one of the monitors back to the point where the communal cursing begins. A still-unknown staffer can be heard muttering *fuck, shit, piss,* etc. Within seconds, as if reacting to a prearranged signal, all the staffers are unplugging their ears and taking part in an act of deliberate provocation.

He advanced the footage to the moment when the mass violence breaks out. Staffers are wolf-packing the guards with trays, bottles and chairs, and suddenly the entire cafeteria is engulfed in savagery.

"This was no spontaneous combustion," said Lukas. "It was planned. Look at them—they've already decided to create anarchy. They're simply following a script."

Really?

"Why? Why stage a riot? To give you more bad publicity?"

"In part, I suppose. But the ulterior motive is more devious. They've been instructed to create a diversion."

"From what?"

"A theft."

I should note at this point that Lukas no longer resembled an eccentric hippie. He was looking more like a schizophrenic on cathidrone.

"A theft."

"Exactly."

"Of what?"

Bottom-of-the-lung breath. "I'm sorry to tell you the PIB is missing again. Its absence was discovered right after the outbreak was quelled. It's *gone*."

Aside from that, Mrs. Lincoln...

"And who's behind all this? Cascadian?"

"Obviously one of the unfriendlies. And who's unfriendlier than that flimflam old fuck?"

So much for the cursing ban.

"Exactly how di—"

"Pay offs, promises, perhaps even plants. What's certain is that the old raisin plotted against me. He exploited my workforce for some subterranean revenge."

"Pretty good for a conspiracy theory."

"Oh it gets better. He's gone double down this time."

"Double down?"

"My wife is missing as well. Both disappeared at the same time. We've searched every square centimeter. The PIB is gone and so is she."

Contextual note: There was no spousal outrage in his voice, no grieving wound. He sounded like a homeowner writing a letter of complaint about the trash pick up times.

"Trimshaw?"

"I'm expecting a ransom demand—something else to deal with. This whole place is falling apart, and please, spare me any analysis. Just get in touch with Roots."

"You want them found."

He looked back at the lacquered screen, at the monitor showing his employees destroying the cafeteria equipment. "I don't understand. How can they stoop to this? These people are like family to me."

Yeah, well, that was the problem.

>>>>>>

Grave Information

I was just about to contact Roots when I got a text from
Belinda—*need 2 c u asap*. Her office was a tiny cubicle
made of partition walls. It screamed *temporary, don't get
used to it*. She'd tried to warm it up with talismans, amulets
and a small candle-covered altar.

Cito Spangler was sitting there, close to breaking
down. He'd been fired for the ASSET assault. Lukas was
still deciding whether to press criminal charges.

"I got kids, a family," he was telling Belinda.
"Much as I hate this fucking job, I *need* this fucking job."

"I'm sorry, but this isn't the end of everything."

"I don't know. I'm thinking this must be what the
ground feels like when they open it up for a grave."

He looked as near to killing himself as I'd ever seen
him. The first netless roof he could find, he was jumping.

"I need to talk to Quinn. Can I leave you here for a
minute?"

Out in the hall Belinda took a quick look around,
making sure no one was in earshot.

"It's about him?"

"No, it's something else."

"What?"

"I don't really know if I know. There's a story
going on about Sabreena. She disappeared?"

"I can neither confirm nor deny, but yes."

"Kidnapped?"

"That's what Lukas says."

"I'm not so sure about that."

"Why?"

Another nervous look around. "I don't want to betray a confidence."

"Why not? Join the party."

"Sabreena told me she's been...*associating* with one of the staffers. A guy named Dustin, I think he's in Information Assurance. He grows moonflowers too."

"How much *associating* has been doing with him?"

"They're pretty friendly."

"She's sleeping with him?"

"I don't know. But she's been acting strangely lately."

"How can you tell?"

"Kind of anxious, kind of panicky. Less *distracted*."

"Like she was planning something?"

Belinda nodded. "I think she might've run off with him."

Place Foot Near Ass, Insert

My plan going back in was not to say anything about
Belinda or about what Sabreena told her. My story: I'd
developed my own sources on the campus. I'd heard the
rumor from them. Turns out I didn't have to worry about it.
As soon as Lukas heard the name Dustin he went all stink-
eye and couldn't care less about the source.

"It's Mathis. *Dustin* is Dustin Mathis. An analyst in
Information Assurance. Not the most brilliant mind, but
tolerably competent. No question it's him. I've been
thinking he might be a risk for quite some time."

He called for a status check on the analyst. Forty
seconds later Lukas had learned that:

(1) Dustin Mathis never showed up for an
emergency meeting to discuss the riot.

(2) He'd failed to attend the daily Information
Assurance staff meeting.

(3) His workspace had been cleaned out. All he'd
left behind was four dozen packages of Saltines in a desk
drawer. He liked soup.

Not exactly signs of unblemished innocence.

"I've always suspected he might be compromised.
He's been interviewed several times with multiple-scale
anomaly tests. A number of his responses raised questions.
I've had some of his messages and conversations scraped
for content. He's earned a place on the Most Watched list."

"What're we talking about here?"

Dustin Mathis, he said, was another Trimshaw
Dawson, a sour employee clogging the feedback channels
with endless, tedious, nursing-home-lobby complaints
about the company's corrosive work conditions. Yes, he

always used official reporting channels to register his objections, give him that, but his remarks were always, in Lukas' view, tiresome, pathetic and blissfully fact-free. Lukas finally had to cut him off. He told Dustin that while he was free to submit an occasional constructive criticism, personnel matters were not in his purview. If he wanted to transfer to HR, speak up now.

The grumbling stopped. Message received, Lukas thought. But apparently Dustin was simply brooding in silence. Weeks later, a series of subversive and—Lukas' word—*bizarre* comments began appearing on blogs devoted to disruptive tech updates. The writer's identity was untraceable, but the comments struck familiar, asthmatically whining chords, attributing the suicides at [0+X] to a failure of management. Even worse, in describing the Steinbrennerish atmosphere at the company, the comments made passing references to classified information. Top secret databases were mentioned, along with event logs, steganographic decryption projects and anonymized computer-intrusion programs. The comments weren't just filled with complaints but *leaks*.

"I don't know what bothers me more, the security breaches or the malicious tone." He called up a file. "Look at this."

Leadership techniques at [0+X] are bad for the health and useless for the soul. They're opposed, in short, to the most obvious laws of mental hygiene and administrative science...

Scratch any problem at the company, and you'll find Lukas Lister-Bertozzi's foot up its ass...

The place continues to be run like a dungeon, and let this stand as a warning: If it doesn't begin to embrace a more healing, human-centric approach, the results will be karmatically disastrous.

"Right," said Lukas, "and from what I understand, we all live in a yellow submarine. This is the puerile work of a *mole*, a classic, deluded *mole*. This was written by someone who's still eating his own pick-nose and has no other weapon but his own obsessive hate."

"And it was definitely written by Dustin Mathis, who definitely took the PIB and ran off with your wife. That's the logic train, right?"

More stink eye. Lukas called for another check: When was the last time Dustin Mathis had been seen in the complex? It took 20 seconds to get the answer: Just before the riot broke out, just before Sabreena disappeared and the PIB vanished.

"I don't know what kind of pinky-swear he made with my wife, but this is sabotage. Ever see pacifists turn homicidal? This is what it looks like."

I could see an image of Sabreena in my mind—basket case. "Your wife's capable of that?"

"My wife hides a great deal of rage. She sometimes overwhelms me with her hostile indifference. A few months after my daughter died, she joined a support group for bereaved parents. An online forum, using a different name. She hated the other members—people who'd gone through the worst kind if grief, and she *despised* them. She tried not to show the contempt in her messages, but the venom was dripping."

"How do you know?"

"I hacked the account, how else?" He swung his hand in a wiping motion—enough. "Get together with Roots and track them down. I want the PIB back. You will think, please, about nothing else."

"I can help you out, on one condition."

"Condition?"

"Give Cito Spangler his job back. Punish him if you have to, but don't fire him."

"Give *who* his job back?"

"Cito Spangler, the guy who beat your robot up."

"Fine, whatever, just get the PIB back from those two. People like that—God. I know certain critics object to the way I keep my staff relevant and awake. Fine, I accept that. We can't be loved by everyone. Look at Jesus—they even crucified *him*."

>>>>>>

"...but on one condition," I said. "You've got to promise not to kill yourself. You do, all bets are off."

Cito was having a hard time with this one. "I'm *back*?"

"But only if you promise. You kill yourself, no bennies for your family. That's the deal."

"You want me to die *peaceful*?"

"We want you to *live* peaceful," said Belinda. "Work might suck, but that doesn't mean the world does. The world doesn't hate you."

"It feels like it. Every day it feels like it."

"That's *you*," she said. "That's a reflection of how you feel. If you think the world hates you, that's just a reflection of your hate. If you think the world loves you, that's a reflection of your love. Truth is, the world isn't either hateful or loving or even indifferent. It's *you*, it's what you really are."

"I don't know. Sounds like a lot of responsibility."

"But you're already doing it," I said. "You're already there. We all are. We want to kill ourselves, we want to escape life, what we really want is to escape our *feelings* about life. But feelings aren't facts. They can change."

"You better believe it," said Belinda.

We gave him a five-day spiritual weather forecast. Me: Despair is like dying of thirst in the rain. Her: If you can think it, if you can dream it, you can be it. Me: Shit can happen to you, but only you can let it get to you. Her: All you need is faith in God and a sense of humor.

Eventually we budged him off it. We tag-teamed him into feeling a little better. "God's cool, I guess," he conceded. He promised not to kill himself. Or he promised, if he heard the dark call, he'd come to Belinda first. That wasn't bad. Under the circumstances, that was probably as good a get as it gets.

>>>>>>

The Silent Enemies

They were busting it up in Red Hook, in the old abandoned
house near the Upper Bay, in the hipster bingo parlor
downstairs and especially in the hidden back room where
the night traders sat at their tatami tables, trading ideas,
making suggestions, sharing data, talking tech (*it's a well-
made piece of crap, but it's a piece of crap*), geeking on
pop-culture (*that's the problem with reality shows—people
mistake them for reality*), trolling Tolkien sites or, in one
case, studying a web page called *The Silent Enemy*, a
treatise on masturbation and how to give it up.

"They've vaporized," said Roots, referring to the
two runaways. He was limping a bit from the burn on his
right calf, the memento of our Cascadian trip. No more pain
patches, though he was popping eight Tylenol at a time.

Searching for a renegade employee and a woman
with dissociative amnesia who looked like she might
poison her husband if the mood was right wasn't as easy as
it sounds. Since they'd disappeared, neither Sabreena nor
Dustin Mathis had used their phones or their credit cards.
Roots had personally searched Dustin's apartment on
W.101st. Not a clue. He and Sabreena were really using the
tools of the fade.

I thought about her and Lukas, what a strange
couple they were. Keeping separate greenhouses, growing
different out-of-season plants. Living in separate galaxies
that never came within 400 million light-years of each
other.

The one glimmer of good news: After he'd gotten
Dustin's cell number from [0+X], Roots had been able to
identify the phone's manufacturer and its operating system.

A few of the night traders were now sucking the digital content out of the OS memory. At least they could build a picture of what Dustin had been doing up to the moment he took off. I watched them working with all their can-do, all-nighter, Zuckerberg energy. They were like young coyotes on the attack—they hadn't yet learned to fear humans.

I asked if they knew anything about cathidrone. Some—they'd heard it was showing up, going by the street name of cath. Dangerous stuff. Where was it coming from? Nobody knew. One night trader thought it might be trickling in from a source in Sco (which I now knew meant San Francisco), but who knows for sure? That's one thing about these otherwise hyper-conscious folks. If it has nothing to do with silicon chips, they don't know shit.

A pair of rumpled cargo shorts attached to a stiff dress shirt was standing next to me. Robbo Fragaruccio. He said they'd been putting together a dossier on Dustin Mathis. Want a look? He took me to a computer and started typing a password, stopped, deleted three of the characters and kept typing. No, he hadn't made a mistake. Typing three wrong characters, erasing them and typing three right ones—that was all part of the access code.

>>>>>>

I looked at the photos first. Dustin Mathis was a humorless black man, unnaturally white teeth, unsure yet angry eyes, as if the air around him was presenting a challenge. Going by the pix he was in constant contemplation of something troubling, like he'd eaten some bad soup. He was part Jamaican, part German, part Indonesian, part Sudanese. A racial profiling nightmare.

He'd grown up in the small town of Elksville, Tenn., population 826 and many of them, apparently, bigots. Dustin was teased by other kids for being a gaming nerd, needled for being a black non-jock and, later, compounding the already alien horrors of adolescence, bullied for being gay. (So his link with Sabreena was ideological, not romantic.)

When his father found out about his sexuality he gave his son a choice: Renounce it or get the fuck out. Dustin sometimes lived out of his car while using minimum-wage jobs to work his way through college. Eventually he was employed as a project manager for Allied Sustainable Security. Former co-workers remembered him as a consummate outsider, a lost soul, desperate for acceptance but too defensive to make any friends. Whenever he thought someone wasn't listening to him or couldn't understand his point of view, he'd go off on desk-pounding tantrums.

He fell in love while he was working at [0+X]. The guy's name was Kirk Hammond, a born-again bisexual banker who introduced Dustin to his wide network of friends, including members of a tight-knit community of Christian social activists. It was around this time, evidently, that Dustin began feeling morally conflicted about working at a soulless company like [0+X]. It was around this time that he began filing those formal objections about the life-destroying, shabby-at-best treatment Lukas was giving his staffers.

He and Kirk had just celebrated their third anniversary together when Kirk collapsed from a heart attack on his way to work, and despite chest compressions applied by a good samaritan, he was pronounced dead at the scene. As it happened, this was right after Lukas has warned Dustin about the complaints. The two events were hardly of equal weight, but taken together they pulled him into a new path. Weeks later he began planting the anonymous attacks on [0+X].

Some of the calls the night traders had retrieved dated back to that time. I listened to one, heard Dustin's voice. He spoke in a carefully measured and metered tone with no trace of a Tennessee accent, every vowel and consonant lined up in a perfect row. He was like Barack Obama—he spoke white better than white people.

I have to take sides, he was telling someone. *After what happened, I have to make a choice. They have the ability to make changes. They have a ROBUST CAPABILITY to make improvements. But he won't do it.*

*He just won't. That bombastic madman just keeps
torturing us with his godless schmutz.*

Later in the sequence of calls he says he's reaching
out to Sabreena. *I've been isolated so long, she's the only
friend I have there. She's the only voice in that wilderness.
She's the only warm flame in that whole block of arctic ice.*

In the most recent messages, he and Sabreena are
setting something in motion. *We've found someone to help,
a kind of crucial mover I guess you could say... Yeah, I
still... I'm still having issues with it. I'm still having doubts
about, I'll be a thief, no one will trust me, no one will ever
talk to me. But she says it'll be all right, the damage is on
Lukas, and she's right. He's going to have a coronary.*

Interesting choice of words.

*I'm just a wreck. I'm emotionally fractured. I'm
self-medicating like crazy. But she's saying we'll be fine.
She says we've walked all this way, let's go through the
door. She's my rock, really, She's my backbone. I don't
know what I'd do without her.*

Hard to miss the mommy echo ringing through
those calls.

How Meta Can You Get?

No grim, sticky coffee shop in Manhattan looks more like every other grim, sticky coffee shop in Manhattan than the Aragon Coffee Shop on Ninth Avenue, between 24th and 25th. We hadn't picked the place at random. A lot of Dustin's calls had been made to a Pauline Capra and an Evan Dowd. Both names, as Roots discovered, were fake, but those calls had all bounced to somewhere among the 2,800 apartments of the Penn South Co-ops across the street.

We sat near the front window, drinking very good coffee while our eyes swept the brick buildings—build in the 1950s by a garment workers' union—and the avenue. People walking their babies, their dogs, their elder-care patients. A dull sun like a cataracted eye in the sky. A homeless guy strolling down the street yelling, *Glucose is the devil!*

Waiting for something to happen—something that might, in fact, not happen at all—held all the thrills and excitement of a spring training exhibition game. Roots wondered why there were no more comedy duos in America anymore. Laurel and Hardy. Abbott and Costello. Dean Martin and Jerry Lewis. What happened to all the double acts? He'd seen them all on YouTube—Burns and Allen, The Smothers Brothers, Rowan and Martin, Bob and Ray, Wayne and Shuster, Allen and Rossi, Jack Burns and Avery Schreiber, Mike Nichols and Elaine May. What happened to the *and?*

"Could be economics," I said. "Tough enough for one to make it these days, let alone two."

"Or there's no more of those big variety shows, you know? No more *Ed Sullivan?* But I think it's more meta than that."

"Something about the culture? The value of the individual?"

"Something like that. Something like…"

I think we might've gotten somewhere with this if we hadn't spotted a somber black Jamaican, German, Indonesian, Sudanese-American swing around the corner of W.24th, where the street finished curving through the Penn South complex.

Dustin wasn't alone. Three BUBS—Big Ugly Bastards—were walking with him. Interesting escort— asses cocked, faces made for mug shots.

"If they're Christian social activists," I said, "God help the rest of us."

"I think I know one of them."

"Least they're only three."

"No, four."

Roots pointed to another BUB in front of a tapas bar, standing by the curb and looking up into the downtown traffic. Dustin and the others joined him, also checking the avenue, glancing at their watches. Waiting for a pick-up.

"I'll get the car." Roots left and walked around the corner. I followed him out 30 seconds later and lingered near the Aragon, pretending to read my messages, watching the group across the street without watching.

A minute later a gray Range Rover Evoque pulled up. I called Roots. "Their ride's here."

So's yours.

Just as the Evoque was taking off, the original crankshaft of a fully restored TorqueFlite transmission pulled a '59 Chrysler Imperial up to me. Wherever we're going, we're on our away.

The Evoque maneuvered across Ninth and made a left on 23rd heading east. We followed.

"It occurs to me," I said, "this might not be the most inconspicuous vehicle in Manhattan."

"It is if you know what you're doing."

Roots' technique was to stay well behind the
Evoque, safely out of their paranoia range. Which was fine
until the SUV suddenly swerved into a turning lane and
took a quick left. Roots had to shoot the gap between a
truck and a bus and drop both our kidneys to make the turn,
flooring the Imperial like a rocket to Russia.

We were on Sixth, merging with the uptown traffic.

"I know where I know him from," said Roots,
referring to the BUB. "FMP Protectional. He works there."

"Private security?"

"He's one of their people. I've seen him before."

"Somebody hired private security? Sabreena?"

"Somebody."

He steered the big boat past Herald Square, Macy's,
late-lunch crowds. The sky was turning dark gray, looking
so much like slate you could just about walk on it. Ahead
of us, the Evoque traveled a few more blocks, then turned
right on W.40th.

By the time we took the corner the SUV was double
parked across the street from Bryant Park. We kept moving
east, looked behind, saw Dustin and two of the BUBs get
out, leaving the other two in the car. Roots drove a few
more feet toward Fifth, then double parked across from the
New York Public Library.

"You're gonna keep it here?"

"That's what they're doing," he said as he put the
flashers on. "Tit for fucking tat." He took something out of
his pocket and slipped it on his finger. A ring with a dime-
size onyx stone. A wireless camera.

Dustin and the two BUBs were crossing the street
and entering the park. We walked back on 40th, passed the
Evoque, and once Roots snapped pix of the passengers
inside, we cut over and followed.

Bryant Park used to be a decent place, an oasis for
dealers selling beat rock, dried-out weed or baking soda
disguised as coke, speed or heroin. Now it was littered with
law abiders, crowded—despite the graying skies—with
people eating lunch and playing chess and quietly reading.
Just *vile*.

Dustin and the BUBS—remember that hit song they had?—were cutting through the tables and benches , navigating a fairly steady course toward the pink granite Memorial Fountain. The security guys were as cool as the other side of the pillow. Dustin, though, was all nervous head twitches, looking for something or someone.

Someone. Now he was locking eyes with a woman who was walking in the opposite direction across the Fountain Terrace, carrying a laptop under her arm. A heavy-set woman wearing a short skirt and a pair of chunky boots that added like 200 pounds to her frame. Obviously not Sabreena.

Still looking at her, Dustin took his phone out, ready to make a call. He and the woman approached each other like they were about to say hello. But just before they reached the meeting point their heads turned—the old last-second look-away—and they kept on walking their separate ways.

"There it is," said Roots. "The exchange. They just made a transfer. Near-field beaming app, his phone to her laptop."

"The PIB?"

"Could be anything."

Roots photographed the woman as she moved off. Dustin and his BUBs, meanwhile, proceeded out to Sixth Avenue and back to 40th Street. Minutes later they were driving past 42nd and Grand Central, taking Madison up to 57th, 57th over to Eighth Avenue, Eighth into Central Park West. We were discreetly behind them, Roots regaling me with an enthusiastic discussion of near-field transmissions, unlicensed radio frequencies, magnetic field inductions and Miller coding versus Manchester coding.

A block before the Museum of Natural History, the gray Evoque pulled over to the right and let Dustin and the same two BUBs out. We saw them walk into the 77th Street entrance to Central Park as the SUV moved back into traffic.

Roots dropped me off at the same spot. "I'll find a place to park."

"Let's keep in touch."

Inside the park I caught the threesome turning off West Drive and crossing the Bank Rock Bridge, heading into the Wiccan wildlands of The Ramble. Was Dustin looking to get laid? With those pair of BUBs around, gonna be some *safe* sex.

They took a maze of pathways through tupelos, sycamores, oaks and bands of bedrock until they came to a stone arch built in the cleft between two outcroppings of rock. Dustin stopped, took out his phone and made a call. He nodded, asked the BUBs questions. They pointed southeast, further into The Ramble.

My phone vibrated as they continued walking. Roots was at the 77th Street entrance. I gave him whispered directions to the stone arch.

More paths, more woods, more rocky cliffs, more quiet directions. Roots caught up with me just as Dustin & co. were approaching a small log-built bridge stretching over a stream. The stream fed into the park's big lake, and through the budding trees we could still see its 22 acres of water.

A man was standing on the other side of the bridge, crew cut, butch wax, XXX raincoat, phone in hand, a face not even a mother could love. Something frightening about it, terrifying, like photos of Judge Judy smiling.

Whoever he was, Dustin seemed happy to see him, and the man seemed happy that Dustin seemed happy to see him.

As Dustin and his escorts began traipsing over the bridge, Roots and I moved in closer to take photos. Maybe a little too close. The trio was halfway across when the man held up a hand—*wait*—and pressed a single key on his phone.

A moment later three nasty guys jumped out from behind the trees and rocks off the path. Not professional security. Sun-bleached jocks, vicious amateurs charging at us with telescoping batons. Gay bashers? Rough traders? Maybe *these* were the Christian activists.

One of them ran up to me and with no introduction outside of a tennis-court grunt swung his baton at my head. Fortunately, my brains aren't that big of a target. As I ducked he tore a chunk out of the red oak behind me. I came up with a frankly perfect uppercut, a shot so solid I could feel and even *hear* several of his ribs cracking apart. He doubled over and wobbled on his feet for a few seconds before getting up close and personal with the ground.

Then everything outside and inside my eyes went blurry. I never saw the second guy sneaking up to me from the side. But I felt the baton smashing into my backbone like a spinal tap. Between the pain and the sheer surprise of getting hit I found myself sprawled facedown on the path.

I tried to scramble up but only made it to my knees. The second guy dropped his baton in front of me and used it to pin me from behind, locking my shoulders while the dude with the cracked ribs staggered over looking for payback.

I was really sorry I'd left my third arm at home today.

Prince Cracked Ribs planted himself in front of me, raised his baton and took careful aim at my face. He looked like he wanted to kill me.

No, he looked like he *had* killed me. He'd killed me, been arrested, been arraigned, been tried and convicted and sentenced to die in the electric chair and now had 2,640 volts (as required by law) burning through his body and fatally disrupting the rhythm of his heart.

He looked like he could actually *see* electricity.

Roots was pointing that early-model cell phone at him, that high-frequency microwave device he'd pulled on me that night on Canal Street. He was toasting the guy with enough electromagnetic radiation to paralyze him until he wilted and fell over.

The third guy, the one he'd already microwaved, was still thrashing on the ground. Roots aimed the device at the gentleman holding me. Dude let me go, jackrabbitted away with a nasally yap and skittered off into the bushes.

I looked back at the bridge. Dustin was gone. The man with the crew cut was gone. The BUBs were gone. It was a mass exodus, completed when the two remaining baton twirlers ran their fried asses off in opposite directions.

Not exactly an award-winning handling of the situation on our part. Still, Roots found a bright side. "Maybe getting that close to them was a dumb move," he said. "But nobody makes dumb moves smarter than we do."

Global Impact

Lukas was his usual bawdy self. Rattled, depressed, roaming through the long miles of some internal darkness. The view from the Cenacle—360 all-glass degrees of the grounds, the Sound, the sky—was completely lost on him. Despite the 10-foot elevation, he was caught in the lower depths. He might not be eating the Last Supper, the way Jesus did in the original Cenacle, but he sure looked (to continue the execution theme) like he was eating his last meal.

Something I said? In this case, no. All I told him was that Roots and I had turned up some contacts and leads and were pursuing them with all due diligence. Lukas was too out of it to press for details. We were following a strict don't-ask, don't-tell policy.

So why the long face? It was all on him, not me. He'd gone off-campus earlier in the day, traveling with a security team to Stony Brook University, where an audience at the Humanities Institute was waiting to hear him talk about the go-backs.

All went swimmingly at first. He opened by discussing the Anthropocene era, a term used by some researchers (and he would add himself to that number) to describe the current period in the Earth's history. Exactly when it started no one knows with any precision, though many point to the late 1700s and the Industrial Revolution. In any case, origins aside, Anthropocene refers to the time frame when human actions create a significant impact on the multi-systems of the Earth itself—and who, as Lukas asked, can deny that such a global impact is indeed taking place? Every step today equals 100 steps of the past. The point is beyond dispute. And yet, incredibly enough, there are those among us who fail to see the enormous Anthropocenic changes happening everywhere we look. There are those who cling to the old and reject the new, who persistently refuse to climb out of the cauldron of the past. They're everywhere among us, thriving like colonies of ants under the floorboards of our homes...

He'd gone on for 20 minutes and was just getting warmed up when it was brought to his attention that he wasn't addressing an audience in the Humanities Institute. This was the Javits Lecture Center, the next building over. And those among us listening to him weren't expecting to hear a talk on Adolph Hitler and Lee Harvey Oswald and the ultimate import of the go-backs. They were education students, attending a required lecture on *Monitoring Comprehension and Creating a Dynamic Interactive Learning Environment.*

Embarrassing enough, but what really killed Lukas was that the fault was his own. His security people had told him when they first arrived that he was walking into the wrong building. He'd ignored them and insisted he knew exactly where he was going.

"I don't know what's happening to me," he said. "My mind seems to be plotting against itself. The forms, the shapes, the patterns—I can't see them clearly anymore. My wife is doing this to me, that much I know. My wife is upsetting me. My wife and Dustin Mathis and I don't know why. Why've they turned against me? Why don't they appreciate my suffering? Why don't they understand what I'm trying to do?"

"I'll have to check this carefully," I said, "but they might not be living inside your head."

Pentagrams

Some good news: The photos Roots had taken of the BUBs paid off. All four of them worked for FMP Protectional. No IDs yet on the woman in Bryant Park or the man in Central Park, but knowing who the BUBs were was a big step up. A few of the night traders had hacked the FMP systems and were now tracking the men's movements. That's how Roots knew they'd taken Dustin to a church in Prospect Heights. Since Janiva's Gowanus studio was only a couple miles away, he suggested waiting there for the next move.

Janiva had a new project going. Gigantic circuit boards—9 x 12-foot grids of precisely etched copperfoil lines—were resting against the walls of the loft. Only one was fully functional at this point. She'd installed hundreds of LEDs in each of the board's round contact pads. Programmed with maps from the Human Genome Project and synced to the heartbeats of the audience, the LED clusters sent out fractals of light that looked like the whorls of a seashell or sun rippling on water before resolving themselves in perfect, five-point pentagrams.

Which came close to matching the pattern of tearstains on Janiva's white shirt.

She and Roots were in the thick of it.

"Are you trying to say you're sorry?" she said, furious and weeping. "Is this what passes for an apology these days?"

"She's angry with me," he said as I walked in, "because I won't answer her angry texts."

"I'm *angry* with you because of what you're *doing* to yourself."

"She wants me to do something where I get paid in money, not gems."

"I want you to *do* something where you don't get *killed*."

"Someday I'll change—I told you that. Someday I'll get into something else."

"Why is it taking *so* long?"

"Why're you getting *so* angry?"

She looked at me. "See, I don't think he *can* change. I don't think he has the inner tools for adaptation and change." Back to him. "Do you have the inner tools for adaptation and change?"

"Fuck you."

"Fuck *me*?"

"Fuck you if you think you can lead me around by the dick."

That was it. No more. She'd had enough of his shit. She wanted him out—out of here, out of her life. She broke up with him with me standing there, LEDs forming peaceful, hypnotic images all around us.

"Why can't we have an honest discussion?" she wanted to know.

"We *can*," he said. "Just change the fucking *subject*."

Closing Time

Roots took it hard. He looked like all the days had fallen off the calendar. "I'm tired of this, I'm tired of all this bumfuck twaddle. All we do is fight like this. It's always all this I-heard-you-twice-the-first-time shit."

We were heading north on Flatbush Avenue, Roots keeping one eye on his phone propped up on the Imperial's push-buttoned dashboard. Robbo Fragaruccio was intercepting the call-ins to FMP and texting what he'd heard. Dustin and the BUBs were on the BQE, approaching the Brooklyn Bridge.

"First time you've broken up?" I said.

"I've broken up with her many times before, though she never seems to know it."

"Has she ever broken up with *you* before?"

"Many."

"And what usually happens?"

"We break up, say it's a Friday night. Saturday, Sunday, I'm plunged in depression. Monday, I meet someone else. Wednesday, I'm back with Janiva. Friday night, we break up."

We took the exit just past Nassau Street and got on the BQE. The midnight traffic wasn't heavy at all.

"You think you're bad," I said, "I should tell you about my marriage."

"Yeah, well she never— Wait, I think I'm *bad?*"

Robbo text: The BUBs were tasking the FDR north.

He disagreed—he didn't think it was *bad*. Not normal, maybe, but not *bad*. In fact, he wished things *were* normal. He was always telling her that—he wished things could go back to the old normal. But then he'd think, well, which of the old normals am I talking about?

The speed limit on the Brooklyn Bridge was 45. We were doing 70.

"That's what it is," he said, "everything gets caught up in retrograde. Everything gets caught in all this *backtowardness*. And she thinks it's *funny*. I tell stuff like this to her and she *laughs*. If she wants to be post-humorously awarded for it, fine, but it's not *funny*."

We swung into the FDR. Again, not much traffic at all.

"This is what can happen when you're young," I said. "Feelings can run really high. You're young, you're so desperate for happiness you can't let anything get in its way."

"I *know*. That's *exactly* the problem. She gets so intense about it, it fucking *scares* me. Just throws me off. I can't function. I can't function with all that destrunction."

That *what*?

According to Robbo, they were turning off on 34th Street. Probably going back across town to the Penn South Co-ops.

"Who the fuck is she to question my core competence? By what right? What happened to a sense of fair play in this country? What happened to a man is presumed innocent until charges are brought against him? I'll tell you one thing, though. I can tell you *one* thing. The hen is mightier than the ford around here."

This was dangerously amusing. The manic half of his bipolar muddle was taking over.

"*Life*! Fucking *life*! Makes all the world of sense, doesn't it? And you know what I'd say to her if she were sitting here right now? You know what I'd say? Frankly, my dear, I don't *give* a fuck!"

We'd just gotten off on 34th when Robbo's next text came in: The BUBs were turning north on Madison. They weren't heading to Penn South.

Interesting that Roots tended not to flip out like this when Janiva was around. He got aggravated, sure, but not demonic. He only went completely non compos when he

was without her. It was almost as if opening the lunatic
floodgates was the only way to make up for her absence.

We made a right on Madison, caught up with them
as they were passing the old Roosevelt Hotel, the first hotel
in Manhattan to feature a TV in every room. The gray
Evoque was five cars ahead of us.

They turned left on 47th, going west. We followed,
Prince Myshkin next to me manically muttering the whole
time. His monologue was just slightly irritating, like a full-
blast mariachi band performing *Cielo Rojo* on the subway
at eight in the morning.

We stayed a few cars behind as they passed through
the diamond district and crossed Sixth, finally hitting
serious traffic at Times Square. The Seventh Avenue
intersection in front of us was rat-trap gridlock. The
Evoque wasn't moving and neither were we.

We saw Dustin get out by the Pig 'n' Whistle. He
had three BUBs with him this time. They started walking
toward Seventh.

"I'm tired of all these paranormal bisexuals," said
Roots. "All these thieving bums and ineffectuals."

He double-parked by the side of the Doubletree. His
disregard for NYPD parking rules verged on the shocking.

We hooked a left and followed the group on foot
down Seventh. The streets were packed with pilgrims on
their way to a late-night Canterbury. Fourteen million neon
signs were all saying the same thing: *Here's More Crap
We're Trying To Dump On You.* There was a good, shouty,
rapturous something about everything.

Dustin and the three BUBs were crossing 46th.

"All these chicks with dicks and their refrigerated
underwear," said Roots. "No sex before six? I get it, I get it.
Keep me abreast? I'll save you a wing."

A biker was standing on the corner of 46th, handing
out fliers for a tattoo parlor.

"God made our skin to be inked," he was saying.
"That's from the Bible."

Right, the Book of Needlemiah.

Dustin was staring in the windows of Forever 21,
former site of the Virgin Megastore. How many pre-iTune

hours had I spent in there? Now it was a massive Mall-of-America size fashion store where you could shop without dropping until 2 a.m.

My view was blocked for a moment by a middle age woman and her elderly mother walking in the opposite direction.

"It's time," the mother said.

"It's not. You just went before we left the restaurant. It's not time yet."

"It's later than you think."

As they passed I saw the DustBUBs nearing the corner of 45th, heading for the Swatch shop. But they stopped, turned around and started moving back toward Forever 21, the BUBs eye-checking the entrance and the street.

"It's a pass," said Roots. "A blatant pass. They've got a meeting and they just made a make-sure pass. Are they kidding me with this? Are they challenging my expertation?"

He was right. The DustBUBs slipped into Forever 21.

"You okay for this?" I said.

"Just a little bipolarish, that's all. But I'm fine. I'm prepped. Solid. Right as rain."

I believe I was the only man in America at the moment who was looking for a renegade Information Assurance analyst in a Forever 21 at one in the morning with a madman who, as we walked inside, was mumbling something about *monkey spots* and *fancy-pants who fart like Greeks*. But I could be wrong about that.

I didn't see our guys on the main floor. I saw woven plaid shirts and skinny jeans and knit hoodies and cargo capris and flare-leg jeggings and fitted skirts and leatherette jackets and glass partitions and high-gloss fixtures and salespeople with pre-printed smiles and kids, kids, kids. Our boys would've stood out in this crowd.

"Four floors here," said Roots. "A hundred and fifty-one fitting rooms. I read about it."

"Plenty of places to hide."

"Priced to sell, going to hell."

We took the escalator down: Acres of makeup and jewelry, all vibrating with electric color. Nice place for a rendezvous disguised as a shopping trip.

"Vicious, delicious, nutritious," quoth the Roots.

Third subfloor: A children's department, dwarfed by a giant's treehouse. And men's clothes—21Men the section was called. I spotted something familiar—a giant's raincoat, a butch-waxed crew cut. The guy from The Ramble, standing over by a rack of toggle-button jackets. He wasn't at *all* out of place, like a rollercoaster built on the surface of the moon.

Something in the air was giving off a chocolatey, sweet-rubber smell.

Somebody was coming up to us—one of the BUBs, face made for a mug shot, curious look in his eye. He semi-whispered to me. "Are you Eddie?"

"Not yet. I'll let you know when I get there."

Roots backed me up. "Zero due on signing."

The BUB was confused, yes, but not enough to leave us alone. Instead he glanced at The Ramble Guy and coughed. The Ramble Guy looked at him, then looked at us.

I'm not exactly sure what happened next.

There was panic and movement everywhere, unexplained crashing noises. The other two BUBs were charging in from another part of the department, knocking over mannequins in their rush. The BUB next to me grabbed my arm. I let my energy drop to my legs and head-butted him in the chest. The glass partition behind him cracked in four pieces as he fell through it.

Customers were screaming and scrambling and hitting the floor. Forever 21 guards were shouting and running over. Roots was yelling *Inny or outty? Inny or outty?* Everything was collapsing in criss-crossed chaos.

The Ramble Guy was suddenly in front of me, loading up a punch like he wanted to kill me eight times over.

I shook my head and pointed to my shoulder. "I can't fight. Bursitis."

"You should've thought of that before you—"

My toes landed directly on the spermatic cords in his nut sac. He wouldn't be reproducing for the next few weeks.

Roots had the other two BUBs crippled on the floor. He was microwaving them both at the same time with a sweep technique that's still being discussed by students of electromagnetic radiation.

The Forever 21 guards, hungry for action, were ready to tackle the both of us. Roots stopped them, holding up—Jesus save us—a fake NYPD badge. And just as he was saying *We're cops—somebody call 911*, I saw a brown blur bolting out of a fitting room by a table of Okeh crewneck tees. Dustin, making a run for it.

He sprinted for the up escalator. I took after him. Climbing three steps at a time, he got to the second subfloor, made a sharp turn and jumped the escalator up to the main level.

Halfway there, he stumbled and grabbed the railing to stay steady. Or he seemed to stumble. As he straightened himself up his body shook like he was sobbing. There was something uncertain about the movement, something involuntary—he could've been yanked by invisible wires. Then he swayed, lost his balance and tumbled back down to the second floor.

This was happening? Dustin Mathis (no, impossible, don't even think it) was finally landing in my lap? Or by my feet?

Not quite. His face was sick and livid with heavy shock. His expression was stunned, wide open, as if cataracts had just melted from his eyes. His mouth was fringed with thick white strings of cathidrone foam.

I knelt beside him. He looked at me like he was looking at winter.

"I don't feel very good," he said.

"How much cath did you take?"

"How much what?"

"Cath—cathidrone. The drug you took."

He yawned. "I didn't take any drug. I don't do drugs."

"Did somebody give you something?"

"I'm freezing. I'm very cold."

Roots and the store guards were here, gathering around us. The silence on the second floor was scary.

"He bit off more than he should chew," said Roots. "Call for an ambulance too."

"It's cath," I said.

"*Shit.* What about the PIB?" He leaned over Dustin. "Where's the PIB?"

Dustin looked up at him. "Aren't you cold?"

"Tell me about the PIB. Tell me about Sabreena."

Dustin smiled. "I love Sabreena."

"Beautiful. *To Love Somebody*, the Bee Gees. Where *is* she?"

"She's my angel. Sabreena is my…" He took a deep breath, smiled one more time and closed his eyes. He never opened them again.

I stood up. Love to stay, but… "You know, it *is* later than we think."

Roots nodded but kept looking down at the body. "Who can answer the mysteries of the tongues?"

You could hear the first sirens somewhere outside. "Let's book."

But Roots didn't move. He couldn't stop staring at Dustin. "What's in *your* wallet?" he said.

Synchronicity

It was like make-up sex, only we hadn't been fighting. It was pure lust but more than lust, our bodies fighting for cleansing, healing, salvation. My hands moving over her warm body, kneading her shoulders, the back of her neck under the long white hair, gently brushing her purple-swollen nipples. My tongue tracing the terrain of her belly, her navel—an inny—then traveling downward, making her hair bristle, making her pussy purr with the original meaning of the term *lovin' spoonful*. Her fingers rubbing the tip of my cock, putting me inside, groaning, her hips moving up and down, slowly at first then harder and faster and beyond control, searching for the depths, desperate for the final flood of freedom and ecstasy, the final moment of Easter release. Which, as we all know, is a seminal event in the life of the spirit.

The sex was good. The talk we had after, maybe even better. At least more peaceful. Moonlight pale on the hanging talismans, erection night results in, her bedroom had a kind of Sunday-morning calm to it.

I needed it after the night in mid-town.

Basically, Belinda picked up her story from the time she escaped her mother and fled Vegas on a bus. She told me about going back to school, becoming an emancipated minor, studying pastoral counseling at the Uncharted Waters Ministries in Santa Monica and getting her chaplain's license. She worked her way through a lot of texts before she discovered the Old Trickster known as the Buddha. That's where she found the spiritual essence of the world, the magic sense at the root of all life. That's how she came across a timeless, spaceless, eternally joyful realm that at the same time is this world of remorse, anxiety, despair and fear.

"It was the paradox that blew me away," she said. "Every truth contains an untruth. Every statement holds its opposite. Everything in zen *is*, and yet it *isn't*, and yet, when you come right down to it, it *is*."

"We all need stuff like that. We need everything we can get. We're all crazy in one way or another. We all need help."

A change of mood. I could feel it in the dark, feel a shadow crossing over her face. Yes, something I said.

Belinda turned over and lit a candle on her nightstand. "I want you to listen to something." She got up, came back to bed with an iPod and a set of earbuds. The iPod was engraved with the [0+X] logo.

"I just started looking into this," she said. "You've seen the staffers listening to these."

"Like everywhere."

"I'm starting to wonder if they might be connected to the suicides."

"I think the cath—the cathidrone—is a big factor."

"They weren't *all* taking cathidrone. But they were all listening to these."

"Must be some *bad* music."

"They don't play music. They only play this."

Which wasn't much. Nothing but synthesized tone clusters droning between the earbuds, repeating themselves with minimal variations in frequency, volume and sound location.

"It's patented as Auralsynch," she said. "Designed to enhance productivity by synchronizing the brain waves. I found out Lukas created it."

Sounds familiar—no pun intended. I was thinking about the MIXEX, the software programmed to induce communal thinking, to persuade people to share the same thoughts and opinions. The software Rj Delgado had slipped into the *Real Story* app.

"There's something generally creepy about it," she said. "I don't know why, but somehow it reminds me of my mother."

I don't know about that. It was not unpleasant. In fact, there was something very relaxing, almost narcotic, about all these smooth sine-wave oscillations. I could feel myself sinking into the bed.

"You can stop now, if you want. You get the idea."

Why would I want to stop? I could see why this was such a big draw on the campus. It was like a mild pot high, with a little zesty meth tossed in. Speedball hypnosis.

"Quinn? I'm not sure if you should be listening too long. It could be dangerous."

Dangerous? This? This was just a trance, that's all. Just serial vibrations. Incantatory. Carnatic. I could feel the sounds looping through my head, altering my thoughts. Okay, maybe there was *some* potential danger. You're always taking a chance when you let yourself fall under a spell. Sometimes, you know, there's not much difference between heaven and hell.

"Are you listening to what I'm saying? Quinn, can you hear me?"

"No. No, I can't."

I Heard It Through The Grapevine

What we knew so far: NYPD was continuing to investigate the fatal drug overdose of a current or former [0+X] employee (the status was uncertain) at Forever 21. Four possibly related arrests had been made involving a scuffle at the store that immediately preceded the victim's death. Meanwhile, the police were searching for two men who'd claimed to be plainclothes detectives and whose images had been caught on the Forever 21 surveillance cameras. Which meant that whatever Roots and I did next, we'd be doing it with one of those abundance-of-caution approaches.

Of the four men arrested and released on bail, three worked for FMP Protectional. The fourth was a Lawrence Broonzy of Hartsdale, N.Y. Presumably this was the big bruiser from The Ramble. But no. Lawrence Broonzy of Hartsdale, N.Y., turned out to be a 5-1 featherweight who taught social studies at Woodlands High School and whose wallet had been stolen while he and his wife were attending a Broadway show earlier that night.

So what we *didn't* know so far included who the guy from The Ramble was and where the fuck Sabreena and the PIB were. The night traders worked their asses off to fill the gaps. Tapping into FMP no longer helped—the agency had evidently been fired from the Sabreena job and cut out of the loop. That left checking Sabreena and Dustin Mathis' backgrounds, looking for anybody who might've aided and abetted their disappearance. But no go. Not even slow go. It was like trying to sell diet programs in Darfur.

Then my man Roots came through. Hacking with some form of Konami cheat code, he found that Dustin had visited a medical clinic when he first arrived in the city.

He'd listed a *Greta Slocum* as his emergency contact on
the patient form. More searching yielded Greta Slocum's
connection with Dustin—she was his aunt on his mother's
side—and her address: 36A Leroy Street, in the Village.

Roots was on the heat.

One of the greatest things New York City has ever done
was to allow its master-plan grid system of streets and
avenues—a vision of progressive precision conceived in
the early 19th century—to skip over Greenwich Village.
This let the area keep its Old World charm, its rambling
roads, its bucolic mews, its quiet side streets. By the late
1820s this countrified maze, an oasis in the middle of
verticals and horizontals, had turned the Village into a hot
piece of real estate. We could see the symbol of its status
looming ahead of us at the end of Fifth Avenue—the arch
of Washington Square Park. Since 1797 this rectangle of
land had been used as a potter's field, a public burial
ground for the poor, the unclaimed and the victims of
yellow fever. But by 1828 the new-money residents of the
Village decided the stench of death somehow clashed with
their gentrified values—NIMBY—and they petitioned the
city to build a park over the remains of 20,000 lost souls.

"I'll tell you something," Roots said as we stopped
for the light on Eighth Street. "Something a lot of people
don't know. Shakespeare was terrible at crossword
puzzles."

A fascinating statement under any circumstances,
but two things took a bit of its sting away. (1) Crossword
puzzles weren't invented until the 19th century—the era of
the grid—so it wasn't true. (2) We hadn't been talking
about Shakespeare or crosswords or anything remotely
resembling Shakespeare or crosswords.

"Crossword puzzles?"

"Known fact. Too much protein, that's the thing.
Too many fatty acids. Man cannot live by fish oil alone."

Bold, jumpy, disjointed associations. He was
drifting again.

"You've been thinking about Janiva," I said as we drove around Washington Square.

"Not at all. Two or three times. A minute."

"That's bad."

"I wouldn't say it's bad. I'd say it's not good."

"So this is a not-good fight you're having?"

It was a fight, period. They fought all the time. He told me how they fought on Facebook, posting battle reports on their walls, trying to convince their friends to take their respective sides.

Interesting dichotomy. Guy was so secretive he wouldn't take money because it could be traced. But he didn't mind broadcasting his love life to the world at large.

We left the Imperial in a parking garage on West 3rd and walked over to Sixth Avenue. The evening downpour had let up, though forecasters were warning that we were going to get a month's worth of rain in 24 hours.

Sixth Avenue was Sixth Avenue. A woman walking by with a parrot on her shoulder. A young couple, second date going well. A woman kissing another woman's fist. Over by the video newsstand, two juicers arguing with each other. *You lost my fucking keys!*

What happened to the happy drunks of yore?

The Village, of course, has a rich history of gin mills. Take The Grapevine, a 19th-century spot once located up on Sixth Avenue and 11th Street. Place was such a fount of gossip and news it gave birth to a phrase: *I heard it through the grapevine.* Or Chumley's, a Prohibition speakeasy on Barrow Street. Whenever the law rushed in through the front door, the patrons would flee through the back exit at 86 Bedford Street, turning *86'd* into shorthand for over and out.

We turned the angled corner of Sixth and Carmine, heading for Bleecker and then Leroy.

"I'll eat any yogurt," said Roots, apropos of exactly nothing, "as long as it doesn't taste like yogurt. That's how I do it—that's what I do. Bacterial fermentation, active cultures, all that. All of us—it runs in the family."

"*What* runs in the family?"

"Eating yogurt." He started sing-songing:

My father's name is Rudy
He's always really moody
Cause he don't get no booty
And he can't make a doody

Odd thing to hear from someone who came home from school one day and found that his father had eaten a bullet in the front seat of the car.

"Can I ask you something?"

"Absolutely, absolutely."

"About your father?"

"Shoot."

Jesus.

"What did you think when you saw him in the garage?"

"Think? Nothing."

"What did you feel?"

"Not a thing."

"Were you at least *surprised*? Had he been depressed?"

"I don't know. I saw him that morning, he was acting a little weird, I guess. He was standing in front of the mirror in the living room, by the front door. He was looking at himself and saying, *I feel like a fucking Puerto Rican.* That's the last thing I ever heard him say. *I think I'm turning into a fucking Puerto Rican.*

I was thinking we had the wrong address. 36A Leroy Street wasn't a residential building. It was a set of ancient, moss-covered steps leading down to a basement door that simply said *Gypsy's*. Had to be a mistake. Nobody's aunt lives here.

Roots verified his research on his phone. No, 36A Leroy Street. Yes, in Manhattan.

Let's check it out.

Roots' first reaction: "Christ in a boat."

Couldn't blame him. We were standing in a crowded, upscale cabaret. A feather-clad woman was performing on a low stage, spinning the tassels on her breasts around like the blades of a Eurocopter TwinStar. She was doing plenty of bumping, though not much grinding, as a five-piece band (The Injectable Potatoes, according to their bass drum) played next to her.

As she slowly peeled one of her feathers off and tossed it to the tables, the crowd hooted, cheered and stomped. Who were they? Bachelorette parties, aging frat boys, brigades of vibrator queens, all happily overpaying for the booze.

This wasn't a strip joint. It was a burlesque revue. No cock-teaser poles here, no lap dances. The show was peek-a-boo flirtatious, more risqué than raunchy.

Not exactly Jack Ruby's Carousel Club.

A smiling, tuxedoed man with a tiny head and a huge tummy came up to us. He was a one-man Laurel and Hardy—Stan's face, Oliver's body.

"Welcome to Gypsy's, gentlemen. Twenty-dollar cover."

"I think we're lost," I said.

"Not here, you're not."

"We're looking for a Greta Slocum."

So much for the smile. "She knows you're coming?"

"I doubt it."

"She know who you are?"

"The *w* in *know* is silent," Roots said helpfully, "as in *saloon*."

The man gave him a steady look. "You want to see her, I suggest you make—"

"It's about her nephew," I said. "Dustin Mathis."

LaurtelHardy understood. He stepped away and made a call on his cell.

We watched the woman on stage remove another one of her feathers.

"Saloon?"

"Crazy Guggenheim," said Roots, "early 60s. It's on YouTube."

A black guy with gold caps on his teeth was weaving away from the tables. He was as tight as credit.

He stumbled over to us and zeroed in on Roots. "If you can't satisfy your woman," he said solemnly, "I can."

Roots went apeshit. "What do you know? What do you know?"

"I can tell you're a little lax in the slacks."

"Fuck you! Fuck *YOU!*"

Another guy—white dude, ponytail sprouting like a scallion out of an otherwise clean-shaven head—rushed over, pulled the black man away and took him back to the tables.

"Who was that son of a bitch?" Roots wanted to know. "What was he talking about?"

"Just messing with your head."

"My head doesn't need any more messing with."

Truer words.

LaurelHardy returned to us. "Greta's the owner. She lives upstairs."

He took us through a side door and into an ancient, moldy, tottering hallway. Not so upscale. I thought I'd see weeds growing out of the baseboards.

Greta had owned this place for many years, LaurelHardy said. It'd been many things—a bar, a comedy club, an after-hours joint, a tranny bar—at many different times.

We took a set of stairs. It felt like we were falling *up* into a rabbit hole.

Apartment door. Knock. "Come on in."

Aunt Greta was an old, disheveled woman with a rag-mop haircut, as thin as *The Anthology of Nazi Humor*. She was smoking a cigarette, wearing a muumuu and circling around the apartment with a deliberate shuffle of her thick white socks.

"Just give me a minute," she said, "while I dust the floor."

>>>>>>

The Bible Ho

She was a woman of hard-bitten dignity, bohemian to the point of dysfunctional, and so she never got along with her sister's in-laws and all those other people down in Moosehead or Elksballs or whatever that town in Tennessee called itself. "I was hip to their shit as soon as I met 'em," she said, wiping down the table where the three of us were sitting with a sponge she'd been using for the last 25 years. "When Dustin said he wanted to get away from his fucko father, I said sure, you can stay here, long as you want. It was pleasure to have him. He talked a lot—there was that—but he had so much he wanted to get off his chest of course he was gonna talk a lot. But he never fucked around with drugs, I can tell you that with some certainty. This overdose shit? Not him—he was a good kid. The stove over there? He cleaned off the top of that stove *every time he used it*. He was *clean* kid."

"We don't think he popped the drug himself," I said. "That's why we're here. We're trying to find out who killed him."

"I wish you would."

"What was he doing lately, past few months?"

Greta chain-lit another cigarette. "Really don't know. We had a drifting apart there, sadly. We *had* been close, bosom-buddy close I'd say, until he turned fundamental. Until he met that Bible ho, Kirk Hammond."

"Didn't get along?"

"Well he didn't get along with *me*. Him and his friends. Kirk—and rest his soul, you know?—but him, his weasel friends, they're the first to point fingers, the last to admit they're wrong. They didn't approve of *me*. They didn't approve of what's going on downstairs. They're looking at a future so glorious and majestic they can't see the world. They didn't make *me* feel blessed, put it that way."

"So they caused a rift?"

"What am I saying? What've I been telling you? Those people turned Dustin's head around. Those holy-rolling, motherfucking martyrs pulled my own *nephew* away from me. You understand? Have I expressed myself strong enough?"

"R.E.M.," said Roots. "Every biddy hurts."

"What?"

"He ever mention a Sabreena?" I said quickly. "Sabreena Lister-Bertozzi?"

"His boss' wife? *Mention* her? He talked about her all the fucking time. He was very *fond* of her. I wouldn't know myself, of course. I never had the privilege of
meeting her."

"When was the last time you saw him?"

"Few weeks ago. Came over with one of his hallelujah buddies, tried to leave me some born-again crap from their group."

"Born-again crap?"

"Pamphlets, whatnot."

"You save them?"

"You kidding?"

"Did you know the buddy?"

"Wouldn't want to. Big ugly bastard. Used rudeness to hide his nastiness. We had some choice words. Then we had some *choicer* words."

"Big *ugly* bastard?"

"Total ass-face, with an idiot crew-cut to match."

"Crew cut?"

"The worse."

"Butch wax?"

"Every fucking hair."

The guy from The Ramble.

"You know his name?"

"He never said."

"You remember the name of their group?"

"How could I forget? PUFE. Praisers United For Ethics. They had it stamped all over the literature. PUFE. PUFE. PUFE. Ridiculous name. How gay can you get?"

How much of a *clue* can you get?

Three Times Faster Than The Sun

The rain was picking up as we walked back to the parking garage. Roots already had his phone out, running searches on PUFE, muttering, mostly to himself, "you know how skeptical penguins are." Right—indeed. As we were passing the video newsstand on Sixth, I caught a story on the display panel. *Naked Man Saying He's Jesus Sets Off Three-Hour Traffic Jam.* Not an unusual headline for New York, but it disturbed me. I don't know why, but it did.

"Hold up."

I watched. The incident happened on E.161st Street. Around 8 p.m. police received reports of a nude man running around Concourse Plaza, yelling and screaming that he was Jesus Lord and Savior. The man fled as the cops arrived on the scene and dashed into traffic on the Grand Concourse. A car in the northbound lanes swerved to avoid him, crashing into two other cars. The third car struck a pole and brought a street light down across the roadway. The first car, meanwhile, was leaking fuel and creating a fire hazard.

Hello—what's this? In the periphery. A guy walking behind us, clean skull with a ponytail, head like an onion growing a shoot.

The guy from Gypsy's, the one who pulled the black dude off Roots. He had a phone to his ear, talking away, looking at us—then looking away, veering a bit off to the side, when he saw me looking at him.

Like he'd been staking out he club, just in case we showed up?

The tail shagging the dog?

190

I turned back to the video. Naked Jesus had been apprehended on the Grand Concourse, uninjured but taken to Montefiore for psychiatric observation.

Okay—got it. I walked away, caught up with Roots, took a few more steps then stopped and wheeled around. Scallion Head was still looking this way, still trailing us, still yammering on the phone.

I have no idea why I did what I did next. Temporary insanity? Permanent? I knew we were supposed to be going careful, but it didn't seem to matter at the moment.

There's a star, HE 0437-5439, that comes from the center of the Milky Way. It's one of 16 known hypervelocity stars, called that because it's traveling at 16,000,000 mph, three times faster than the sun. That's what I felt like, like HE 0437-5439. My mind was moving three times faster than the sun.

I pulled the Glock out and shot him.

Right there on Sixth Avenue, the street loaded with traffic and witnesses. He spun in a half-circle as the bullet hit his shoulder. The phone clattered to the ground as he dropped it but he didn't pick it up, deciding, wisely, to start hobbling away. Have legs, will run.

"What the fuck?" Roots yelled. "What the fuck, I say. You can't do that!"

"I know."

"They're already looking for us. Forever 21. You blew it! You *superblew* it!"

"I know."

"It takes *time* to become what you already are!"

"Do me a favor? Grab the phone."

All Things Can be Measured In Time

We waited in the parking garage, sitting in the Imperial's swivel-out seats until whatever police action taking place on Sixth and Carmine or thereabouts had died down. At least we had Scallion Head's cell. A real find—repeated calls made over the last hour to the same number. This was better than looking for PUFE. Roots was talking geek-speak to the night traders as they used GPS and other tools of direction detection to triangulate the location.

He looked over at me for a moment. "Man," he said, "you been counting some nasty sheep."

Well said, I think. Actually I didn't know what to think. The fuck had I done out there? What kind of thrill-kill compulsion had taken me over? I was trying to understand it and trying not to think about it at the same time.

Need a diversion—check your messages. Banal, useless tweets. No, I needed something more *challenging* to take my mind off this. I called up *Interzone Quantum Time Differentials6B*. Give it another shot, so to speak. Sure, it takes about 800 pages to get started, but once it does...

I doubt if any reader will be surprised—or, for that matter, sorry—if we refuse to engage at this point in a thorough discussion—comically or otherwise—of the questions raised by Khilnani and O'Reilly and their agnostic speculations about the measurement of time. I will confine myself to simply laughing at them and dismissing the Titanic stink of their conclusions with an irrefutable statement: ALL TIME CAN BE MEASURED, AND ALL THINGS CAN BE MEASURED IN TIME.

I stand corrected: I'd always told my ex-wife that sex can't be measured by time.

Should anyone require a more extensive refutation of their noxious hypotheses—and a
confirmation of the theories we are currently examining—allow me to point to the formative work done by Chi'en, Podgorni and Malkin. What, you say? What does the Chi'en-Podgorni-Malkin research have to do with wrapped-string incongruities? I submit that the two approaches
are, in reality, different interpretations of the same fundamental theory.

Everything is, and yet isn't, and yet is.

Take the example, if you will, of Calabi-Yau shapes. It matters not their size, their configurations, the number of their holes, the variety of their holes, the extra dimensions ascribed to them. The physics of any Calabi-Yau shape is unequivocally identical to all other Calabi-Yau shapes. In the same way, the properties of wrapped-string incongruities—which at first blush may seem wildly divergent—are in fact different translations of the one and the same Chi'en-Podgorni-Malkin theory. Think about it.

I *was* thinking about it, whatever it meant, and it was pissing me off. I was getting irritated, frustrated. I felt like my ex-wife when her Facebook chat function goes down.

I called up a word count for *Interzone Quantum Time Differentials6B:* 398,547 words. Round it off to 400,000. That means it would take 40,000 people to read this shit without wanting to kill themselves.

"The gods of the underworld," said Roots, "are closer to the surface than we think."

"The fuck did you say?"

"Nothing. Just thinking out loud."

That was it—that's why I was so knife-blade edgy. I was picking up contact craziness from *him.*

But why now? Why didn't it happen earlier in our esteemed relationship? Something else in play here? Like the Auralsynch? Those repeating subliminal drones? Designed to stimulate productivity, but creating destruction

instead. So Belinda believed. Jesus, was my tolerance
that low? I'd only listened to five minutes of it. Or 10. Or
15...

There was a digital clock in the parking garage:
1:49 a.m. Something was wrong with it, like when they
switched to Daylight Savings somebody forgot to reset the
circuit. Because the colon between the numbers kept
flashing. On-off, on-off. *Two-dots. Two-dots. Two-dots.* It
was driving
me nuts.

"We've got it," said Roots. "We know where to go.
We've got a location."

Send My Regrets

And one with some history attached to it. By the time we got uptown to Sutton Place I'd found a little background on the building. According to the *hiddenhistorynyc* site, Nelson Rockefeller once kept an apartment here under a different name. Why? So he could slip through the service entrance around the corner and meet his girlfriends. No, not Megan Marshack, the one who was pinned under him when he died. That happened close by, in his townhouse on E.54th, near the garage where we'd left the Imperial.

Hard rain on Sutton Place, long slanting lines of wet. Along with townhouses, a communal garden, a bankside view of the East River. Up until 1875 this had just been a northern extension of prosaic old Avenue A. But then a Gold Rush prospector named Effingham B. Sutton built a block of brownstones and decided the street needed a more affluent name. And what better than his own? Still, it took a while for the wealth to spread. See the River House, that art deco apartment building down by 53rd, where Sutton Place begins? There were still tenements on that block when the building was constructed in 1931, the same slums where the Dead End Kids were always getting in trouble.

Our building, the Nelson Rockefeller Nooner, was a 14-story prewar with red bricks. We glanced in the entrance as we passed under the canopy. The doorman was blissfully asleep. Rest in peace, my friend.

The street around the corner was nice and quiet. No traffic, car or foot. I'd forgotten how Sutton Place Sutton Place can be.

We stopped by the service entrance. Roots produced the device he'd used to break into door number ED8 at the [0+X] complex and began connecting wires to the lock.

"There was a philosopher," he said. "I forget which. Plato, Spinoza, Ibn Rushd. He said, *for those who marry and for those who do not, I predict regret.*"

"This have anything to do with the lock?"

"Indirectly. I keep thinking about Janiva. I'm having trouble concentrating overall."

"Like the guy said, regret either way."

"I don't care. I'd rather be miserable with her than without her. I need to get back with her."

In the driving rain he's telling me this.

"So get back with her."

"I don't think it's gonna be that easy this time. I think I need some help. I think I need you to intercede."

"*Me?*"

"Long as you don't shoot her."

"Why *me?*"

"She won't listen to my friends."

"But she'll listen to me."

"I'm just throwing it out there."

"Throw it back."

"Just have a talk. I'm not gonna be right until we're back."

He was working on a broad definition of *right*.

"Do I look like eHarmony? I don't have enough on my mind? Now I'm running a lonely hearts club?"

The lock popped open. We shut up and stepped inside like a pair of Rockefellers.

Elegantly ancient hallways, dark, filled with rarified heat and the woody smell of wet fall leaves. Roots was walking with his phone held in front of him, using some kind of app to find the sweet reception spot for Scallion Head's calls.

Nothing on the first floor. We took the service stairs up. Roots Geiger-countered the second floor, the third. Zip.

I was getting light-headed, weird-headed. Things were turning druggy and hallucinatory, like I'd been watching too much news.

A month's worth of rain in 24 hours.

Fourth floor, fifth—not getting any warmer.

Everything is, and yet isn't, and yet is.

Sixth floor—paydirt.

"I'm getting a hit," Roots whispered as we came off the stairs. "It's getting stronger."

We walked half the length of the hallways, him holding the phone like a dowsing rod.

"This is good," he said. "This is good."

Then it wasn't. He stopped.

"I'm losing it."

"No," someone corrected, "you've *lost* it."

We never heard the door open behind us. The Ramble guy was standing there now, in front of one of the apartments we'd passed, crew cut, butch wax—the works. Oh yeah, and a big Buck Mark rimfire gun pointing at us. With a silencer on the barrel, the thing was an easy foot long.

"You two fucks are really getting tedious," he said.

Roots' response: "Ugly black-sky unloved scumbag don't-like don't-like don't-like."

Ramble was not amused. "What flavor of shit you been eating?"

Contrary to popular opinion, he was not one of the authors of the King James Bible.

"Huge motherfucker bastard-face can't-fuck can't-fuck can-he?"

"What's wrong with him?"

"He's nervous," I said.

"He should be." He motioned with the Buck Mark. ""Everything on the floor."

I took out the Glock and placed it in front of me. Roots divested himself of his phone, his break-in instrument and his microwave device.

Ramble pointed to the latter. "That fucking thing. Shove it over."

Roots nudged it with his foot and slid it across

the floor.

Ramble picked it up. "What the hell is this thing?"

"Dumb diphtheria clueless fuck-face."

He squeezed the unit in his large hand. "I said what the hell *is* this?"

"Don't touch that *key!*" Roots yelled.

As Ramble's eyes jumped down to his fingers I gut-rushed him. Stupid thing to do? Oh way beyond stupid. Dangerous. Hashashin delirious. *Suicidal.*

He raised the Buck Mark at me—not very Christian-like. I didn't hesitate, I didn't care. But he was swinging his arm too fast and too far and when he pulled the trigger the shot spit past me.

My tackle caught him in the chest. We staggered down together in one big fucking pile of bodies. His arms and legs were wrapping around me—he was octopussing me. I jammed my thumbs in his eyes and gouged them with kamikaze rage. He screamed, let go, but then went to smack me with the gun. I grabbed his hand and sank a deep-tissue bite into his wrist.

As the gun fell I scooped it up and smashed it into his head so fast he didn't have time to protect himself. I hit him again, then again, flashblooding, beating on him in some rabied-brain frenzy.

"Back off it, Quinn!" Roots yelling. "That's enough!"

I couldn't stop. It was like the time I killed that junkie, deliberately put a bullet between his eyes. I just couldn't stop.

"Do you mind not killing him?" said Roots. "That's fucking *enough!*"

Blood was everywhere. I'm thinking this isn't happening. This is *big-time* not happening. But it kept happening. I kept on—

Latex.

Electrified latex.

Something out of nowhere had struck me with like 8,000 pounds of pressure and everything was going polymer. The world was turning into hot gummy rubbery latex.

Canal Street, caught in a power field of electromagnetic radiation.

Roots. It was Roots—he was paralyzing me with those high-frequency I-fucked-your-mother microwaves. No muscle movement. Pufferfish polio. Houdini-chained with no chance of escape.

Eighteen hours went by. He dialed it down. Least I could speak now: "Really? You *had* to?"

"You're going lunatic, man," he said. "You're going fucking *psycho.*"

"*Me?* You're talking to *me* about psycho?"

"Yes, *you.*"

The Unwanted

Sabreena barely paid attention to us as we dragged the unconscious Ramble through the apartment door. She was sitting at a desk at the far end of the living room, a single lamp keeping her from drowning in the dark. She blinked at us with minimal interest, then went back to reading her iPad.

I walked over to her as Roots began talking flash photo of Ramble to send to the night traders. She sat still, in quiet concentration, like she was receiving messages from the dead. It felt like visiting hour at the sanatorium.

"Time to go back," I said.

All she did was hand me the iPad. "Look at this."

In a way she *was* getting messages from the dead. She was reading another story about murdered children, only this one wasn't about an Ohio midwife who'd killed her own newborns. This one was a nearly 2,000-year-old mass infanticide.

Archeologists digging at the site of a Roman villa had discovered 97 infant skeletons buried in a yard area. The deaths had taken place over a period of 50 years in the first centuries of A.D. time. Bone measurements showed that the babies had all died at about 40 weeks gestation, suggesting they'd been deliberately killed soon after birth. No one knew why for sure—no signs of illness or deformity could be found on the remains. Some archeologists were speculating about sacrificial rituals, but most saw more practical reasons. They were probably laborers' children, put to death to keep their mothers working. Or the villa could've been occupied by a brothel, and the infants had been born to prostitutes. Either way, the babies seem to have been slaughtered simply because they were unwanted.

"The Romans would've appreciated Lukas," she said. "He thinks the human race would be better off without people."

Point taken.

"Still, we have to take you back."

"I'm not going back. Not under any circumstances. I might've lost Dustin, but I'm still going on."

"Where's the PIB?"

"I have it, but I'm not giving it up. You can do anything you want to me, I'm not."

"I'm not going to hurt you."

"It doesn't matter. I'm tired. I'm tired of my husband. I'm tired of his gift for strategic humiliation."

She took the iPad back, summoned a slideshow of a child's photos. Her daughter, Samantha, selected images from the first and only four years of her life. Between her mother's angel face and her father's slate gray eyes, Samantha had been a beautiful little girl.

"It's hard for me to look at these sometimes," Sabreena said. "It all floods in." She pointed to one of the photos. "I could never get her to eat fruit. Grapes, cherries, apples. Wrinkled nose. One day I was slicing a lime—it was right after this was taken. She asked if she could smell it. She liked it because she started *eating* it. She *loved* it. She'd take a bite, offer me one, take another bite. She ate the while thing. From there on in she loved limes. Sweet fruit, never. She loved her limes."

The photos disappeared. She took us back to the home screen.

"Despite what Lukas wants, I don't *know* what happened. That day, the fire. The day she...became invisible. I just don't know."

"He said he's tried to get you help."

"Yes. Lots of help. Lots and lots of help."

"You ever talk about it with him anymore?"

Weak smile. "Something Emerson said: *What you are speaks so loudly, I cannot hear what you say.* I'm pretty sure he had Lukas in mind."

Roots came over. He had the stats on Ramble. "His name's Ronald Branca. He's a mercenary. He started contracting with Cascadian a few months ago."

Sabreena squinted at him, as if the apartment was getting darker. "Cascadian? Trimshaw? He works for Trimshaw Dawson?"

"Hired gun, yeah."

"No, that's not right. That's not true. He's a Praiser. He belongs to Dustin's group."

"We know, PUFE. But he's been scamming you. You, Dustin—probably manipulating all of you."

"No, things didn't happen that way."

"A question," I said. "Whose idea was it to take off with the PIB?"

"But it was a *good* idea. Dustin liked it. Everyone went along with it."

"How about the riot in the cafeteria? Did this guy start it?"

"I don't know, but he knew it would happen. He knew when, and how."

"See?"

She saw. She didn't look like she was getting messages from the dead anymore. She looked like she was *sending* them.

Even my crazy heart was cracking open.

She gazed around the apartment. "So none of this has been real."

"I guess it's real, but not like this."

"Right, right, I've been fooled. So what do I do now?"

"Will you come back with us? With the PIB?"

"I guess I have no choice."

"I'm sorry."

She nodded, but in a kind of dizzy, abstracted way. She looked like she'd been staring at the sun for too long. "There's no way to get away, is there? No way out."

"We'll take you back."

"It's like what the dummy said to the ventriloquist. You can't escape the sound of my voice."

CHAPTER 8

NIRVANIVA

Dark Matter

Given the gothic claustrophobia of his office, it was odd to see Lukas sitting there with his pants off. He had electrode patches stuck all over his legs, a necessary step when you're giving yourself an NCV—a nerve conduction velocity test. To detect any nerve damage, he was stimulating his leg nerves with electric impulses from a handheld probe. The attached electrodes, hooked up to an electromygraph, were measuring the length of time it took for the impulses to travel. He routinely performed NCVs on himself, he said. He found them very relaxing. Though not as relaxing as the peace and solitude of a closed MRI.

Lukas needed some decompression. He was angry about the subversion of that asshole emeritus, Trimshaw Dawson. He was angry about the betrayal of his wife and the late Dustin Mathis—a betrayal that, in his mind, compared favorably to the ones perpetrated against Caesar and Christ.

On the other hand, he was happy about the return of the PIB. Especially since he was actively planning for a third go-back. He was now in possession of a drawing by Kurt Cobain, a piece of paper rife with DNA. Turns out one of the [0+X] employees was a huge Nirvana fan and collector and had sold the drawing to him.

"One of my *own* people," he said as he checked his readings. "One of my own *staffers* trusted me enough to sell it to me." His point: Despite the complaints of his wife and Belinda Halestre and all the others who are prone to moan, the sale proved that not all his employees hated him.

He was going to use the DNA to determine once and for all whether Cobain had been a victim of suicide or murder. He was going to address the many death theories, take the mystery out of the history. It would make a perfect third in the go-back series, a perfect trifecta of the past.

"It's like baseball," he said. "It's hard to improve on three up, three down."

He was right. Adolph Hitler, Lee Harvey Oswald, Kurt Cobain. You've got your turdunken, you've got your cherpumple, now we'd have a Hitleebain.

But I really had to bring up another subject. I mentioned the possibility that Auralsynch might be contributing to misery, depression and DIY deaths.

Lukas dismissed the notion. "It's just a little experiment in binaural beats—which were first discovered, if it makes anyone feel any safer, in 1839. Auralsynch was simply a side project in auditory processing, interaural time differentials and critical bands. Believe me, if I wanted to force people to kill themselves, there are better ways to do it."

Quite a statement from a man sitting in his underwear.

I warmed the River of Jordan oil in my hands and rubbed it into her neck and naked shoulders. Just a little oil, enough to still create some friction and deepen the pressure of smooth rhythmic stroking. I started at the back of her neck, making small circles with my thumbs to release the tension at the base of her skull, then moved down the sides of her neck, using pressure to stretch the muscles, and continued out along the tops of her shoulders with slow, soothing, full-finger strokes. Her body was so beautiful I wanted to shoot myself.

I'd told her what happened—about shooting at the guy on Sixth Avenue, about beating Ramble so bad I had to be turned catatonic to stop. I had to tell her the truth—there was no other way to spin this record. I told her I felt like I'd downed some evil Kool Aid, like someone had bugged my brain, like life had been going downhill ever since we

discovered hills. Scientists are looking for dark matter?
Shit, let 'em train their satellites on me.

"I'm sorry I let you listen," she said underneath me,
face down, white hair swept off her back. "But you
shouldn't have listened so long. Your addictive personality,
you got off on it right away."

I told her what Lukas said. She dismissed his
dismissal. "Wouldn't be the first time technology came
with unintended side effects."

Maybe, actually, it wasn't all so bad, I said. I told
her about Bill Wilson, the founder of AA, as I worked the
heels of my hands in circles up and down her back. A failed
stockbrocker, caught in the middle of the Depression,
Wilson had been fighting booze for a long time. He was
doing his fourth bid at a New York City detox center with
nothing to show for it when he agreed to try the Towns-
Lambert cure, a treatment whose main medication was the
poisonous plant belladonna, aka deadly nightshade. As he
was tripping on the hallucinogen that night, as he was
peaking on his desperate paranoia, Wilson suddenly saw a
white light fill his hospital room. *It seemed to me, in my
mind's eye, that I was standing on a mountain and that a
wind not of air but of spirit was blowing. And then it burst
upon me and I was a free man.* He never picked up a drink
again.

"You're not on belladonna," said Belinda. "You're
on something weirder."

"So where do you go to detox from sound?"

"Not sure that place can be found on any map.
You're going to have to look somewhere else."

"And that is?"

"We all live by an invisible sun inside us. You're
going to have to look for yours. You're going to have to
watch for it and listen for it and move in tune with your
dreams." She groaned as I ran my fingers along the
trenches of her spine. "And for a while, maybe, you
shouldn't be meddling in your own affairs."

>>>>>>

Better To Burn

They were going nuts at *Real Story* over the Cobain go-back. Why not? From the moment it happened, on April 5, 1994, his death had slipped right into mythology. The body of Nirvana's lead singer had been found in the spare room above the garage of his Seattle home. A Remington M-11 shotgun was resting on his chest, a handwritten note was laying under an overturned flowerpot nearby. The wound in his head was consistent with a shotgun blast fired inside his mouth.

His fans were riven with shock. But surprise? Not so much. At 27, Cobain had been long haunted by clinical depression and heroin addiction and had just bolted from drug rehab seven days earlier. Factor in the frustrations and instantaneous exhaustion of fast fame and the prince of grunge darkness seemed like a natural candidate for biting the bullet.

But some observers took refuge in a different interpretation. Among the arguments they raised:

•According to the toxicology report by the King County Medical Examiner, Cobain had a heroin level of 1.52 milligrams per liter in his blood, an amount that would have killed most junkies. Unless he'd built up an extraordinary tolerance, he was too stoned to pull the trigger, let alone get the barrel in his mouth.

•Reportedly, no legible prints were found on the Remington M-11, not even on the trigger. Would've been difficult for anyone, even someone as talented as Cobain, to shoot himself and then wipe the shotgun clean. In addition, the gun had been loaded with three rounds, an act more suggestive of self-protection than self-destruction.

•Never quite a bower of bliss, Cobain's marriage to the much-maligned Courtney Love seemed to be crashing to an end. The nuclear nature of their relationship lead some to speculate that Love—maybe acting with the male nanny who looked after their daughter, Frances Bean—had conspired to murder Cobain.

•As soon as the police found the handwritten note at the scene, they labeled it as a suicide note. But was it? From its first thoughts

I haven't felt the excitement of listening to as well as creating music along with reading and writing for too many years now. I feel guilty beyond words about these things.

to the Neil Young tribute near the end

I don't have the passion anymore, and so remember, it's better to burn out than to fade away.

Cobain never talks about killing himself. He sounds more like he's getting ready to walk away from the music world rather than the world itself.

So what really happened in that room above the garage? *Real Story*'s audience was about to find out. The dotcom staffers began seeding the site with teasers about the go-back to come, promising that history would be rewritten, that the way we'd think about Cobain and Love and Nirvana from now on would be determine by genetic regression.

That's progress for you.

Notes From The Underground

Roots wouldn't leave me alone about Janiva. He wanted me to call her on his behalf, try to get these two kids back together. He said I'd promised to call her, and even though I definitely hadn't he kept telling me that I had. Yes, she was a pain in the ass, scathing, faultfinding, taping and analyzing every move they made in bed—by the way, is it dull as dishwater or ditchwater?—but he wanted her back.

"I'm so lost. I'm so out of control fucked up. Took a shower last night. Really, really should've taken my clothes off first. I need her in my life. You talk her into it, I'll be soaring, man. I'll be singing. Like the song says, if dogs can fly, so can I."

"Dogs? Not doves?"

"Doves? Where's the challenge in that?"

I called Janiva. No, she couldn't talk. Too busy. Way way way way way too busy. She had to go check out the new TunneMall, see if it would work as an installation site for her current project, the one with the huge circuit boards and the LED clusters.

I wouldn't let it go. I begged her for some time— although I had no idea what I was going to say to her. He needs you to keep from going crazy? Not all that romantic. I was going to treat it like I was speaking at an AA meeting—just show up, feel the room and let inspiration take over.

I wore her down. Please, please, please. Okay, okay, okay. Meet me by the Leonard Street entrance.

>>>>>>

West Broadway. A blurred, haloed day. One of those
spring days with summer temps. I had a heat headache.
Maybe that's why I was thinking about the Atlantic Ocean.
That's right, the Atlantic Ocean. Created 190 million years
ago when the supercontinent Pangea began to rupture.
Water rushed in, broke the land mass into the seven
continents and pushed them all apart. Still doing it, too.
Even as I'm walking down the street the Atlantic is
growing wider at a rate of an inch per year.

Water. Water water everywhere. And if not, well
you *bring* it there. That explains the TunneMall. It was an
old water tunnel, abandoned for decades. Burrowing under
West Broadway, it became so well known to underground
explorers the city decided to stop trying to keep people out
and start inviting 'em in. With Manhattan running out of
real estate, the city was looking to squeeze utility out of
every square foot of space. So they opened the tunnel up
for six blocks, from Leonard down to Warren Street, and
zoned it for retail.

Maybe a month old, the TunneMall was a mecca of
subterranean shopping, vendors selling video games, footy
pajamas, relaxed fit jeans, DVDs, turquoise necklaces,
kimono tops, boxer briefs, lash revitalizers, books,
magazines, adjustable wrench sets, zirconia earrings,
polarized sunglasses, cable knit sweaters, crew socks, nail
tips, scoop tees and butterfly rings, among other flea-
market things.

Janiva was standing by a display of shapewear
lingerie, her black clothes in contrast with the pastel colors
on sale. She liked the space, she said, pointing to the
tunnel's kiln-fired green brick walls. But was it the right
venue for her art? At this stage the TunneMall was
considered tacky, yes, but tacky in a hip, unconventional
way, so maybe so, maybe so.

We were walking through the catacomb when I
started singing Roots' praises. Turned out to be a short
tune. As long as he was going to keep doing what he was
doing, she cut me off, there was nothing to discuss. The
night trading was nonnegotiable. It was going to get him in

trouble or worse and she loved him too much to let that
happen.

Case closed. She went on studying the tunnel,
wondering where her big circuit boards might go, what
gave her the best projection space. Feeling the room.

I stopped next to a rack of Borsalino Panama hats.
Beige to off-white, the same shade as the lighter tones of
skin on the woman's back in Matisse's *La Coiffeur*. The
hats brought back memories. An old friend of my father's,
Frankie Olson, always wore those Borsalino Panamas. I'd
see him around every once in a while in the later years.
Frankie would always ask how my father was. I always had
to tell him my father was dead. *What? What happened?*
Killed himself—jumped out of a window off Houston
Street. *That's terrible, terrible.* Next time I'd run into him,
same thing. *How's your father doing?* Finally I gave up,
just told Frankie my father was fine. *Glad to hear it. Give
him my best.*

He'd walk away happy, content, screaming…
Screaming?

There were three of them. Three long-armed,
squinty-eyed, wall-pissing, malevolent pervs had grabbed
Janiva and were dragging her toward the Warren Street
exit. She was giving them royal shit, trying to fight them
off with echoing screams. The shoppers had paused in their
bargain hunting to get seriously worried.

A random snatch? Fuck no. Somebody knew she
was coming here.

I took off and got my hands on one of them. A
baby-faced dickwad, his features a testament to arrested
development. I gripped his jacket and went to sling him out
of the way, but his legs held steady and instead of budging
he swung his arm and back-fisted me in the face.

I staggered away. Pissed me off. PISSED. ME.
OFF.

I came at him again, going for his jacket again. His
arms went up in defense, and as they did I stopped, pivoted
on my left leg and hooked the instep of my right foot into
his ribs.

Pretty decent UFC strike. He folded and fell to his knees. I kicked him in the pit of his stomach. He flattened to the ground, covering himself as I drove my foot into his abdominal oblique, his deltoid, his latissimus dorsi.

There's a reason the Good Lord gave me two legs—to cripple this motherfucker.

I just kept kicking him, thinking of a song.
Gonna drink all day, dance all night,
Doin' wrong till I do it right.

I wondered if I'd end up killing him. I wondered if he believed in reincarnation. See ya later, alligator. After a while, crocodile.

Wait, stop—this is just self-indulgent. C'mon, maybe a wee bit more? No, stop—there are two other numbnuts to deal with.

No there weren't.

No numbnuts, no Janiva. I'd gotten so lost in my attempted-murder opium fugue I'd let them get away.

I ran up the gut of the tunnel, shoppers scattering out of my insane way. Stairs, street, corner of Warren and West Broadway. The fuck are they?

My eyes were jump-cutting in all four directions. A nail spa. A music store. A music school. A liquor store. A video game place. A check cashing place. The Smyth TriBeCa Hotel. The Mysterious Book Shop. The Raccoon Lodge bar.

No sign of the two guys. No sign of the dyed blue streak in Janiva's black hair.

She was gone. Solid gone.

I Don't Currently Want To Die

It took us three hours to find out what happened. Roots, in the meantime, wasn't all that happy about my protective abilities. I was leaning hard on his disappointment button, he said. I was fucking up right and left. I'd taken a big steamy shit this time. He was losing blood just *thinking* about what happened.

There were plenty of questions to be asked. Why hadn't I gone back to check the guy's ID? Because the people down there were already calling 911 and the police were still looking for us, remember? Still wanted to talk to us about the death sale at Forever 21?

Who knew Janiva was going to the TunneMall? Like everybody. Turns out she'd tweeted it, she'd blogged it, she'd Facebooked it.

Why did you keep kicking on that guy? I tried to explain about these dream swoops I kept falling into, these Auralsynch brain fades. It was like waking up on a groggy morning and the dream juice is still flooding your mind. No matter what I do, I can't get the shit out of my head.

"I'd be looking into self-decapitation right about now," he said. "You're starting to sound like me."

Not good news.

Roots was choking on his own questions, like the more he asked the more he'd clear things up. Dialysis by analysis. Who could've taken Janiva? Why? Where? And, more to form, how come there's no cigarette smoking in cigar stores? Why is there a Manhattan Beach in California? Either he didn't know it or couldn't help it, but he kept asking the same questions over and over again.

Three hours of this later, he got a strange message on his phone. A video icon, labeled *Insurance File*. He opened it up. It was a copy of the Zapruder film, 26.6 seconds of eight-millimeter grain showing the presidential motorcade gliding through Dealey Plaza in Dallas, JFK's head snapping as he's hit by gunfire, Jackie Kennedy scrambling over the trunk of the car, pleading with the Secret Service agents for help.

The fuck does *this* mean?

Nothing, said Roots. It had to be a stego video—embedded with hidden content. The size of the file was a lot bigger than a mere 26.6 seconds of footage. Thing is, he couldn't decrypt it on his phone.

He sent it to Robbo in Red Hook. With better equipment and interconnects, Robbo could detect and reverse the protocol controls, the staganalysis algorithms, the linear collusion, the pattern recognition, the binary message vectors. Well sure.

Robbo sent it back. Janiva was sitting in front of a bare wall, a background with no identifying details. She looked spooked and angry and terrible, flesh closer to the bone, like she'd lost 10 pounds in three hours.

I'm okay. They haven't hurt me. Physically. They just grabbed me. Grabbed me and took me. I don't know who they are. All I can tell you is, I don't currently want to die.

She moved her hands as she spoke, every gesture precise and deliberate. An artist, everything tactile. I watched the hands like I'd watch a priest's saying the Mass, trying to determine if they had any meaning.

I'm supposed to tell you something. It's a message from a Trimshaw Johnson. (Someone in the room said something.) *Dawson. A Trimshaw Dawson. He wants you to get rid of something called the PIB?* (She glanced off-camera for confirmation.) *The PIB. Get rid of it. Destroy it. Demolish it. That's what you're supposed to do if you want me to be all right.*

The video abruptly ended. A cold cut to black.

Roots was shaking, shivering like he was walking naked on an Antarctic ice floe. "He can't do this, son of a

bitch. Little old son of a bitch. This breaks all the rules.
I'm never working for him again. I'm dropping him as a
client right fucking now."

Good move. The hell was wrong with Trimshaw? If
he can't trick people into joining him, like Sabreena, he just
hauls them off the street?

Trimshaw Dawson's recipe for margaritas: First,
steal a bottle of tequila…

>>>>>>

The video message had been so onion-routed—sent
through so many disguised proxy networks—it would take
days to trace its source. But as Roots noted, three hours had
passed between the kidnapping and the arrival of the video.
Three hours—roughly the drive-time you'd need to get to
the Cascadian headquarters up in Salamanacki, a.k.a.
Salami City. The night traders mobilized. They dropped
their individual projects and banded together to train their
secret arts on the Cascadian complex.

I asked Roots if he was going to tell Lukas about
the PIB demands. Never, he said. If Lukas knew I was even
tempted to damage the PIB, he'd never trust me again. He'd
dump me, lose me on the spot. With Trimshaw off the
roster, I can't afford to lose another big account.

Forty minutes later one of the Red Hook buccaneers
got a hit. A Cascadian car was scheduled to take Trimshaw
tonight to the Cedar Crown Cemetery in Salami City.
Arrive time: 8 p.m.

A cemetery at 8 p.m.? Who holds a funeral at night?

>>>>>>

We took the same Eurocopter TwinStar upstate, only this
time we were flying on Roots' own ruby. Same chopper
pilot, too—leather bomber jacket, white silk scarf, Ray-
Bans shielding his eyes from red sun setting on our right.

You could feel the tension building with every mile
north. Roots responded with more frantic word-churn,
recounting the highlights of their screaming matches and

arguments. The time she woke him up with her hands around his throat. The time he tried to run her over with his Imperial. The time she chased him around her studio with a knife. The time he had to tie her up. The time she tried to set him on fire with a welding torch. Still, all in all, when it was good it was good. He should remind himself to remember that. She had 17 million colors in her computer—surely he could've designed workflows for her palettes and been happy doing it.

"She always saying I can never make up my mind. I can never make up my own damn mind. And it's true—I'll cop to that. I *can't* make up my mind. And why *should* I? It's stupid. That's what we have experts for."

He was a particularly fine example of push-to-talk technology.

Me, I was completely focused and concentrated. Did you know that Hitler was spying on the Nazis when he first joined their ranks? The truth. He was working as an informant for the German Army and got assigned to monitor a meeting of some little known political group. But he liked what he heard, and once he opened his mouth, they liked what *they* heard. He was a mesmerizing public speaker. He signed up as a Nazi a week after that first meeting, realizing he'd found a fellowship. *They like me, they really like me…*

Okay, Roots had his affliction, I had mine. His was a possession by bit-torrents of thought that operated as a show unto themselves and didn't necessarily need to be connected to anything going on in the outside world. Mine was a real drift from the outside world, a lapse into some Bardo plane of memory where I was doomed to wander.

Between us, we made some pair.

>>>>>>

And Still They Frown At Cedar Crown

The car rental place was downwind from a Dunkin'
Donuts. Nice coffee smell in the air. But why was I picking
up the taste of the ocean underneath it? We GPS'd for the
Cedar Crown Cemetery, a direction that took us away from
the empty warehouses along Route 87, past the main source
of local employment these days, the Salamanacki
Correctional Facility, and into Salami City's modest
downtown. Thrift shops. A fur shop. A Christian Science
Reading Room. Chinese and Mexican take-out. Lots of
auto supply stores. *Get the shocks of your life*, said one
sign. Another asked, *How Safe is Extended Lubrication?*,
which seemed inappropriately sexual to me.

A deep pit-of-the-stomach fear was growing on
Roots. "She's all right, right?"

"I'm sure she is."

"They haven't hurt her."

"She's collateral. You don't fuck with collateral."

"If we can find her and get her out—"

"Not if, *when*."

"Either way, she's gonna be pissed."

That would be the least of our problems. The most?
I could hear Belinda's voice. *We all live by an invisible
sun. You're going to have to find yours.*

Give me that GPS.

"I need to know you won't go psychopathic," said
Roots. "Don't unhinge me. Don't heebie-jeebie me."

"No, no heebie-jeebies."

Truth was, I wouldn't put anything past myself.

>>>>>>

Nor would I put anything past Cedar Crown Cemetery.
There was no nocturnal funeral ceremony taking place
here. We caught that hint as we were driving through the
open gates, saw a skydiver jumping out of CASA plane
flying overhead and heard cheering from the other side of
the crowded parking lot by the chapel. They had an old-
fashioned, street-fair, grave-hopping party going on—a few
hundred wired-up kids and adults frequenting the bounce
house, the inflatable obstacle course, the air slide, the face-
painting tables, the game and contest stands, the crafts
stalls, the food and booze booths. Over by the Reflections
Pond,
a pair of pyrotechs were spraying jets of potassium sparks
15 feet in the air. A DJ was set up in front of a balloon-
bedecked mausoleum, cranking out *Le Freak, Get Down
Tonight* and other blasts of discorata. Everybody was
boogying. Even the headstones seemed to be tapping
their bases.

I'd heard about these things. Cemeteries across the
country were adopting a new promotional strategy and
trying to lighten up their image. With the demand for
cremation up and the market for burial plots down,
cemeteries were opening their gates to concerts and fashion
shows and wing-dinging revels. The message: We're not
just a somber, distant, rarely visited place to grieve. We're
a warm, happy part of your family—now and forever.

There's soda pop and the dancin's free.

Roots and I stayed off to the sides of the crowd,
moving through the shadows. We stopped next to a
monument of some sort. *The Tomb of the Unknown
Furrier.* The pride, Roots said, of Salami City.

He pointed Trimshaw out to me, standing away
from the general population. I saw an old stooped-over man
with white hair and a blazer, but I didn't recognize who it
was until I saw the shorts, skinny white legs and red knee
length socks under the jacket. He was holding a friendly
conversation with people in suits who looked like high
school principals. Probably Salami City officials, the
mayor, trustees, the head of the Chamber of Commerce,

220

thanking the head of Cascadian for coming out tonight
and showing community support.

Thirty feet away his skull-shaven bodyguards, the
kneeheads, were gathered in front of a crypt, eating fried
chicken and drinking like Republicans.

Neither he nor they were gonna be leading us to
Janiva any time soon. He was holding her on the premises,
with all these people around? Not likely. Or if he was, she
was grooving to the sounds of Shirley & Company and
Shame, Shame, Shame at the moment.

Roots was muttering something about the farmer
and his paraplegic daughter and how most guys just leave
her hanging there. I didn't know what he was saying, but I
agreed. Hard to take, but this had been one wasted effort.

We both got the same idea at the same time. There's
Trimshaw, surrounded by the jolly citizens of Salami City,
separated from his guards and not suspecting a thing. He'd
kidnapped Janiva? We'd kidnap him. If one of us could
distract the kneeheads, the other would slip over to
Trimshaw, quietly put a gun in his back and walk him
away. From there we'd negotiate a prisoner exchange.

Roots pointed to the Reflections Pond and the bank
of spark-fountains shooting in the air. He knew something
about those things, he said. They're called gerbs, and the
two guys over there are setting them off with a remotely
controlled electrical signal that ignites the e-matches.

Which was interesting, according to Roots, because
he had an app on his phone, built by one of the night
traders, that had something to do with electromagnetic
interference, harmonic content, receiver chains,
synchrotron sources, circuit degradation and modulated
noise.

I don't know what was happening to me, but I
almost understood what he was talking about.

At least I got the gist: He could wreak us some
havoc.

Let's cook this thing.

He headed for the pond. I took off in the direction
of Trimshaw & Company, doing a casual stroll, careful not
to attract attention. Halfway to closing in on the weenie

meanie, I felt somebody touching my arm. Tall, pale
man, mortician thin, looked like ZaSu Pitts during her
television years. He said I didn't look familiar to him. I said
I was from out of town. He said his name was Wes Huey,
assistant cemetery superintendent, and he hoped I was
enjoying the festivities.

"It's a way to get people here," he said, "but not in a
grim way. We like to say we're taking the frown out of
Cedar Crown."

Yes, talk to me—tell me more. Wes would make
good cover while I worked my way over.

"It's part of our outreach program. It's a way for us
to, you know, reach out."

I nodded and took a step toward Trimshaw. Wes
followed.

"We're hoping that if we can get people here they'll
look around and say, This is a nice place for my family."

Nod, step, follow.

"You know, a hundred years or so ago, cemeteries
were social gathering places. We're trying to get back to
that time."

More dancing—me leading, him following.

We all live by an invisible sun inside us.

Over by the pond I saw a few of the gerb-jets
suddenly conk out. A few of the others, however, were
spritzing sparks 25-30 feet into the sky. I could see Roots
standing nearby, his phone out.

"Back then, cemeteries were sometimes the most
beautiful places around. People would come out to take
rides, have a picnic by a loved one's grave."

Okay, Wes, enough.

The gerbs continued flaring up and shutting down.
The two guys running them started yelling at Roots. *Are
you fucking doing that?*

A commotion. The kneeheads looked over at the
pond to see what was going on.

I should've known—nobody gets away from a sales
pitch. I took a step toward Trimshaw. Wes blocked my way
with a wall of words.

"Course some people don't like it. There's a
woman over there, I was talking to her, she said cemeteries
are made for the dead. I'm thinking what's her problem?"

Shut up, Wes. Shut up, shut up, shut up.

The kneeheads spotted Roots—*hey*—and began
moving, hands reaching for weapons.

I wasn't close enough to Trimshaw to make my
move.

JFK once slept with a girlfriend of Hitler's, a
possible German spy named Inga-Binga. That's right,
Inga-Binga.

No—I wasn't going to get lost. Not this time. No
repeats of the TunneMall slip. I'm *here*. I'm fucking *here*.

"Excuse me," I said to Wes, then I pulled out my
Glock and as desperate as a vampire at high noon I started
firing.

Everything went dizzy and hallucinatory, as
hyperventilatory as a scene out of The Apocalypse,
kneeheads jumping for cover, hitting the deck at the base of
the mausoleum wall, 8,000 lightning flashes of screams,
people floating away in panic, running through the
frightened geometry of the headstones, where's Trimshaw?,
white flashes of gunfire, a red suicidal hailstorm of bullets.
The nuclear option. Invisible suns. *Move in tune with your
dreams.*

Roots was grabbing at me, trying to siphon me out
of there, pull me away from this clusterfuck of jet-spraying
gunfire and stampede confusion and Inga-fucking-Binga
madness. I'm gonna run to the city of refuge I'm gonna
run.

As we reached the parking lot Roots gave me a look
that was bitter and angry and filled with condemnation.
"Well *that* was fucking lively," he said.

>>>>>>

A Deal-Changer

The chopper ride back was not a pleasant one. I'd said no heebie-jeebies, Roots pointed out, and what the fuck was that back there *but* the heebie-jeebies? Why did I open fire like that? I couldn't think of anything else to do? Sure, the kneeheads had seen him and were set to attack, but I couldn't come up with any other way out? A shootout in a fucking *cemetery*? And now what do we do? *Now* what? We're down to our last cigarette and I just lit the filter. The woman he loved was still a hostage, and we'd done nothing to further the cause. I should be sent in for head repair, get my irregular bissextiles straightened out.

I was exhausted. I was out of it on a subatomic level, my quarks too pooped to populate. I had no excuses—I'd just up and out lost it. Still, I wanted to say something to him, so I sat there waiting for inspiration.

Instead of inspiration, I got Lukas.

More glum news.

His tone on the phone was apologetic—or as apologetic as he could get. He said he was sorry, but the go-back might have to be pushed back. He was aware that delays didn't sit well in the world of mediathink, but he had no choice. They were having difficulties with the Cobain DNA and he simply didn't think he could deliver the package on time. They hadn't been able to reconstruct or re-deconstruct the right memories yet. No, the PIB hadn't been compromised—it had been rigorously tested and retested and it was everything you'd want a Pangenic Illumination Beam to be. He blamed his researchers in the *Gengo* lab instead, basically saying they were as lazy, shiftless and incompetent as Albany politicians. In any case, the go-back at this point was a no-go.

Don't ask me why, but as his call ended I started thinking about a guy I once knew, Big Tuffy Abbate. He went to the bathroom one day, voided his bowels, flushed, stood, turned around and making sure the flush was complete, bent down to pull up his pants. What happened next, according to the police reconstruction, Big Tuffy must've lost his balance, fell face first in the toilet, hit his head on the rim, knocked himself out and drowned in the bowl.

The chopper was somewhere over White Plains when the kicker arrived. Roots got a message, another coded video. He sent it to Robbo. Robbo sent it back. Janiva was sitting in the same room as before.

What did you DO? she said. *How did you fuck things up THIS time? Whatever it was, whatever you did, you've got your friend Trimshaw in a dither. He says he's upping the demands. He doesn't care about this PIB anymore. Don't bother destroying it. He wants you to destroy Lukas Lister-Bertozzi instead. Can you hear me? I can't believe they're making me say this. He wants you to kill him. If you want me to stay alive, he says that's what you have to do. You understand? He wants Lukas Lister-Bertozzi DEAD.*

A Masturbating Moses

Speak of the devil. Lukas wanted to see us the next day. It was a matter of urgency, he said, of extreme, uttermost, *radical* urgency, so urgent he couldn't even tell me what it was over any digital medium that could be captured and transmitted to others. Which only left writing a letter and he wasn't going to do that. *Get out here—I need you.*

Roots wanted no part of it. He wanted to find Janiva *now*. He was going to devote his time and energy to getting her back and to nothing else.

And where does that leave me? What am I supposed to tell Lukas? What excuse should I give? Oh by the way, Roots can't make it today—Trimshaw's kidnapped his girlfriend and, guess what, he wants Roots to kill you.

Roots fought it—he didn't want to waste time on Lukas.

"Look at it this way," I said. "You show up at Zero-plus-ex, someone from Cascadian's gonna know about it. They'll think you're setting something up. You'll be *buying* time."

Roots gave this considerable reflection. "Don't give me any good ideas like that," he said. "You're just gonna get me to do what you want."

Lukas was acting like a man who'd just caught his wife cheating on him. Which was something he *didn't* do when Sabreena ran off with Dustin Mathis, but he was making up for it now. His eyes were searching for explanations everywhere they could look—in every corner of his office, in every square inch of my face, ditto for the simmering Roots. He'd just made a discovery, he said. Kurt Cobain's DNA was not, in fact, Kurt Cobain's DNA. He didn't know whose it was, but it wasn't his. And the alleged source of the DNA? The alleged Cobain drawing? A freestyle sketch of what could've been Moses playing with himself? It was a rank fake, a crafty forgery. The treachery was bad enough, an untimely piece of timing, but what made it worse was that one of his *own employees* had sold it to him.

Her name was Sioux Zeckendorf, a group manager in Preventive Maintenance. He wanted to confront her. He wanted to find out why she'd tried to deceive him, why she'd engaged in this insidious duplicity.

I didn't get it. "So ask her."

"She's not answering her messages."

"So go down to Preventive Maintenance and ask her."

"She's not there, she's not at work. Apparently she's getting married today."

"So ask tomorrow."

"This can't *wait* until tomorrow. I know where she's holding the reception. I'm asking her now."

"You're crashing her *wedding?*"

"I don't care if it's her funeral. I'm going to confront her, I'm going to scrape the truth out of her and I'm taking you two with me. I don't trust anyone else. I know there's a certain last-minutedness to this, but it can't be helped."

Call me crazy—and why wouldn't you?—but I didn't like the way Roots was looking at Lukas. That steady, laser-like anger was just a little disturbing. Lukas was oblivious to it, of course, but there it was. A constant contemplation of something bad.

Probably just resentment. He'd been expecting a quick meeting, a quim, a fast in-and-out. We both had—I really wanted to see Belinda. He really wanted to find Janiva. He wasn't expecting getting dragged into somebody's time-consuming nuptials.

But how angry was he? I couldn't see him doing harm to one of his biggest accounts. On the other hand,

Janiva's life was on the line. Did he resent him, or want to kill him?

Maybe venturing off the premises with these two wasn't such a fine idea.

"You can't go to the wedding," I said to Lukas.

"Can, will."

"She's probably invited plenty of co-workers. You won't be welcome, to put it mildly."

"Ridiculous. That's something Sabreena would say."

"They'll tear you limb from limb if you're lucky."

"I disagree."

"Really. How often do you mingle with your employees?"

"Never."

"So how do you know?"

Lukas didn't answer. He just stared at me like I was some quantum equation he couldn't grasp. "Interesting," he said.

500 Miles Per Hour

He was the strangest looking Islamic woman I'd ever seen.
Still, give it to him, by swapping his old dead-dog frock
coat for a burqa, he'd fashioned a fairly decent disguise.
With the hijab covering his head, you couldn't see his
beard or long hair, just the gray eyes. He'd get away with
playing *Undercover Boss*.

The wedding, he said as we rode in his limo, gave
him an opportunity not only to interrogate Sioux
Zeckendorf, but to find out what his staffers really thought
of him. He was confident he'd prove Sabreena, Belinda and
his other critics wrong. His song: To know know know me
is to love love love me.

The limo was a security special—armored with
steel plates, five layers of bulletproof glass in the windows,
tires that would keep rolling even after they'd been shot
out. He always used this car, keeping himself safe from
outside attack. But inside?

Roots kept glaring at him, rambling in a whisper to
himself. *Toes turn black and fall off. Penance is the only
way to reach the heart.*

Lukas wasn't paying attention. He was busy telling
us that technological innovation is rarely predictable and
never inevitable. Take the jet plane. You'd think that once
the jet engine was invented, the airlines would be
scrambling to give their passengers faster travel. Not so.
The first designs were patented in the 1930s and ignored
for years. Even after World War II, when Nazi prototypes
for jet fighters were found, no one thought about adapting
them for civilian use. It wasn't until 1952, when someone
finally built a jet and began breaking speed records, that the

airlines said, you know, maybe flying 500 miles per
hour might bring us some advantage. So you never can tell.
You just never can tell.

All Apologies

Built to the highest mob specifications, the Sunrise Party Parc sat on a piece of flat South Shore Long Island land that had once been a potato farm. But around the time jet engines were being patented, the area was invaded by a pest called the golden nematode, a greedy little bastard that bores into the roots of potato plants and feeds off their juices. Crops failed, land values sank. Developers eventually sucked up the cheap real estate and turned it into suburban housing developments and baby-boomer breeding grounds.

And many of those kids celebrated their life rituals at catering halls like this, a building clouded by enough garlic odors to resemble downtown Pestovia. Somehow the Sunrise Party Parc reminded me of my friend Kelvim Bowser. He'd gotten married on Jan. 2, 2003—1-2-3—and he *still* couldn't remember his anniversary.

The place wasn't the Plaza, but that was okay. You wouldn't find the Zeckendorf-Quattrone reception in the Plaza anyway. Nothing terribly elaborate here—probably a second or third marriage for both parties. A healthy crowd of people, half Zero-plus-exers (the bride's side), half bacciagaloops (the groom's), everybody liquored-up on house wine and dancing to the Ray Conniff Singers. Lots of bad wigs and open flies, enough polyester to fill all our gas tanks.

We started circulating, me keeping watch on Roots with paranoid eyes. Lukas' burqa drew quite a few stares, but everyone was too loaded to much care. I spotted Cito Spangler across the room. He waved, surprised to see me here. I noticed he wasn't wearing his earbuds.

Sioux Zeckendorf was an amphora of a woman—long, narrow neck, broad rounded bottom, hands on her hips. A living vase. A sturdy, attractive, happy but slightly weary gal.

Her huzbo's name was Boy William Quattrone (his mother, it turns out, was a big Culture Club fan). He was a heavy soul, short on height and short on breath, stuffed into a bright green suit.

I kept staring at that suit, the greenness of it. You can tell when a quasar has died somewhere in the universe when you see a massive cloud of gas that same color. A green gas cloud is a delayed optical echo of a dead quasar.

No, no, no, no, no—don't start with this shit.

Lukas was having a little trouble dealing with the crowd, and not necessarily because of the burqa. Usually he never went anywhere unless he was the star attraction. But he adjusted to the anonymity and was soon making small talk with the Zero-plus-exers.

"So you work for Lukas Lister-Bertozzi," he said in a soft, accentless voice. "I'd be interested to know what you think of him."

No you wouldn't. He's an insane scumbag.

"That's not what I heard. I heard he's just like everyone else. He smiles, he dances. Sometimes he even sings. From what I hear, being Lukas Lister-Bertozzi isn't much different from *not* being Lukas Lister-Bertozzi."

He's insane, trust me. If he's like everyone else, then we're all insane.

"I respect your right to be wrong."

We stuck with Lukas as he made the rounds. We heard the same litany.

He's such a lame.

They need a special complaint number on the voicemail menu just for him.

He's a human zit.

He gets high on his own farts.

He's a revolutionary? Revolutions just make people miserable and put them out of work.

He thinks his cock is so big he can use it as a belt.

He's done quite a lot, it's true. Which is quite an achievement, considering he's got his head up his ass.

Lukas pulled us off by a side door. He was visibly upset, and that's just going by his eyes behind the hijab. "I went through all this trouble to become me, and what's the point? Just to be hated? I don't mind telling you, this is very discouraging. If someone wanted to kill me, today would be a good day."

I glanced at Roots. *Well?*

No time for follow-through, though. One of the Zero-plus-exers, a man with fleshy ear lobes and a nasally yap, had the mike in hand and was toasting Boy William. He was sending his best wishes to the groom and, of course, to all his Eye-talian family and friends.

A nice sentiment, though Boy William felt constrained to point out that while many of his friends were indeed Eye-talian, he himself was Sicilian. His parents had come from Sicily, and so, following the custom of these things, he was Sicilian. He hoped everyone could appreciate the difference.

Apparently they couldn't. Someone on the [0+X] side said something like, *It that why your tits are bigger than your wife's?* Maybe the remark was meant to be funny, but it didn't go over well. Suddenly both sides were exchanging drunken choruses of shouts and insults and the whole thing was turning as raucous as an Irish poetry reading.

The uproar was such that Boy William felt compelled to take the mike. "Easy, easy. No need to get hopped up. All we had here was a poor choice of words, that's all. Like thanking a one-armed fireman for single-handedly putting out the flames. Just words. So, you know, any hurt feelings? I'm rebuttaling them. We're here to have fun. I'm saying this to the house, we're *here* to have fun!"

It was a heartfelt speech, moving enough for anyone listening to swear mayhem off. Unfortunately, nobody was listening. As soon as Boy William was finished someone broke a wine bottle, someone pulled a knife, someone grabbed a chair, and within a few mad, chaotic moments a gang-banger brawl had broken out. It was pretty bad, even for a wedding.

If someone had told me a couple of hours ago I'd be watching a rumble in a South Shore catering hall today and helping a man disguised as an Islamic woman pull a bride away from her own wedding, I never would've believed it.

Believe it. We took advantage of the confusion and yanked Sioux through the side door like we were dragging her out of harm's way.

"It's okay," she protested. "This happens at all my weddings."

Lukas was leaning over her like he was checking her for dust. What she'd done to him, he was saying, was deliberate sabotage, ugly, venomous and mean. Sioux, staring up at him from a chair in the dressing room, was clearly upset by the sight of her boss with his hijab down, but she was sticking to her story: She was a Nirvana fan, a collector of Cobania and she'd only sold him the drawing to pay for her wedding.

"*No*. The drawing is what's known in the vernacular as a *plant*. You sold it to me knowing it was fake, and I want to know where you got it from. You don't think something like that matters?"

"Sometimes it matters, sometimes it doesn't. I'm sure of that."

"Who gave it to you? One of my enemies?"

"Another collector."

"You're sure."

"To the best of my knowledge, yes."

"To the best of your knowledge? You were *there*."

"It's a bad figure of speech," she allowed. "Yes, another collector. He knew how much Nirvana meant to me. He knew I also collect, I had a lot of—"

"I already know you collect."

"I'm trying to make a point."

"What?"

"The pull of the past is very strong."

"Well, yes, that's true, the pull of the past *is* very strong at the present moment, but that doesn't give you the excuse—"

The door opened. Sounds of the melee still in progress blew in—along with a pink, sickly, caved-in face.

"Excuse me," said Cito. "Saw you all come in here a while ago." Lukas' burqa only gave him a little pause. "Sioux, you in trouble again?"

"I'm getting my ass grilled off in here," she replied.

"We're just trying to find something out," I said.

Cito walked over to the bride. "I don't know what's going on, but Quinn here's a good guy. I owe him. Tell him what he wants.'

"It's none of your business," said Sioux.

"You owe *me* a few favors."

"Shit."

"Tell him."

She let out a breath like she was giving up the ghost. "I did if for Trimshaw."

"How could you *do* that?" Lukas wanted to know. "Trimshaw? He's a *parakeet.* I'm an *eagle.* "

"I like him, I respect him. I only came to your stinking company to work for him."

"What happened?" I said.

"I'm not a Nirvana fan. I'm not a collector. I never even liked their music. Though *All Apologies* is nice. The acoustic version? With the strings?"

"What happened?"

"Trimshaw asked me to do it, said he'd pay me. I don't know why, I don't know anything about the drawing. I'm almost innocent."

"You got it from him?"

"No, somebody who works for him. Some big galoop with bandages on his head."

Roots took out his phone, showed her a photo of Ramble—Ronald Braca.

"That's him," she said. "That's the one who gave

me the drawing. And the money."

"This is vile and revolting," said Lukas, "and it doesn't go unpunished. No way. This does *not* go unpunished."

She sighed. "God, I hate my life."

"I hate *all* life." He went off by himself to make a call and put her termination process in motion.

Some day for Sioux—gain a husband, lose a job

I stepped closer to her. With what I knew about Trimshaw, coming across a fan of his was a real curiosity.

"You said you only came to Zero-plus-ex to work for Trimshaw?"

She nodded. "He's the best boss I ever had. I wanted to go to Cascadian with him, but he asked me to stay put. Said I'd be doing him a favor, letting him know what was going on."

"You worked for him before."

"Active Denial Security Systems, the job I had before I came here. Best job I ever had."

"Doing the same thing? Preventive Maintenance?"

"No, much more interesting. Tracking Development. One of his clients was the FDA. He had a contract with them, develop ways to track designer drugs on the street. Usage levels, distribution channels, all that."

It felt like all the gods had withdrawn at the same time.

"What drugs?"

"Everything. MDPV, mephedrone, premazepam. Anabolic steroids, of course. Even some of the melanotan peptides, the tanning drugs."

"Cathidrone?"

"That was one of the newer ones back then, but yeah, cathidrone."

I was thinking about Rj Delgado, the way he used to carry a scale around to weigh himself.

I was thinking about Dustin Mathis, dying at the foot of an escalator.

I was thinking about Trimshaw Dawson. I don't care how great of a boss he was, he was gonna pay the price.

Destroying The Sun

Two hours later Roots got another video message. Janiva's eyes were tear drained. She looked like she'd been doing a lot of praying.

He says this is the final warning. You had your chance. What are you waiting for? I don't know what to tell you what to do, Roots. They seem to be operating on some tight margins here. He says this is the final notice. He says the price of my art will go up—that's the affect of posthumous value. Please, I don't know what to tell you. I don't.

I used to know a stoner named Bobby Stakes. He was a dealer, but he and his wife, Caroline, were often too fucked-up to negotiate business. At one point or another, everyone who knew them resorted to using the phrase, *The Stakes are high.*

The night traders had continued their surveillance of Cascadian HQ. In the course of it, Robbo had picked up something weird. Every four hours a Mazda RX-8 would leave the building and come back about an hour later. Then leave again, come back again. He'd seen it happen repeatedly over the cycles. Always the same car, departure every four hours. They seemed to be taking consistent care of some off-complex business. Like keeping tabs on a hostage? Robbo didn't know, but some kind of douchebaggery was going on.

>>>>>>

We were waiting in a rental with the front gate in sight, waiting for the next four hour shift to begin. Another hot spring day, nothing in the air but the strangled gasp of a breeze. Perfect weather for murder.

Roots was telling me about the night he'd spent, no sleep, went out for a walk, didn't know where, bought himself something to eat, never ate it, kept pacing the apartment for hours wondering how he could be having a nightmare when he was wide wide wide awake.

He glanced down to road. "*Cascadian.* What kind of name is that? Why name a company Cascadian? Something to do with the mountains? Waterfalls? Volcanoes? Rain?"

I agreed. "When you name something, you want to get it right. You want to have the right ring to it. Like titles. Literature. I mean *The Importer/Exporter of Venice? The Tell-Tale Liver? Moby Richard?* Not the same."

Roots was uneasy. "You can't go kerblooey, you understand? Don't get confused."

Heebie-jeebies, right. All these fragments and fissures of thought. No, I was cool. I wasn't giving in to them. My resistance to temptation was so strong that whenever I burst out shouting I only said positive and inspiring things.

Stay calm. Check the messages. Catch up on the news.

An environmental group is calling the River Jordan unsafe for baptisms. When you've got Israel, Syria and Jordan siphoning off 98% of the fresh water, and raw sewage and farm run-off seeping in, the results are too unhealthy for human immersion. The river where John the Baptist anointed Jesus 2,000 years ago has slowed to a dirty, sludgy trickle and should be declared off-limits for now, said the group.

"It's happening."

The Mazda RX-8 pulled out of Cascadian, sticking to its schedule. It was painted Velocity Red Mica. Shouldn't be *too* hard to follow.

The car headed for downtown Salami City but
swung north just before getting there, avoiding the heart of
the town. It only took us minutes to get into
deep woods, thick, shadow-mouthed clusters of pine and
oak. This was what New York State looked like on the last
day of creation.

A forest, thought the kid in me, filled with monsters
and beasts.

I remembered something Belinda said, talking about
the suicides. They reminded her of what seismologists call
a silent earthquake. Instruments start recoding faint tremors
and slips. Nobody feels anything, nobody reports anything,
but after a few weeks you realize the silent but steady event
has released as much energy as a 7.0 magnitude quake.

I missed her.

I could smell her body.

I could smell the musk of her pussy out here.

The red car turned off the road and drove for
another minute along a rumbly path. We could see a
structure up ahead—a cottage lodged in a cavity in the
woods. A fixer-upper, cramped and ramshackle, warped
joints, swollen wood, flaking paint, the whole thing on the
verge of collapse. It looked like no one had been there in a
century.

The Mazda stopped about a hundred feet away from
the house. And just sat there, nobody moving. Why not go
all the way to the door? They've made us?

A window in the cottage slid up. So did another
one. They stayed open for three seconds, then closed.

A signal. The Mazda proceeded to the front of the
house. Two kneeheads got out. Two more came out of the
cottage. They started talking to each other, discussing
something.

We got out of the rental, and as we moved closer
one of them popped the Mazda's trunk. Nobody took
anything out. No, they were getting ready to put something
in.

"Shit," Roots whispered. "They're taking her
somewhere. They're taking her away."

"Adds up to a dim sum."

"*Where?* Taking her *where?*'

"Let's do it. Take my shoes."

"Quinn, not now. No time for your shit."

"It's not shit. Hold my shoes."

I slipped off the path, barefoot-quiet, and worked through the woods along the side of the house, looking for some desperate shit-into-gold alchemy. Two of the kneeheads went back inside the cottage—which, Jesus, from this angle was in worse shape than I thought. Place really should've been boarded up.

Something Belinda said: Whenever you try to go to one extreme, your mind swings back to the other. You're thinking about how different things are, the back of your mind is saying they're all the same. You're trying to find the unity in things, your mind is telling you they're not at all alike.

It's all too zen for me.

I was about to start around the back of the cottage when I heard the door open, saw the kneeheads dragging Janiva to the Mazda.

I pulled the Glock.

So clean and beautiful out here.

So how come the air smells like death?

I waited until they shoved her in the trunk and slammed the lid shut. I started firing at the back of the cottage, just blasting it, trying to fucking *ignite* it, send it up in flames like an Afghani suicide. I felt a lot like Bill Wilson on belladonna—poisoned, possessed, hemlocked in a half-dream, world collapsing in terrified traces of burning phosphor. That's right—*exactly* like Bill Wilson on belladonna.

Running, moving, semicircling the back of the house while I kept firing. Invisible suns. Every day is doomsday.

When I was a kid I always wondered: If nuclear bombs are so powerful they can wipe out all life on earth, will they also destroy the sun?

I stopped shooting when I came to the return leg on the other side of the cottage. It felt like my mouth was filled with ashes. Gunfire started from the back of the house. All four kneeheads had been drawn inside and were pumping through the rear windows, spraying bullets into the woods at the places I'd been.

Keep moving, silent run to the front. Zen again. A line from Basho: *There is nothing you can think of that is not the moon.*

Roots had the trunk open and was pulling Janiva out. She was pissed, as predicted, but not at him. "*Punish* them," she whisper-shouted. "I want you to *hurt* them. I want them to fucking *pay*."

"First we get out of here," he said.

Least I'd gotten them back together.

There is nothing you can think of that is not the moon.

The kneeheads were still shooting at the trees at the back of the house. Roots and Janiva started running for the rental. I didn't follow.

He turned. "*What?*"

"Go ahead."

"Go ahead? What's *that* mean?"

I glanced at the open trunk. "I'm taking the ride."

CHAPTER 9

RIMFIRE

Thoroughly Dead

My phosphene images—those patterns spinning through your vision when your eyes are closed—were going as nuts as I was. Swirling clouds of jeweled pixels, twirling crystals conjured up in the darkness of the trunk, joining in a demented dance with all their other little molecule friends. Whirling, manic, confused—a clear mirror of my mental state while I rode curled up in the trunk, hot, carsick and cramped. Apparently, the storage space in the Mazda RX-8 wasn't built for human transportation.

Good sound system though. Music blasted through the back panel. *Let Me Hear You Scream. War Pigs. Suicide Solution.* The kneeheads were on an old-time Ozzy Osbourne kick.

Actually *any* music was fine. I could gauge the time passing by the songs. *Crucify*, approximately three minutes. *No Easy Way Out*, closer to five. I was adding the minutes and counting the nauseous turns the car made. If I ever had a chance to reconstruct the route later, at least I had a shot.

About 25 minutes into the ride the phosphenes became more elongated and thready. Like filaments of hair-thin laser light. Like the light needles of a meteor shower. Like one of Janiva's sculptures.

Scientists using extremely sensitive electronics and software can detect the sound individual neurons make as they transmit information. They're faint, staccato sounds. I could feel them popping in my head.

Right, nothing you can think of is not the moon.

Or another zen saying: *Be dead, be thoroughly dead, and do what you will.*

The car came to a stop. Ozzy off, engine off. Doors opened and slammed. Wherever we were, we were here.

The trunk unlocked and lifted into a sudden influx of light. The two Mazda kneeheads were surprised to see I wasn't a woman with a streak of dyed blue hair and a background in the arts. They were also surprised by the Glock in their faces.

"Back off," I said. "*Off*—over by the wall."

We were in a huge, sterile vault of a place walled with tiny green and white tiles. It looked like a public restroom and smelled like a climate-controlled crypt. I recognized the décor. Roots and I had stumbled through here, him with a burn on his leg, as we were taken to see Trimshaw. This was the main Cascadian building.

"Where's Trimshaw?"

"Where's the girl?" one of the kneeheads said. "The fucking girl?"

"Probably on her way home by now. And Trimshaw?"

They didn't say.

I went to climb out of the trunk, got my leg over the rear bumper. Shit—wait.

One of the kneeheads moved, jumpy. "Who the fuck are you?"

I re-Glocked him and got out. "I'm sure you've got other plans, but you're taking me to see Trimshaw."

"Yeah, but who *are* you?"

"His name's Quinn McShane and he's a major piece of shit."

A size XXX voice, coming from the side of the car. Ramble—Ronald Braca—was standing there in all his sneaky-bastard glory, his Buck Mark rimfire gun leveled at my head. Bandages were still wrapped around his.

"Put it on the floor."

I set the Glock down.

"Shove it out of harm's way."

It skittered across the floor.

He turned to the kneeheads. "How did *this* happen?"

"We had a thing at the cottage," one of them said. "An *incident*. Must've happened then."

"An *incident*. When were you gonna tell me about it?"

"Right now."

Ramble was too disgusted to go on with it. "Feel him."

One of the kneeheads moved behind me, slipped his hands under my armpits and clasped them around the back of my neck, locking my arms over my head. The other one patted me down from the front. Outside of my phone, I was clean.

The patter stepped out of the way as Ramble came into my space, up close and impersonal. The other kneehead kept my arms fixed in the air.

Ramble gave me a long assessing look, head to toe. And back to toe. "Where're your shoes?"

"It's a long story."

"Trust me, you won't have time. Remember our first meeting? Central Park?"

"Couldn't be more romantic."

"I've discovered a few things about you since."

"Such as."

"I've discovered you have no likeable qualities whatsoever. I've discovered you're an interfering dipshit who really, really needs to be shut down."

"When you discover soap, let me know."

He hit me so hard he knocked me loose from the kneehead's grip. Was like a pitcher red-balling a brick into your gut from 60 feet away. My legs buckled—my *soul* buckled—and I splattered down, the phosphene images running rampant in the cosmos.

Tried to get up, couldn't hold it, staggered over to the car, scraped my hands on the license plate as I fell into the open trunk.

It's like your brain's selecting images in a dream. You're thinking this is bizarre, this is insane, and yet it feels just right.

My hands fumbled around the trunk well. It was still there, the loaner from Roots, the thing I'd dropped when I was climbing out.

I turned it on them, hosing them with high-frequency microwaves, jackhammering Ramble and the glue-footed kneeheads with paralyzing beams of electromagnetic radiation. They froze, they went limp, they collapsed. I stood over Ramble, giving him an extra dose, keep him incapacitated for a good long while.

I felt a sizzle cutting across the flesh of my shoulder, heard a gunshot muted by the space. It burned with force. I landed on Ramble's body and twisted around.

Some white-haired specimen of magnified mouse was standing behind me, wearing suspenders, shorts, knee-high socks and holding my Glock in his hand. Trimshaw's eyes were swollen and inflated like they were being squeezed out of their sockets, but he still had that chummy smile on his face.

Be dead, be thoroughly dead, then do what you will.

I struggled to get to my feet, kept trying to push off Ramble, but my hands for some reason kept slipping away. Made one more grand effort, lost my grip on a wet slick and flopped over on my back.

Why is everything I'm touching soaked with liquid?

Ah, cause I'm bleeding all over the fucking place.

Trimshaw came closer, chuckling to himself. "It's like Mel Allen used to say, how *about* that!"

>>>>>>

"I shouldn't be firing off weaponry," he said, walking like a bent twig 10 or so feet behind me, the Glock at my back. "Not at my age. My age, the body breaks down at the slightest."

"Least your aim's still pretty good," I said, shifting my hoodie again. Thing was all lumpy from the rags I'd found and stuffed inside, trying to sponge up the blood.

"Well, shooting a gun, it's like riding a bike. At my age, all you get is a hernia."

He was taking me down some kind of service corridor, absolutely featureless except for the blue Barbicide walls. Every blank square foot of it was vibrating in my eyes with halos.

"You interrupted my snack," he said. "Now I've got a headache this big."

"I'm supposed to apologize?"

"Not your fault. That's another thing that comes with age. You can never miss a meal."

Don't ask me why, you got me, but the corridor had me thinking about the flat, marshy borderlands between Germany and Russia. Thanks to the combined efforts of Hitler and Stalin, 14 million Jews, Poles, Ukrainians, Belarusians and others were killed there during World War II. All citizens, no soldiers—shot, gassed or deliberately starved to death, and not one of them had ever fired a gun in the war.

"Now you being here," said Trimshaw, "yes, that *is* your fault. No offense, but you're a poor substitute for Roots' girlfriend."

"Taking her was too much, you know? She had nothing to do with your shit."

"I respect your right to be wrong, but you *are* wrong. And now you've been compromised. I'm afraid you've taken what we call a bidet-proof dump. No matter how hard you wipe your ass, it'll never come clean."

"Got it. I understand."

"Just curious, were there things you wanted to do before you died?"

"I don't know, visit Tibet. Finish reading *Finnegans Wake*. Learn how to use Saran Wrap without getting then ends crinkled up and stuck together."

"Can't help you with any of that. By the way, where are your *shoes*?"

>>>>>>

The Last Supper

It didn't strike me this way the first time, but sitting here now in Trimshaw's office, taking in the lava-green walls and the stripped-down furniture, it reminded me of the bunker in the Hitler go-back. The place was as happy as a mineshaft, as overdecorated as a rock. Sitting here, I was caught in Hitler's cave.

Only one thing saved the view from total boredom: That blown-up NASA image of two spiral galaxies colliding. Blazing golds and reds setting fire to a battleground of blue, locked in a 100 million-year-old death match.

Trimshaw was gobbling down one of his prune sandwiches, restoring his vitals with strained fruit, whipped cream and chopped walnuts while holding the gun on me. He'd taken Roots' phone-like microwave generator out of his pocket and placed it on the desk.

"Can I offer you one of these?" he said. "No problem making it for you."

"Not much appetite."

"Just seems rude, like *I'm* eating your last meal."

I had a better look at the old fucker now. Blossoms of broken veins on his face, networks of fine wrinkles laced around the sockets, blue eyes shimmering with the weak, eerie glow of a night light.

"When's the last time you actually talked to him?" I said.

"When I left. I haven't spoken to Lukas since. Unless you want to count the times I've muttered at the screen."

"Yet you're still waging guerilla warfare."

   "I don't think there's all that much mystery to
it. It's payback for those who've taken their own lives. It's
revenge for his brutalizing management style. I think I told
you how it went. I came there as a guide to good business
practice, a sherpa to enlightened governance and
management. And everything about the company was very
woo-woo back then. Conventional wisdom said it was a
smart move to make."

   "Like most conventional wisdom, it was about half
right."

   "I'll say this, his mental illness has done him a
world of good. He created a very exciting product range.
And Lukas himself, there were times you could think he
was almost human. But I could see there were problems.
He'd get trapped by his own brilliance, by his own
theories. He'd lose sight of the people around him, get lost
in the labyrinth of his own ideas. I thought I could bridge
the divide, broker the gap. I thought I could be the
smoother over."

   "But Lukas is smooth-proof."

   "Exactly, mon frere. It hadn't escaped my attention
that staffers were miserable, they were crawling and
crying through this workplace Siberia, they were choking
on his rules and regs and insanely demanding suspicions,
they were jumping off the roof because of his bubbly
affect. I tried to address it. I tried to pull him into cold,
clear reality. I showed him the predictive models—the
suicide rates would only get worse. I suggested installing
programs, hotlines, counseling, employee assistance,
anything to help. Every proposal I made, he called them
ridiculously impractical and blissfully fact free. *There are
no provisions for anything like that in the original plans.*
Everything I said left him cursing like a Russian and
accusing me of accomplishing the miraculous feat
of not appreciating his talents. So he ignored it all.
He ignored *me*. He just went on pontificating and
pompostulating like everything was fine and dandy and he
was satisfied being the smartest man who
ever drove people to their *deaths*. What a fucking
hoot *that* was!"

He hurled his prune sandwich and smashed it against the wall.

Get a jump on him?

No, he swung the Glock back on me.

"So I left. I made my decision. I needed to change my life. I told him any organization that holds human life in such little regard is a worthless organization, no matter how much money it makes. He begged me to stay. He gave me all his crap-mouth, pocket-lint arguments. There's innovation here, there's power here, there's creative *glory* here. I decided I was already glorious enough. I left."

He looked raw-eyed and worn down, hurting, almost defeated. A crucifixion face. Kurt Cobain in the garage.

He glanced over at the fixings on the counter—a Tupperware of strained prunes, a can of Reddi-wip, a bowl of chopped walnuts, a loaf of bread.

"Know what the secret to a good prune sandwich is?" he said. "Once you've boiled them soft, you squeeze the prunes through a sieve, then add water and sugar to the pulp. But what I do, I add a little cinnamon to the sugar, just a pinch, mix it in. Then I bring it all to a boil."

"Tell me about the cathidrone."

"The cathidrone."

"Tell me."

He slowly nodded. No point in bullshitting.

"I guess it's just another addition to a long list of regrets, and I wish there were a better way, but it had to be done."

"Really. *Had* to be?"

"Yes."

"You *had* to kill people?"

"I had to punish him for what he did. I had to get back at him for what he did to those people. For what he's *doing*. I had to show him he's not nearly as Number One-derful as he thinks he is."

"Pull him into cold, clear reality."

"Exactly. It's perfectly simple. I need to hurt his plans. I need to hurt his company. I need to hurt his corporate image. I need to hurt *him*. I'll do *anything* to hurt him."

"You hate him."

"Are you *serious*?"

"You hate him because he kills people. So *you* kill people. Logic?"

"Are you *listening* to me? I'm trying to put pressure on him. I'm trying to make his life catastrophically miserable. I'm trying to drive him to suicide—mental, emotional, spiritual, *actual* suicide. I'm trying to give him the justice he deserves."

"The old I-kill-because-I-care defense."

"I *do* care."

"You're a murderer."

"No. Not that. I'm sure you can find many derogatory categories for me, but I don't fit that one."

"What do you call yourself?"

"An *avenger*."

"What kind of fuckass talk is that? It's like what they call bestiality in Arkansas. Safe sex."

"If I'm guilty of anything, I'm simply guilty of being human."

"And lying. You lied to me."

"Possibly. When?"

"First time I came here. Roots and I asked you about Rj Delgado. You said you'd never take an innocent life just to hurt Lukas."

"Not without cause, no. I wanted the MIXEX he had. I thought it would prove valuable. Sorry, I was wrong."

"So you went for the PIB instead. After the first go-back, you made the PIB your target."

"Absolutely."

"Then why kill Dustin Mathis?"

"That wasn't working out the way I'd hoped. You were getting too close to him. Much as I admire his loyalty, he became a liability."

"Just another name. Another patient on the chart."

"I have a conscience. I'm not immune from sadness. I'm already getting ready to feel remorse for you."

"And who gives out the cath? Ramb—Ronald Braca out there?"

"He's very skilled. I'll never say he isn't."

Trimshaw took another look at the prune sandwich ingredients on the counter. He was hungry. I leaned over, adjusted the bloody rags on my shoulder with my left hand. The right I worked around my back and under my hoodie until I could feel the handle of the gun. The Buck Mark I'd slipped off Ramble while I was rolling around on his body. Hard to spot under the hoodie's lumpy folds.

He turned back to me. "There's another factor in play here as well, Mr. McShane. My age. I'm running out of time. If I'm going to do what I have to do I have to do it now."

"You're not that old. What're you gonna tell me, Edna St. Vincent Millay was a great piece of ass? You're *that* old?"

"Old enough to have fewer friends above the ground than below. It's amazing how fast it all goes. You look outside, buds are breaking out on the trees. You take a bite of a sandwich, look again. The leaves are turning brown."

Or gold or red, like the cosmic detonations going off in the NASA blow-up on the wall. I was star-gazing at the photo, my brain running on theta rhythms, learning something, remembering something.

Be dead, be thoroughly dead, and do what you will.

There is nothing you can think of that is not the moon.

"There's something else too," he said. "I'm going to be honest with you."

"Why start now?"

"It's a kind of confession, I suppose. I can't explain it, I don't know why it is, but every time I do damage to him, every time a life is taken, I feel something."

"What?"

"Peace. I know, it sounds strange, but every time one of those people dies, I feel a tremendous sense of peace. *Overwhelming* peace. Each overdose gives me a glimpse of something I've never known before. Do you have any idea what I'm talking about?"

"Yeah. It's what everybody wants. An overpowering connection with the world. An ecstatic embrace of the universe. A return to the oceanic womb, said Freud. Burn like fire and dance with the stars, said the Buddha. Everyone wants the same thing—the only difference is how we get it."

"How do you know this?"

"I learned zen meditation in prison."

"*Meditation.* I prefer my way."

"Yeah, but your way doesn't last, does it? It's never something you can hang onto. It fades cocaine-fast, and then you want more."

"That's true."

"You should find something else. Something more lasting."

"Like what? *Zen*? Prayer? Collecting crystals? Rubbing Tibetan finger bowls?" He laughed. "I can't see myself getting all churched-up about this, can you? *Please.*"

His emphatic contempt was making his gunhand move an inch or two every few words.

"I was going to suggest something else."

"Like *what*?"

"Like this."

His eyes turned a wet red as the hole opened in his head. Bits of bone blew out of his skull. The look on his face: uncertain, frozen, astonished.

His body recoiled off the back of his chair and bent forward, like he was closely examining the surface of his desk. Thick strings of blood and strained fruit spilled out of his mouth, just like the threads of vomit from a cath overdose.

I don't know about him, but I was feeling much better.

CHAPTER 10

Every Truth Carries A Lie

Holy Conspiracy

Belinda told me a story about her mother. This happened before Child Welfare tried to take Belinda away, before her mother smuggled her out of the apartment in a suitcase and went on a ghost-run. Her mother's family knew she was sinking into a pharmaceutical pithole, so they decided to give her a book on sobriety one Christmas. But no one wanted to bear the brunt of the blame, so they made it anonymous. A gift from Santa Claus. When her mother opened it up and saw what it was, she predictably got pissed. They all said no, no, it's not from me, it's not from me. It's from Santa. *In that case*, said Mom, *Santa Claus can go fuck himself.*

I loved that story. I loved the answer—*Santa Claus can go fuck himself.* Repeating the phrase over the next few days helped me on my shaky way to recovery. Once the adrenaline washed away, the pain in my shoulder wound really started cutting against the grain. The doctors recommended a few days of recuperation. I spent much of that time in the honeyed light of Belinda's bedroom, listening to her stories, her narrative incantations, getting big doses of April happiness. Felt like I stayed hard the whole time, kissing her ears, biting the back of her neck, brushing my lips all over her body, the inside of her pussy as purple as Cleopatra's sails.

When it comes to knowing about sex, women don't fuck around.

It helped, it all helped. It helped pull me out of the Auralsynch weirdness, helped finish an act of release that began with Trimshaw's death. I don't know, but the payback for Rj Delgado's murder seemed to purge my mind with some cathartic magic. Whatever hallucinatory blinders the sounds had implanted in my head, they were melting away like cataracts from my eyes.

Belinda thought it was no coincidence. She saw a purpose in the whole thing. Her exposing me to the binaural beats, the sounds hypnotically sucking me in, me coming back. I'd gotten lost in the madness so that my Prodigal Son return would mean that much more.

Everything, she said, is a holy conspiracy.

It's been estimated that the cost of a murder to society runs a bit over $17 million. Factor in the loss of productivity from the victim and other indicators of economic disruption, plus the price of a coroner's report, a crime scene clean-up and a police investigation, then toss in the amount of money the average American would spend to *avoid* being shot in the head with a Buck Mark rimfire gun, and society gets hit with $17.25 million worth of sticker shock.

But the cost of putting Trimshaw Dawson out of commission? Priceless.

Consider the beneficial results. Ramble was arrested for numerous cathidrone deaths, including those of Rj Delgado and Dustin Mathis. I was cleared of all charges—self-defense. Roots and Janiva were reunited and happy together and showing every sign of eventually turning into an old couple who fights over the icepack for their respective aches and pains.

And Lukas was inspired by the permanent elimination of his rival. The expression of euphoria didn't really fit his face—it had the effect of distorting his passionately tortured features—but euphoric he was. Life at [0+X] was no longer the usual strange. Lukas had started calling Belinda in for consultations on how to improve company morale.

He'd been staggered by the comments he heard at Sioux Zeckendorf's wedding. At one point one of the staffers became suspicious about his questions and asked

who he was. He assured the employee he wasn't
himself. For the first time in Lukas' life, he was
congratulated for *not* being Lukas Lister-Bertozzi. That
stung.

"They hate me," he said to Belinda. "They hate
my methods, my goals, my accomplishments. I don't
understand. Yes, I *am* a genius, but through no fault of
my own."

He was interested in her suggestions. Yes, maybe
they should be told there's profound joy in the spiritual life.
Maybe it's true that every moment of our lives is a gift
from God. Maybe holding feng-raisers or whatever you
call them is a good idea. "I have a great respect for
spiritual practices," he said, "no matter how ridiculous they
might seem."

Lukas, in fact, was doubly inspired by Trimshaw's
death. He committed himself to creating another go-back.
He'd promised a third installment and he couldn't let the
world down. To find a sub for Kurt Cobain he was tracking
down controversial historical candidates and their available
DNA, turning himself into a genetic scavenger.

A lawsuit filed by the estate of Lee Harvey Oswald
did nothing to dissuade him. According to their legal claim,
the assassin's DNA was the tangible and intellectual
property of the Oswald family and had been used without
their permission. The estate was seeking monetary damages
plus authorization to use the [0+X] go-back technology to
produce its own Lee Harvey Oswald sequels.

Lukas didn't care. Minor speed bumps never slowed
him down, never discouraged him. He had to come up with
another blast from the past, one that would shine as brightly
in the world's eyes as the tablets on Mount Sinai. Moved
by Trimshaw's cold body, he'd lit a fire under his own ass.

>>>>>>

Something Belinda said to me: Every truth carries an
untruth. Every statement contains its opposite. Every fact
conceals a lie. We know this in our bones. We sense in the
back of our minds that there's something absurd and weird

and self-contradictory about everything. And when we chase this contradiction to the center of life, when the whole world stands revealed, we weep with unstoppable laughter, we laugh with uncontrollable grief.

Risen Into The Light

I still hadn't read all of *Interzone Quantum Time Differentials6B*, but since I was resting up I figured I'd make a run for the end. I was determined to finish the fucking book, operating on the hope that maybe, just maybe, I'd get to a point where something actually *happened*.

Version *6B*. Was it possible that the earlier drafts were easier to read? Was *4A*, say, written in something closer to English? Probably not. I'm guessing they were all as twisting and turning as a colonoscopy.

I didn't read every word, but I skimmed deeply. I made it past his meandering meditations on counterfactual paradox resolution, delayed-choice deviation, Ghirardi-Rimini-Weber reformulation and why certain half-wits disagree with what he's talking about, whatever that is.

Am I blaming the 20th Century? Not in its entirety, no. Of course not. Aspects of the 20th Century were progressive, formative and intellectually wholesome. But once the concepts propounded in this book made their entrance into history—a moment unlike any other in samesaid history—the misconceptions of the previous century should have been laid aside. Unlocking the long-held secrets of the past, of Babylon, Nineveh, Chang'an, Texcoco, Aksum, Thebes and Rome—yes, even of the pre-Adamite lands—is an achievement whose magnitude it is almost superfluous at this juncture to describe in further detail. Indeed, I shall not. To transcribe every musical note of one's own magnum opus is repugnant. I have, perhaps, already said enough.

Enough? Hear that sound? That's the horse choking.

I kept going, and limping, crawling, palms and knees torn bloody, I finally saw the finish line up ahead.

Let my last remark be this: Some day we shall be amazed by what these very words have brought about. As the human race climbs upward, the deep layers of mystery are risen into the light. The whole of human progress tends in the direction of clarity, and these words lend but a helping hand. I record them here not for my own glorification. No, no. I serve only as a harbinger, a messenger. I see myself standing on the border of a vast plain, one whose boundaries extend far beyond my own mortality and death.

But while I live I shall walk that land with the widest stride, shouting the news that the present is bound to the past, that by looking closely at the present we can see the past. The syllogism is simple: The past has already happened, therefore it can be predicted, and if it can be predicted, it can be made to live again. We imagine the past as an ungraspable phantom. I tell you it is not so. I say this to the universe, that which has happened, those who have been taken from us—the one who has been taken from me, the one to whom these words are dedicated—are no longer lost. Some day they will return to the range of our visions. And this is the key to it all.

No mystery. He was talking about his daughter, Samantha. *The one who was taken from me.*

To quote Mel Allen and Trimshaw Dawson, how about that?

Something actually *did* happen.

Dying Is Easy, Supposedly

Lukas was surprised by what I was saying and I was just as surprised by his surprise. Isn't this why the go-backs were originally created? To discover why your daughter died? To discover what shocked Sabreena into a long, blacked-out, colorless amnesia? You said you wandered around for weeks after the fire—that's when you started thinking about the possibilities of the past. Wasn't this the real reason why?

All I was saying was, you want to produce a third go-back? Then go back to the electrical fire in your old residence on the top level. Reconstruct what happened. Find out why Sabreena couldn't or wouldn't save the child. Help her remember what her mind has forced her to forget.

We were standing in the greenhouse built around the small grave. As soon as he heard my proposal, Lukas insisted we talk out here, surrounded by cultivated magnolias and lilies and human-size sunflowers. Today's fresh roses had already been laid in front of the granite marker. *Samantha Lister-Bertozzi*—black words chiseled into black stone, only four years of life separating the dates.

He looked rattled and detached, like a sphinx who's lost track of its own riddle.

"She went through a terrible time," he said. "The treatments for dissociative states are particularly grueling. Even brutal. How far down is this buried? It takes painful probing to find out. To live through what happened again is almost catastrophic. I don't think she can take it anymore."

"Understood. But you really don't want to know the truth?"

"I don't know what she did. I don't know what she *didn't* do. Neither does she, and finding out might crush her. She's suffered in the shadows for a long time. I don't think she can stand the light."

"It's your call. And hers."

"*Hers.*" He sighed like a man with pleurisy, bent over and began pulling brown leaves off one of the magnolias. "There were times when I'd have a bad day, I'd go back to the living quarters, I'd sit down and sigh just like I sighed now. My daughter would sit next to me and say, Talk to me, Daddy." He smiled. "My counselor, my comforter. I'd tell her what was going on, she'd say, Oh Daddy, you act so superior. You really have to stop being so sassy..."

"Four years, still a lifetime of memories."

He straightened up, stuffed the leaves into the pocket of that old frock coat. "After the fire, we had to move what was left. We packed her things up, put them in storage downstairs. I'd go down there, sit with her things in my hand. Her toys, her clothes. I'd sit there by myself, hours. I never felt so alone. I thought I was going to die..."

"You told me. Fever."

"I was all ready for it. I was all ready to die. I thought, it can't be that hard. It can't be as hard as this."

He moved away from the grave, heading for the door, but stopping at the greenhouse's other slab of rock. The one that said, *Lukas Lister-Bertozzi Was Conceived On This Spot*, the one he'd erect whenever he found out where that spot was.

"I can't say yes to what you're talking about," he said. "It's impossible. It has the potential to destroy her. Besides, it's not what was promised. I don't think your people at *Real Story* would be happy."

"I've already brought it up. They're thrilled. It's not what was promised, no, but they think it'll still be big. Maybe even bigger."

"Why? It's not history. It's *personal*."

"Your *child* died. You'll get a huge audience. Different market maybe, different demographic. But huge."

"I don't understand. Why would anyone care?"

"The go-backs have made you a known commodity. They've made you famous."

"I've always been famous."

"With a *wide* audience. They'll care about your daughter. The go-back'll get big hits."

"Big hits."

I nodded.

He stared around at the [0+X] compound through the greenhouse glass. "I supposed there might be some advantage to that. It might help me with the employees, improve my standing. They might understand me better, show me some sympathy. At least hate me less."

"Least no one'll sue you."

"You're right about Sabreena. It *is* her call. It's her decision. It's her culpability, it's her guilt that's at stake. If she thinks she can handle it, fine. See what she says. If she agrees, I'll agree."

"*See?*"

"See. See what she says."

"*Me.* You want *me* to see."

"I can't do it."

"You want *me* to talk to her. Just a *little* passive-aggressive, no?"

"What can I do? I can't talk to her. Too much time has passed. Too much has come between us. Or *hasn't* come between us. What I say I say with sadness, but if the question comes from me, it'll taint her decision. No, you have to ask, she has to answer."

He turned to leave. The scalp under his parted hair glistened in the glass-filtered sunlight.

"Interesting how you absolve yourself," I said.

"She was the *only* one there. The only one who *lived.* Wherever the road leads, she's the only one who can walk that walk."

>>>>>>

Miracle Child

She was in her own parallel universe, her own small greenhouse instead of his, the moonflowers closed up and drooping, waiting for the night to bloom. We found her absorbed, as usual, in her iPad. We? I'm no fool—I went there with her friend and confidante, Belinda.

Glad I did. I hadn't seen Sabreena since the night Roots and I found her in the apartment on Sutton Place. She'd only gotten worse. She looked as sick and decayed as any creature who's never seen the sun. A sleepwalker in the middle of a crumbling dream. Ophelia in the last stages, well beyond rosemary's remembrance.

I'm looking at her and thinking, no way is this gonna happen.

But my powers of prediction, it turns out, sucked to the heavens. She wanted the go-back. No hesitation. She wanted to do it right away.

"I've lost something and I want to get it back. I'm tired of not remembering. I'm tired of living in exile from my own mind."

"No guarantee," said Belinda.

"I don't care. I'll try it. I'm tired of him holding it over my head. Look at me, look what it's done. I used to have *some* good looks. I used to have what people called a kind face. *Now* look."

She'd weighed in, she weighed out. Just like that. Back to the iPad.

"What're you reading?" I said.

"You know what I read." She handed it over.

Body of "Miracle Baby" Found in River.

Yes, it fit the pattern.

Bizarre story: A few days ago a pair of New Jersey fishermen looking for fluke on the Manasquan River pulled out a plastic bag holding the corpse of a 2-year-old girl. Working from her dress, police were able to trace the body to a pediatric hospice in Asbury Park. The child was identified as Elicia Alvarez and, most amazing, she'd died at the hospice three years earlier.

Investigating, police discovered that her coffin had been smashed open—probably soon after her death, going by the three years of vegetation growing over the gravesite. Where had Elicia been between now and then? No one knew, but there was plenty of speculation. The girl had been born with semilobar holoprosencephaly, a condition that prevents brain development and usually results in death soon after birth. Since Elicia had managed to live for more than two years, she'd been called a "miracle baby." According to black rumor, her body had been stolen by members of Santiera or Palo Mayombe or some other dark cult who'd tried to ritualistically siphon off her miraculous survivor spirit for themselves. That's why the corpse was still in such preserved condition, even three years after her death.

"I'm worried about my daughter," Sabreena said, taking the iPad back. "I'm worried about where she is out there. I'm afraid someone might steal her."

"Don't worry," said Belinda. "She's well protected."

"But she was a miracle too. Not a medical miracle, not a miracle baby. A miracle child. Just being around her was a miracle. She had a miraculous effect on me. On us…"

"I heard," I said. "Lukas was telling me. He'd be having a rough time, she'd sit with him and talk."

"After he'd leave work, yes. I remember those times. He'd pour out his troubles to her, she'd get all mock-sarcastic and say, Gee, Daddy, it's really *tough* being you."

She put the iPad down, stood up, started untangling some of the vines of her dormant moonflowers. Tending to her garden, just like Lukas. Amazing how much alike they were.

"There's an old Japanese custom," she said. "An old ritual, it's called *Hesono O*. They'd leave the umbilical on the baby, they'd let it dry and fall off. Then they'd put the cord in a box, a *kotobuki bako*, and leave it there. Forever. No matter what happened through life, the cord in the box meant the child would always be loved, always be remembered."

"It's a beautiful tradition," said Belinda. "But I don't think you need her umbilical cord. You love her. You remember her."

Sabreena didn't answer, just freed a few more vines from themselves. Then she turned to us. "I did something. I never told Lukas about it."

I stared back at her. "What?"

"After she was gone, I wrote her a note. Told her how much I loved her, how much I missed her. I got one of those helium balloons, tied the note to the string and let it go in the air. I was hoping it would find her."

For some reason, although we knew it wasn't possible, we all looked up at the sky.

The Big Bang

That sky opened up the night of the go-back. After a day of uncertainty, the weather finally decided to go for an all-out thunderstorm, a wild and beautiful noreaster that no one would ever forget. But not because of the rains and winds beating against the [0+X] complex. Now matter how *King Lear* crazy the storm outside became, it was still no match for the cataracts and hurricanoes raging inside The Hive.

Everything was atomic. Everything inside that three-story tall aluminum basketball was ferocious and driven and crowded and fluttering and precise and electric and seemed on the verge of total opening-night collapse. Staffers Segwayed across the floor. Engineers climbed the catwalks. ASSETS patrolled for security. Problems were discovered and fixed. Samantha's DNA, easily extracted from the things still in storage, had been transformed by the PIB into a holographic chip, and the quantum cascade lasers were ready to project her last recorded genetic memories on the 360-degree screen of the interior walls and feed the link to the *Real Story* servers for a live transmission on the site. Everything on this sweeping and pressurized canvas was crashing together with the attending marvels of a thousand and one [0+X] sounds and sights.

Sabreena came in, walking with Belinda. She was composed, tranquil. Whatever was going to happen, let it happen.

Not Lukas. He was all nervous emphasis, embedded dread.

As she came up to him I realized this was the first time I'd ever seen them together.

"We don't have to do this," he said. "There's still time to stop."

She reached out for him. I thought she was going to stroke his cheek. Instead she clamped her hand over his mouth. "Do it."

He raised his arm—a signal. Everyone put the protective goggles on. An echo-free voice issued from the dozens of speakers on the walls. *Everything is ready.*

It started with an explosion. Almost a dream of an explosion, some massive, electrical-overload, Big-Bang detonation that made the whole apartment—the current site of the *Gengo* lab—quiver with shock. The little girl with the angel face and slate gray eyes had just gotten to her feet, leaving the stuffed animals she'd been playing with on the floor. She was startled but not scared, concerned but not crying. Samantha was looking around the room like she couldn't find one of her toys.

Alarms went off. Moments later, a fuzzy red glow could be seen in the hallway outside her room—the instant spread of an electrical fire, something titanic and multiple about it.

Now Samantha was confused. Should she run? Stand still? She didn't know what to do.

A shiver of a voice could be heard. Her mother's voice, calling her name. Then footsteps coming from somewhere in the apartment. Sabreena's steps, heavy, landing with full-run force.

Samantha moved in to the hall, running toward her mother's voice. The voice sounded closer now but it kept bouncing off the walls, reverberating from different directions.

Chaotic, quick-cut images followed as the girl dashed down the hall and into another corridor, trying to get to her mother. The floor ahead of her was stairsing up to another level, but just as she got to the steps a star of yellow flame burst open in front of her. The fan of fire was blocking her path, burning like God's punishment.

Samantha jumped back, saw a closet door off to the side. A safe place to hide.

Darkness. Security. Sabreena calling her name in panic. Then a purpling glow lined the doorframe. Tongues of liquid yellow seeped through the spaces around the door, lighting up the closet. Brooms, mops, a vacuum cleaner, bottles of cleaning supplies.

Running steps outside, her mother shrieking and powerless. Samantha went for the door but a Niagra of light and smoke blew in and drove her back. She screamed but her voice couldn't be heard over the burning roar.

The heat was building rapidly. Samantha moved away from the door, backed off as far as she could go. The closet was turning into an oven, a furnace, a crematorium.

And then it blew up. It erupted in a volcano of chemical combustion as the heat ignited the contents of the bottles. The sky seemed to shudder. The screen filled with a whole hell of fire and smoke.

The girl fell down, drowning in smoke. The image began to fade, grow weaker, turn an ash-colored gray. Now you couldn't hear anything, not a sound. You couldn't see flame or smoke anymore, just an emptiness, a hungry darkness, as the child lost consciousness for the last time.

The entire Hive, the entire gigantic three-story balloon, was silent. Everyone knew now. Everyone understood what had happened. Samantha had hid in the closet—that's why her mother had never been able to find her. It wasn't Sabreena's fault. It was no one's fault. Everyone understood that now. Everyone knew what has passed through Sabreena's cloud-tortured mind.

Lukas was disoriented, sweaty, sick with revelation. Accepting what he'd just seen was a challenge he couldn't face right now. He couldn't even face his wife standing next to him.

Sabreena was still calm, sadly serene, like she was holding an invisible umbilical cord in her hands. "You and I have been here before," she said, "a long time ago."

He groped for an answer and opened his mouth to say something, but that was as far as he got.

There's a star in the constellation Monocerus, located 100 light years away, that gives off a sound as it spins through its magnetic cycles. Scientists using stellar seismology say that the star, HD 49933, sounds just like a ringing bell.

I could hear it right now.

The Probability Of Terrible Results

If you happened to be hovering over the [0+X] complex in a Eurocopter TwinStar the next day and looked down through the glass ceiling of the Cenacle, you would've seen the broken sight of Lukas Lister-Bertozzi sitting by himself on the floor and propped up against one of the window-pane walls. You would've seen a human shadow of a man. Although it was morning, it was full night for him. The sun-glistening beauty of the grounds, still wet from last night's storm, seemed to be crushing him with its peaceful indifference.

That's how I found him, flopped on the floor, not even looking up at me once I'd climbed the winding stairs, just staring at his iPad. He was reading *Interzone Quantum Time Differentials*—6B? Yes, 6B—trying to find some comfort in his own words.

Actually, he was *trying* to read his book. Something was wrong with the iPad, he said. The words on the screen weren't holding steady. They weren't staying linear. They kept jumping around instead, rearranging themselves in messages meant only for him.

This sentence, for example, should've read, *Once we've adjusted our dynamical descriptions and obtained the paradigmatic amplitude for a series of events, the probability of possible results becomes intriguingly dense.*

What he was seeing was, *Once we've adjusted our tyrannical descriptions and obtained the paranoic amplitude for a series of events, the probability of terrible results becomes intriguingly dead.*

I took a look. SOS—same old shit to me. He was gone.

"I don't see anything wrong." I handed it back.

"Nothing?"

"Nothing."

"You read carefully."

"Carefully."

He stared at the screen with complicated silence. "I was thinking of writing another book."

Ah Jesus, no. "About what?"

"A history of the dawn."

Interesting topic. "Least it's something we can all relate to."

He put the iPad down, glanced at the unbroken view around the Cenacle—the estate, the water, the sky. Going by his eyes, he was looking at the desert of a lithium salt field.

"You're a fucking mess, you know that."

He nodded. "I got up this morning, all sweaty. Went to wash my face. I looked sick in the mirror. I looked old."

"The mirror didn't lie."

"After the fire, that time, I became very sick."

"Yes."

"I was hoping I'd be diagnosed with Stephen Hawkin's disease. Seemed fitting, you know? Neuro-muscular dystrophy, related to amyotrophic lateral sclerosis? No such luck."

"Sorry for your loss. How's Sabreena?"

"I don't know. Triumphant? Gloating?"

"How *is* she?"

"I don't know. I haven't seen her." He looked at me after a moment's thought. "The go-back was a mistake. You never should've suggested it."

"It's *my* fault you can't live with the truth?"

"It's a *mistake*. A gross error, a travesty. In terms of miracles it managed to turn wine into water."

"Because it didn't show you what you wanted to see?"

"I wanted to know who killed my daughter."

"No one did."

"Not good enough. I wanted an *answer*."

"And you found it. It was a *mistake*."

"I wanted to know who was *responsible*."

"You wanted to know who to *blame*."

"I wanted *certainty*, not some no-fault policy. She was my *daughter*. My beautiful little daughter. For her to die like that? Randomly? Accidentally? With no purpose? No, I haven't worked this hard, I haven't lived all these years for *nothing*."

His breathing rhythm was changing, getting faster, amping up until it was almost a gasp.

"So you think the go-back was faulty."

"Yes."

"Because it didn't give you certainty."

"*Yes*! *Thank* you!"

"But isn't that the problem with all the go-backs? No certainty? They can answer plenty of questions, but not the fundamental questions. They can give you plenty of answers, but not the ones you really need."

"If they can't, I'll find ones that will."

"Not in the past. You can't depend on the past for certainty. Or the future. Only now."

"You don't know me. I'll *find* the ultimate truth."

"But the ultimate truth doesn't exist in the past. You push back far enough in time—you know this—you get to the quasar cutoff, the part of the universe where quasars haven't formed yet. All the answers are still infinite."

"Infinity can't be trusted. What I'm looking for is finite. A simple, tiny, uncomplicated explanation that I can hold onto."

"You can only find it now. It's now or never."

I guess he didn't agree. Because he tore into me with an attack of crazy yammering about how he knew many things, many many things, and he knew there was an irrefutable, undisputable, *mathematical* proof to be found in the past and once he found it he'd give the world a crash course in how to save itself with his irrefutable proof which he was not only capable of finding but which he certainly, conclusively, come hell or high water *would* find. Only it sounded something like, *whichhecertainlyconclusively comehellorhighwaterWOULDfind.*

I gave it right back to him. There's no irrefutable proof of truth in the past that can save you or anybody else. How can there be when everything keeps changing? When *we* keep changing? Every minute millions of our cells die and get replaced. Every minute our hair is growing, our nails are growing. People change with every breath—right, that's Buddhism. Each time we think of something or remember something our brain cells go through a metamorphosis, so even our memories are changing. Only I sounded something like, *soevenourmemoriearechanging.*

Lukas rejected the argument. "I *can't* believe that," he said with a kind of sacred terror. "I *can't*. If I believed that, if I let go of the truth, I'd fall into a black hole. I'd fall into the chaos. I wouldn't know anything. I wouldn't even know if the future will happen."

"Trust me, the future will happen."

He turned away from me, giving himself a break, looking around at the landscape like it was covered with a shroud.

"If there was no answer," he said, "fear would accumulate. Frightening things would incubate. They'd multiply just beyond the range of vision without an answer."

"God isn't found in the answers. God's found in the wonder that leads to the questions."

"Really." He reached down for the iPad but he stopped. His hand never touched it. "In what universe is *that* supposed to take place?"

CHAPTER 11

I'VE NEVER BEEN THIS OLD BEFORE

Say It In The Grave

I slept heavily and got to the local news late the next morning: Investigators were still assessing damage from the rainstorm. An overturned tractor-trailer on I-95 was tying up traffic on the George. Lukas Lister-Bertozzi, head of [0+X], and his wife had died in an early-morning fire at company headquarters.

It was as thorough and in-depth a story as you could get in 18 seconds.

I spent the next few hours finding out what happened. The fire had broken out at approximately 4 a.m. and had destroyed The Hive. External security cameras showed smoke pouring out of the aluminum bubble like an Alamogordo mushroom cloud. Then a tremor shudders through all three stories and the structure suddenly erupts in thousands of white flash points, like the sky was filled with paparazzi.

The charred bodies were found on the floor, underneath what was left of the catwalks. Since both victims' throats had been slashed, the incident was being investigated as a possible murder-suicide.

Not murder-murder? No. When the fire marshals first entered they spotted a knife under Lukas' blackened, pustular arm. A carving knife, taken from the kitchen of the couple's apartment in the main building. They also found a note nearby, fused by the fire to the metal of a storm-proof butane igniter.

Handwritten on [0+X] letterhead, the paper was badly burned, but parts of it were still legible. *...feel nothing but the pain of remorse and regret*, it said near the top. And, at the bottom, ...*all that I have left to say can only be said in the grave.*

It sounded like a confession, and although further analysis was needed to identify the handwriting, police were able to reach a preliminary conclusion. Lukas, in some Black-Mass perversion of grief, had killed his wife and deliberately started the fire before cutting his own throat.

It made sense. Thinking about him in the Cenacle, the last time I'd ever see him, it made perfect pieces-fit sense. He was angry because Sabreena wasn't guilty, because no one was guilty. He couldn't accept the truth of that. He couldn't kick reality. He couldn't live with the way the world was going and it was too late to change the universe. Life was stumbling ahead on its stupid and defiant path as if in total ignorance of Lukas Lister-Bertozzi. And so, like an Inquisitor who saves people from the fires of hell by burning them at the stake, he did something about it. Instead of cutting his early-morning farts like everyone else, he reduced The Hive to a mangled mess, condemned Sabreena and himself to howling deaths and melted their bodies into blobs of pink meat.

How did I feel about it? I was watching the local news on TV. A reporter was interviewing an old man at his 111th birthday party. How does it feel to be 111? *I don't know*, said the man. *I've never been this old before.*

That's how I felt. Exactly. That's how I felt about what he'd done.

Or about what everyone thought he'd done.

Autopsies are to coroners what the go-backs were to Lukas—a careful, meticulous way of reconstructing the past. As the bodies were examined and the truth of what happened emerged, the certainties about Lukas were peeled away like chest tissue under an ME's knife. For starters, a significant but non-lethal amount of Vicodin was retrieved from Sabreena's stomach, This suggested a certain level of anticipation. Whatever her exact reasons for downing the drugs, she was planning on feeling no pain.

Further results revealed the causes of death. Lukas had bled out from the slash wound in his neck. In other words, he'd expired before the fire spread. Sabreena, on the other hand, had died from smoke inhalation. She'd been the last to go.

Then there was the note. Investigators compared the handwriting to the slants and slopes of Lukas' work notes discovered in the [0+X] archives. It didn't match. But it did match the baby journal Sabreena had kept during her daughter's first two years of life. I should've known. The note was too clear and to the point to be Lukas'.

They'd gotten it backwards: Sabreena killed her husband and deliberately set The Hive on fire before cutting her own throat.

Life's ability to humble us never ceases to amaze me.

It had to be revenge. Had to be payback for all of Lukas' rejection and blame—all of it unjustified, as it turns out. Payback for the self doubts that had always denied her own full grief. Payback for the lonely November road she'd had to walk by herself. For the demonic silence of her troubled and power-drunk genius of a husband. For the man who'd send her birthday cards (from what she told Belinda) and signed them, *all the best*.

When it comes to making shit up, nobody beats God.

When I was a kid a woman who lived a few blocks away was arrested for keeping nearly 100 cats in her house. The place was piled with foot-high feces and swimming in enough urine to drown the roaches. As cops with hazmat masks were taking her away, one of them asked how she could stand the smell. *What smell?* she said.

I always took that to mean you can get used to anything, and generally that assumption is true. But there are always notable exceptions. Sabreena was one. Knowing she'd been punished all this time for a crime she'd never committed was too much to take. She couldn't get used to living her choked life anymore. She couldn't find a place in her wounded cosmology anymore.

For her, the go-back was one cat too many.

There's Something There

Lukas and Sabreena were buried in the greenhouse, along with their child. Their remains—or what was left of them after the unsanctioned cremation—would be placed on either side of Samantha's grave. Moonflowers had been added to the garden's summer mix. Their headstones, when they were finished, would be made of the same veined black limestone as their daughter's. His birthplace plaque, I guess, would sit there forever, never finding a home.

[0+X] had stepped up its security for the memorial service. REACTS were fireplugged everywhere, ready for any violent, hysterical or otherwise melodramatic anti-Lukas protests. Strange, since his tyrannical rage and sponge-like self-pity were usually considered such attractive qualities.

But no protests broke out. The company was already a different place. Temporarily taking over while it searched for Lukas' replacement, the board had instituted a number of improvements. Many of Belinda's suggestions for morale building had been put in place. The company was returning its focus to producing security systems and abandoning the difficult, depleting demands of the go-backs. Staffers still wore their [0+X] iPods, but the devices had been reprogrammed to play music. Auralsynch had been banned.

The changes were as welcome as a governor's pardon. Since Lukas' death, no suicides had been reported.

So the crowds standing on the grounds and sloping hills around the greenhouse were all churched-up for peace. Hold a photo of the service in the landscape view and you'll see a beautiful April sun, thin clouds floating below. A good day to go into the earth.

Belinda conducted the service. At times like this, she said, we realize there are certain moments in life that hold a special significance, a special weight. They're almost moments out of time, moments when ordinary living fades and we sense there's a mysterious density to life, a *something*. There's *something* there. At moments like this, it's good to open our hearts and find our connections to a loving God. If we can do that, then all other things can and will flow. The Jews believe that the soul, the *neshama*, hovers around the bodies of the deceased. The *neshama* is the essence of these people, the totality of their thoughts and experiences. We ask God to guide their souls to peace. And we ask God to guide us to peace. Please help us get to the timeless, spaceless world of eternal joy, which is still this world of guilt, fear and sorrow. Help us see the infinite right in front of our eyes, in the touch of cold water, in the hammering of a nail, in the smell of a flower. In the smell of *this* flower.

Yeah, she was mixing it up, pouring a cocktail out of Christian, Jewish, Islamic, Buddhist and Hindu bottles. When it came to religions, she believed in cross-training. She told me that spirituality was like a forest. The named religions were the treetops. She was trying to get to the roots.

Like zen says, if you're holding the Buddha in your mind, tell him to find some other fucking place to rest.

Her words were falling on my ears like drops of honey. Look at her—her eyes embracing everything like a caress, the wind catching her long early-white hair. The wind was in love with her.

She talked about living by an invisible sun inside us. About not blaming Samantha and Lukas for what they'd done, since all our souls are fractured and in need of repair. She talked about people talking, people fighting, people laughing, traffic blaring, the wind roaring and still life holds a mystery. She talked about a world of pain and grief, and still... And still...

I looked around the grounds, the main building in the distance. The old Federated Aerospace headquarters, where guidance systems and mapping cameras for the Apollo mission had been built. The place was lit with history.

Cito Spangler was standing 20 feet away. I squeezed over to him, asked how he was coming along.

"Much better," he said. "Much, much better. Before was like writing code for the Pentagon. Everything you did had 192 rules to follow."

"Now?"

Suddenly this angry, sunken-faced man who not so long ago was asking me to drive a knife in his throat was shy and smiling. "Sometimes I guess there's a reason we forget the important things. It's so much better when you remember."

Belinda was saying that the real work in life is to grow spiritually, and you can't do that if you stay attached to the ego. The only way to free yourself from creeping self-hatred, from loathing, failure and guilt, is to free yourself from your self. When we're dreaming in the deep-sleep stage, she said, we don't experience any sense of self. Gotta be a moral there. The only way to move in tune with your dreams is to dance without your self.

True. It's like getting sober. The paradox of it is, yeah, you're the one who does it, but you can't go through spiritual surrender with the ego and its idiot kinfolk envy, fear and pride.

The self doesn't exist. That's not an objective statement of fact, like water boils at 212 F. It's more of a mantra, a breaking-through, a way to open the mind and go beyond habitual words.

A small altar with lit candles and a silver Tibetan bowl had been set up in front of the greenhouse. Belinda wrote the names of Lukas and Sabreena on two pieces of paper, set them on fire and dropped them in the bowl. As they burned she began a beautiful, shamanistic, Celtic-sounding chant. Ogham, the old language of the druids. She was eyes-closed possessed by the strange words, catching the Holy Ghost with them, all her mother-water flowing forth, praying so deeply and devoutly it felt like she was chanting from the bottom of the ocean.

We all listened in spellbound silence, heads nodding and bowed. The strange words held the hypnotic power of a Latin mass, letting us feel that just for a few minutes we understood the mystery of life and its secret nature.

I was crying. I couldn't stop. Every time I blew my nose I checked the tissue and made sure bits of my brain hadn't come out. Too much, too much. I turned away and worked out of the crowd, moving like the wind was carrying me.

Been a long time since I'd heard a Latin mass. I took early retirement from the Catholic Church—16, to be exact. The decision led to a huge fight with my mother, which in turn led to a bitter argument over the correct pronunciation of Thomas Aquinas' last name. Aqueenas or Aquwhynas?

Jesus Christ, the things people fight about when they're fighting about something else.

Speaking of which…

I heard a commotion over by the trees, two guests in full dispute. Roots and Janiva, going at it again.

>>>>>>>

They were dressed in their best raven black, Roots with that angry, incredulous, overwhelmed look that always came in handy in dealing with his girlfriend. She was yelling so hard at him I started making up excuses for myself.

"So you're disappointed," Janiva was saying. "So *what*? I just wish you'd do a better job of *hiding* it."

"I *can't*. Living with you's like eating rock. It's not only hard, it's *boring*."

"Ooh, I'm so bored—help me, help me. Everything you say is IM. *Immature*."

"The things I say might be childish and stupid, but they're just as stupid as the things you say."

It was just like that night on Canal Street, the first time I met them.

The second I got within 10 feet they started pleading their cases to me, like I'm a walking Appellate Court. They were trying to tell me what they were fighting about, but despite their best intentions they became so sidetracked in detailing the obvious deficiencies of the other person their secret remained safe.

Janiva believed he was dense and pigheaded and she couldn't believe how fucking people *live* like that. Roots believed she was overbearing and egotistical and he didn't believe he was stupid at all. She said she'd never *said* he was stupid—dense and pigheaded and maybe shit-hole dim is what she believed she'd said. If either one of them believed that if they had nothing good to say about someone they shouldn't say anything at all, they'd both be mutes.

"I'm sorry I have to come down on him," Janiva said to me. "I have to do *something* about him. I fucking *love* him."

With her closing argument complete, she left the courtroom and walked 50 feet away.

"I don't know, man, I don't know," Roots said. "She's got me second-guessing so much I'll be stuttering next."

"What's going on? Catch me up."

"Fuck should I know? Everything with her's all quizzical and tizzical and metaphysical. All I know is the elastic on my underwear's gone all loose and slack."

There you go—he was rambling again.

"This is all gothic and freaky and I don't know what," he said. "Is this what the moon smells like?"

Roots, I decided, would make a bad diabetic. He'd never be able to distinguish the light-headedness and confusion of hypoglycemia from his normal condition.

"You don't *love* me," Janiva yelled over. "If you were somebody who loved me, you would've fucking *loved* me."

"Who says I don't fucking *love* you?"

He stomped off—he wasn't letting her get the last word.

There was something comforting in seeing them fight, something almost inspiring. It meant that, no matter what, life goes on.

One of my favorite inscriptions goes like this: *Alpha and Omega. The Beginning and the End. For all things became every day worse and worse, for the end is drawing near.* It was chiseled on a crypt near Poitiers, set in French stone in the seventh century A.D.

We never stop living, even though we know we're going to die. In fact, we never stop living *because* we know we're going to die.

I watched them walk away, every step a shouting match. Everything had changed, and yet nothing had changed. That's it, there it is—that's the key right there. You have to realize two things—that everything has changed, that nothing has changed—to understand this crazy, cracked-loose, beautiful life.

###

Who The Hell Wrote This?

I worked as an Executive Editor at *Entertainment Weekly* for 11 years and (in two separate stints) at *People* magazine and people.com for 12 years. I often speak to young journalists and try to use myself as an example for inspiration—a guy who spent time in jail, rehab and a psych ward and somehow become a successful editor at Time Inc. and managed to stay sane and alive. I've tried to reflect those experiences in this book.

I owe much of my survival to my wife, Laurie. We've been married 41 years. And we still live together! In Garden City, N.Y.

Please feel free to write a short review of this or any of the books mentioned on the following pages. And feel free to contact me @
Facebook: http://on.fb.me/l02cd4
Twitter: http://bit.ly/ii7Kn1
Or my blog, Am I Laughing With, Or Laughing At, Richard Sanders? http://on.fb.me/hsFoa8

Many thanks,
Richard Sanders

Other Quinn McShane Books
[All available at Amazon, Kindle, iPad, Barnes & Noble and Smashwords.com]

SEX DEATH DREAM TALK
The lit-crit take: A genre-bending, character-driven thriller, centering on themes of redemption, revelation and the power of the unknown.

The pure plot pitch: What do you do when clues to an unsolved murder have been coded in a stolen $50 million painting? You try to steal it back. Only you have to deal with corrupt collectors, crazy thieves, lust-powered women, shootouts, betrayals, double-crosses and surprises. And a psychic dog named Hillary. It's not as easy as it sounds.

For a quick taste, please go to: http://bit.ly/p5Cl3Y

THE DEAD HAVE A THOUSAND DREAMS
The lit-crit take: A genre-bending, character-driven thriller, centering on themes of prophecy, mortality and salvation.

The pure plot pitch: He was told he had exactly eight days to live. By a blind psychic photographer. Okay, Wooly Cornell was plenty crazy—not to mention a huge asshole—but he asked me to help him. So I did. And as the countdown to his death started and I found myself facing threats, shootouts, a mysterious scarred woman and weird predictions that somehow managed to come true, I could only come to one conclusion: Fate is one strange thing to fight.

For a quick taste, please go to: http://bit.ly/oQ43KK

TELL NO LIE, WE WATCHED HER DIE

The lit-crit take: A genre-bending, character-driven thriller, centering on themes of celebrity, addiction and survival.

The pure plot pitch: The sex tape of a famous actress suddenly turns up on the internet, showing her on the last night of her life. The full version is being offered for sale, and the reason for its high price goes way beyond celeb voyeurism. The video also contains a clue to who killed her. That's why everyone is--literally--dying to see it.

For a quick taste, please go to: http://bit.ly/orJgQu

THE LOWER MANHATTAN BOOK OF THE DEAD

The lit-crit take: A genre-bending, character-driven thriller, centering on themes of redemption, responsibility and spiritual freedom.

The pure plot pitch: Just before he dies in a downtown hospital, a doctor passes along the half-formula for a powerful new hallucinogenic drug. Find the other half, and you've got a miracle drug—one that can save lives, save the world, and make a lot of money. Which, of course, makes it worth killing for.

For a quick taste, please go to: http://bit.ly/pjE5Sy

THE SEVENTH COMPASS
POINT OF DEATH

The lit-crit take: A character-driven thriller, centering on the themes of terrorism, understanding and hope.

The pure plot pitch: Here's bad day: Guy sets out to rob a bank but ends up pulling a carjacking, and when he's arrested a body is found in the trunk. The victim is a Sunni community leader, and why was he killed? Who killed him? The search for answers takes me into a homegrown Islamic terror underground, into plots, counterplots, deceptions and love affairs, all leading to an attack on a major NYC landmark.

For a quick taste, please go to: http://bit.ly/pjE5Sy

DEAD LINE

The lit-crit take: A genre-bending, character-driven, word-burning thriller about memory, identity and making peace with the past.

The pure plot pitch: Sure, we all know about arrogant, self-centered media executives. But how about one who served time as a teen for murdering her sister? And who suddenly believes she's possessed by the spirit of Indira Gandhi? And now, at the height of her power, a secret from her past is threatening to destroy her empire, while someone from that past is trying **to** take her life. Stop the damn presses!

For a quick taste, please go to: http://bit.ly/kHVjSl

DEAD HEAT

The lit-crit take: A genre-bending, character-driven, word-burning literary thriller about politics, love and the haunting pain of memory.

The pure plot pitch: I didn't know—or care—much about the tight race for governor of New York until someone took a shot at one of the candidates and killed his wife instead. The main suspect, it turns out, was an anti-government crazy (and a devoted quilter—yes, you heard that right) who once did time with me. So suddenly I'm trying to track him down, getting sucked into the panicky heart of a closely fought election campaign, into an affair with a troubled political operative, and into the dangerously surreal world of people who prefer casting their vote with a sniper's bullet.

For a quick taste, please go to http://bit.ly/nVXk6Y

CPSIA information can be obtained at www.ICGtesting.com
Printed in the USA
LVOW041617190712

290767LV00008B/90/P

9 781475 235609